Stars for Lydia

Stars for Lydia

An Amish-Country Mystery

By

PL Gaus

Stars for Lydia
Published by Paul L. Gaus, through
Kindle Direct Publishing
Copyright © 2019 Paul L. Gaus, All Rights Reserved
ISBN 9781796845426

**Version 2, fixing some typographical errors and
resolving some mistakes in pagination.**

Copyright Notice

Disclaimer

Chapter 1

After his first lecture of the new semester, Professor Branden closed his notes with satisfaction. He still could read the faces of his students, to judge with certainty whether or not he had gotten through to them. Were their eyes alive with thought, or were they blank with disinterest? Did his students have enthusiasm for the classroom, or were they seeking only a graduation credit? Professor Branden had always been able to tell. An entire classroom, or each individual student. He could still read their faces as he spoke. It was Civil War History that had always been his subject, and today had been his first lecture of the new semester, a full year after the Fannie Helmuth case.

Over a year ago, Fannie had chosen her own unique solution for her life, and now after the start of another fall semester, Branden knew that he had his life's enduring solution, too. He would always be a professor first. A Reserve Deputy, to be sure, but always a teacher first. He was built for the classroom, and today's lecture had been a ratification for him of something he had long known. He should never have doubted. He wouldn't retire after all. Not any time soon. Maybe never. He was in the right place.

Once or twice during his last academic year, the one following his sabbatical at Duke University, the subject of his retirement had come up. Certainly, Caroline had

1

encouraged him to think about it. Millersburg College had a new president who was putting her personal stamp on things - Dr. Nora Benetti. She had written to him at Duke to introduce herself to him, and once he had returned to campus, she had made a point to engage him about her aspirations and intentions for the college. For the most part, he found that he admired her industry and her vision. Now however, she had a meeting scheduled with him. There had been troublesome rumblings about his museum.

As he fastened the latches on his briefcase, a young Mennonite woman asked at the podium, "Professor Branden? Can I have a moment?"

He looked up as the latches snapped shut. "Lydia. I'm glad to see that you're in the class."

"You'd been away, Professor. This was my first opportunity to take one of your courses."

"Are you OK? You seemed a little distracted this morning."

"Sorry. Trouble concentrating. Family problems again."

"Can I help? I know they aren't very happy with you."

"Not really. It's the same old problem. They don't think I belong in college. They want me to come home and live Amish again."

Branden nodded and smiled sympathetically. "You want to talk about it?" He led out into the hallway, and she followed.

Lydia shook her head. "Not really, Professor, no. But I do have questions about the slaves." They continued down the hallway toward Branden's office, she a half step behind him. "How did they keep a census?" she asked further. "You know, in the slave states?"

Branden stopped and turned. "There are quite a few records, Lydia. What in particular?"

"Babies, Professor. Births. Who kept a record when a baby was born to a slave woman? I mean, who would have known if a slave baby was born on a remote farm? Likewise, Professor, who would know if an Amish baby were born at home?"

Lydia's eyes seemed troubled to the professor. She was fiddling nervously with the straps of her backpack, twisting them in place on either side of her neck. Instead of the severe black dress, heavy bonnet and shawl of the Old Order Amish, she was wearing a long lavender dress and a white day apron, with black hose and soft black walking shoes. These were Mennonite clothes, appropriate for her new non-Amish "liberalism." She had made a successful transition out of a conservative Schwartzentruber sect, into a Mennonite order.

But Lydia appeared somewhat untidy to Branden, as if she had dressed herself in a rush. Her lace prayer covering was a round white disk pinned to the top of her hair bun, but the disk wasn't properly centered. Her concern for some matter of great importance seemed lodged in the down-turned corners of her mouth. It seemed to be set into the rippling tension along her jaw. She turned her wrist to

3

glance at her watch, and then she went back to twisting the straps of her backpack. Abruptly, she slid her shoulders out of the straps and dropped the heavy backpack to the floor at her feet. She closed her eyes briefly with a sigh, then earnestly she looked again to Branden. "Maybe I'm imagining things, Professor. But I need to know about births to slave women."

Several steps behind him, through the open door to his office, the voice of the professor's assistant/secretary, Lawrence Mallory, sounded out on the phone. Branden took Lydia's elbow and ushered her in the direction of his office. She picked up her backpack, shouldered into the straps, and followed him down the hallway.

"We'll cover this in a couple of weeks, Lydia, but we can talk today. Can this wait until later this morning? I have a 10:00 meeting with the president."

Lydia stopped, and Branden stopped, too, and turned to face her. Lawrence Mallory's voice carried indistinctly out of the professor's office, two doors down. Lydia searched the professor's eyes and said earnestly, "My family won't talk to me anymore. I'm worried about my older sister, and no one will talk with me about her. They won't talk to me because I'm not Amish anymore."

Branden gave her his full attention. "We can talk, Lydia. But I have that meeting. Let's take a few minutes, here, and then Lawrence can make an appointment for you. First thing after my meeting. Sometime still this morning."

4

Lydia nodded. She pulled out her phone, looked briefly at the display and glanced anxiously down the hallway past the professor. "I've got a class, now, anyway."

"Can you come back?"

Lydia started off down the hall. She seemed to have been distracted suddenly by a new concern. There seemed to be a new anxiousness that was animating her thoughts. She turned back to the professor, and he saw the stitch of a ridge appear between her brows. Her eyes closed to slits and then opened wide. She turned and began to walk slowly to her next class.

"I'll be in my office most of the day," Branden called after her. He wasn't happy about the intensity in her expression. Or the worry in her eyes.

She shook her head, turned for the corner, and said, "I'll try." There she stopped for a moment, eyes looking briefly down to her shoes and then nervously back to Branden. "I'm really glad I'm not Amish anymore," Lydia said. "The best day of my life was when you gave me that scholarship."

- - - - - - - - - - - - - - -

Inside his office, in Mallory's outer vestibule, Branden asked, "Who was on the phone, Lawrence?"

"President Benetti," Lawrence answered with a puzzled tone.

"What'd she want?"

"She cancelled your 10:00 meeting, Mike. Just like that. Didn't give a reason."

"You sounded cross with her."

Carrying two mugs of coffee, Lawrence followed Branden into the professor's inner office. He set one mug on the professor's desk and took his customary seat in front of the desk. "I'm hearing rumors, Mike. About our museum."

Branden sat behind his desk, picked up the mug of coffee, said, "Thanks," smelled the rich brew appreciatively, and spoke over the rim of his mug. "Just rumors?"

Lawrence nodded. "Grumblings."

Branden smiled, settled back in his swivel chair and sipped at his coffee. He thought a moment and then stood and turned with his mug to gaze out through his office window, into the college's central oak grove below.

Professor Branden was youthfully slender and amply tall, but he was nevertheless half-a-head shorter than his wife Caroline. His trimmed beard and combed brown hair were traced through with gray. Because the summer's unusual heat had lingered through most of August, and because he was the senior-most professor at Millersburg College and could manage the attire, he was dressed rather more casually than most professors – sandals with socks and blue jeans, and a yellow Guy Harvey T-Shirt with no jacket. Years ago, as an assistant professor, he had worn sport coats and ties. Now he was "enjoying the benefits of seniority," as he had lately commented to Caroline. And the benefits of tenure. It was the teaching that mattered to him, not the clothes.

Turning his head back to Mallory, Branden asked, "Can you find out what class Lydia Schwartz has at 10:00?"

"Sure Mike, why?"

"I want to catch her after that class."

"Oh?"

"I don't like the way she was asking questions just now. She seemed worried to me."

Lawrence stood and made for the passageway. "Like what?" he called back from his outer vestibule. "What questions?"

"Questions about babies born to slave women, Lawrence. Census records."

With a puzzled smile, Mallory returned to Branden's inner office. "She was just asking questions?"

Branden shook his head. "She was bothered by something during class. She wasn't really 'in the room.' Like the students you spot who aren't really paying attention. Like the disinterested ones."

"You'd spot that kind of thing better than anyone, Mike."

"I suppose. But this seemed personal to her. She was worried about her sister. She was thinking about birth records for slave babies."

Mallory arched a brow and returned to his outer office. Branden came out from behind his desk and followed him. "Also, Lawrence, try to find out who those professors are. The ones who are grumbling."

Then, stepping out into the hallway with his mug of coffee, Professor Branden turned back to face his door, and with pleasant satisfaction, he read the titles that were posted there.

Dr. Michael Branden
Chairperson – Department of History
The Arden S. Beaumont Distinguished Professor of
American History

Mr. Lawrence Mallory
Director and Curator
The Millersburg College Museum of Battlefield Firearms

There in the hallway outside his office, Professor Branden pulled his phone and called the college president's office. The woman who answered the call was well known to him - Pamela Stone, recently promoted from secretary in the history department, to Executive Assistant in the president's office.

"Hi, Pam," he said, once she had answered his call. "Why'd I lose my 10:00 with Benetti?"

"Hi, Mike, I really don't know. But she's in her office with a couple of professors right now. Talking with an architect about your museum."

"Really? An architect?"

"Yes."

"OK, Pam. Can you let me know if this grows into something that I should worry about?"

"Sure, Mike. But right now, I think it's all rather preliminary. It's not a secret, really. You know – this new major in neuroscience. We're trying to find a place for the labs. Benetti says she wants you to be kept up to date."

"But can you let me know about meetings like this one? It's important."

"Yes, definitely. When I know something. Probably yet this morning, after this meeting with the architect."

- - - - - - - - - - - - - -

Five minutes before the end of Lydia Schwartz's class on British Poetry, Professor Branden was waiting for her in the hall outside the classroom. He watched carefully for her when the students began to file out into the hallway, and then he looked for her inside the room, as the last few students left for their next classes. Lydia was not in the room. Instead, there was only Professor Karen Byrne, shuffling her notes together at the lectern.

"Lydia Schwartz?" Branden asked as he came up to Professor Byrne. "Wasn't she in class?"

Byrne consulted her class list. "No, Mike, I don't think so. She didn't make it."

"A young Mennonite woman in a lavender dress?"

"Definitely not. Do you know her?"

"She has one of our scholarships, Karen. From Caroline and me. Really, it isn't at all like Lydia to skip a class. Not on the first day."

"Sorry," Byrne said as she took up her papers.

"It's OK, I suppose," Branden said. *It really isn't like Lydia at all*, he thought.

Back in his office, Branden took out his class list and found Lydia's cell phone number. He punched it in, and it rang several times before it switched to voicemail. Branden heard Lydia's greeting.

> *"Mary, if this is you, please come up to campus. Call me, or just come see me, OK? I'm worried about you. Anyone else, please leave a message."*

After the beep, Branden spoke for the recording. "It's Professor Branden, Lydia. Please call back."

After he had switched out of his call, the professor decided that he wasn't satisfied with his message, so he called Lydia again. This time the phone went straight to voicemail. Carefully, he said, "Professor Branden again, Lydia. I am eager to speak more with you. Your questions are important to me. Please call me back as soon as you get this. Any time of the day. I'll make time for you. As much as you need. Let's talk. Just as soon as you are free."

Chapter 2

After attending to some electronic and paper correspondence in his office, Professor Branden left the second floor of the history building and passed into the college's oak grove, walking along one of the shaded brick pathways that laced the campus. He walked at a decent pace for his age, but he knew that his legs had lost a bit of spring in recent years.

At the edge of campus, Branden crossed the road near the main entrance to the college grounds, and he walked down the sidewalk of his street, where he and Caroline lived in an older brick colonial, with a wide backyard that overlooked a serene Amish valley, spreading out luxuriously beneath the cliffs at the edge of Millersburg. Lost in his thoughts, he walked absently past his own home and realized his error only after he had circled the cul-de-sac and found himself headed back mistakenly toward campus.

He stopped, shook his head and smiled at his absent-mindedness. *Occupational Hazard*, he thought, scolding himself. Then crossing the cul-de-sac at an oblique angle, he paced deliberately over to his short front walk, climbed up onto the shallow stoop, opened the door, and entered the cool front hallway of his home.

11

The lights were out in the living room to his left. The curtains were drawn there against the late summer heat. To his right, the hallway to his garage was shaded, too.

Down the hallway to the kitchen, Caroline had the ceiling fan running over their curly-maple kitchen table, and at the table, back-lit by strong light from the kitchen windows, Pastor Cal Troyer was sitting as if haloed, with a small cup of coffee and a delicate porcelain saucer, under the cooling breeze of the fan.

Branden stepped into the kitchen and asked Cal, "Something up?"

Cal shook his head. "Caroline called," he said. "I'm getting a free lunch."

Troyer's white hair and beard were growing long again. His hair was down to the tops of his ears, and his beard was starting to show some need for a trim. The strong light from the windows seemed to put a glow into his features. He had a broad and rugged face, large knotted hands, and a strong workman's build. Shorter than average, he was a pastor at a small Christian church in town. It had always been impressive to the professor that Cal took no salary from his congregation, instead earning his way in life as a carpenter. They had known each other since kindergarten, and together with Sheriff Bruce Robertson, they were the most respected trio of friends in Holmes County. And maybe the most notorious.

The professor angled left toward the coffee pot, took a mug out of the cabinet and poured out the last of the brew. He switched the pot off and started back to the kitchen table.

But Caroline put a hand out to his arm and asked, "Well, Professor?"

Branden smiled, moved on past her, and took a seat across the table from Cal. "I guess I'll stay there a while, yet," he said. "Teaching suits me, really."

"Oh, please," Caroline crowed. She carried sandwiches to the table. "Like there was ever any doubt? Really, Michael, I don't know why you won't consider cutting back. If you retired, you could still teach a class or two as an Emeritus."

"What are you talking about?" Cal asked. "You wouldn't stay on at the college?"

Branden turned to Caroline. "Is this why Cal is here? In case you needed an ally in our retirement dispute?"

"What?" Cal asked.

"Don't be ridiculous," Caroline said, with a conspirator's smile. She gave a shrug to let the matter drop, and she turned back to the refrigerator, saying, "It's not a *dispute*, Michael. I just have a different opinion than you."

Shaking his head at Caroline's ruse, the professor changed to a different topic. "We've got a new president, Cal. She appears to have some issues with my museum."

Cal sipped at his coffee and passed a glance to both Caroline and the professor. "What's wrong with your museum?"

Branden chuckled. "Nothing. But she needs space for a new major in neuroscience."

Caroline put out three glasses of milk, sat at the head of the table and said, "Really Michael, I don't understand why a small Liberal Arts college needs a major in neuroscience."

Caroline's light auburn hair was done up in a bun at the back of her head. She was a slender but sturdy woman, with a fair complexion. She had been a free-lance editor for many years, but with their recent sabbatical at Duke, she had set that aside. She was 'slowing down as the years speed along faster,' she had explained to her husband. 'Slowing down because time doesn't.'

"Isn't neuroscience rather specialized?" Caroline continued. "It's certainly not part of a Liberal Arts curriculum."

"I don't know," Branden said. "Seriously, I don't know." He started on his sandwich and added, "It's all just preliminary."

"What can they do, Mike?" Cal asked. "You've had your museum in place for decades."

"Don't know," the professor said. "Look, Cal. Lydia Schwartz spoke to me after class. I thought she had a good first year while we were on Sabbatical. I didn't see much of her last year. But she's troubled about something now."

"Haven't heard anything," Cal said.

"Who would know?"

"Ed Schell, I imagine," Cal said. "They've been helping her make the transition out of Amish culture."

"I know him pretty well," Branden said. "It was the Schells who first introduced us to Lydia."

Caroline said, "Light-Path Ministries, right? They have a church."

"Yes," said Cal. "Light-Path. Ed and Donna Schell. They help people who want to leave an Amish sect."

"That'd take a lot of help, I expect," Caroline said.

"Everything," Cal agreed with a nod. "Checking accounts and credit cards. Utility bills and driver's licenses. Budgeting, groceries, clothes and legal matters. Amish people sometimes need help with everything about modern life. Especially if they come out of one of the conservative churches. Like Lydia Schwartz. From the Schwartzentruber sect."

"Well, I'm worried about her," the professor said. "She was talking about slave babies and Amish babies as if the two belonged in the same sentence."

- - - - - - - - - - - - - -

Later in the afternoon, the professor edited a rough draft of an article he was submitting to *The Journal of the American Civil War*. He also held meetings with two students. At 3:00, Branden taught his second class, on nineteenth-century American history. At 4:00, he met with an assistant professor new to the history department.

At 4:30, he retrieved his small white pickup truck and drove down off the college heights, to the old red-brick jail on courthouse square. He parked in the bank's parking lot just south of the jail, and he climbed the worn concrete

15

steps into the back of the jail, just as the out-rigger clouds of another late-summer storm began to slide in from the west.

Down the long first-floor hallway, past the busy squad room on the left, Branden entered Sheriff Bruce Robertson's office at the front of the jail building, and without greeting the rotund sheriff, he took a bottle of water at the credenza behind the office door, and he slumped into a low leather chair in front of Robertson's battered cherry desk. Legs stretched out in front of him, Branden sipped at his water and contented himself with the simple luxury of sitting together in silence with his old friend, Holmes County's irascible top lawman, sometimes inscrutable, sometimes impulsive, and always as large and indelicate as a bulldozer.

Rain began to pelt the west facing windows, and thunder broke immediately behind an overhead lightning strike. With his sizeable belly pressed tightly against the edge of his desk, Sheriff Robertson cast a moment's glance to the advancing storm outside his windows, and then he continued to shuffle papers back and forth mechanically on his desk.

He was sporting a full and bushy gray beard, which everyone knew covered the long scar on his left cheek, a ragged battle wound that he had earned in the fight with old Earnest Troyer, near the conclusion of the search for Fannie Helmuth, at the end of summer, a year ago. The sheriff's hair was also gray, and it was cut with his customary Korean War flat-top style, which made him look, with his eyes weary from the day's paper grind, like a fifties-era state trooper who had been out on traffic patrol too long. Except that now he wore a beard, covering a scar that lay beneath it.

Robertson worked with his papers at his desk, sighing occasionally with an end-of-the day boredom. He edited some of the papers and gave his signature to others. As he worked, he sorted the papers into the various document trays on his desk, and without looking up, he said simply, "Mike," to acknowledge the professor.

"Bruce."

"First lectures?"

"Went fine."

"You get caught in this storm?"

"No."

"New president?"

"Yes."

"She any good at it?"

"I suppose."

A long, multiple flash of lightning strikes lit the windows to the sheriff's left, and thunder rumbled forward as the light of day was wrangled down to a dim and desultory gray.

"You seem distracted, Mike. Are you down here for a reason?"

"Lydia Schwartz. One of my students. Do you know her?"

"No. Why?"

"I'm worried about her."

"I don't know her, Mike. She hasn't been through here."

"Then do you know Ed Schell?"

"Light-Path," the sheriff said. "Sure. He's something of a fixture down here. Tries to help the Amish kids who get arrested. Why?"

"Cal says the Schells have been helping Lydia Schwartz."

"You were down at Duke when she started college?"

"Yes, and I didn't see much of her last year. Was she any trouble for you here?"

"No. Schwartz?"

"Yes, Lydia Schwartz."

Robertson shrugged his shoulders. "Ed Schell is easy enough to find."

"I know. Church on Perkins."

"Yes, and a boarding house. They came here from Ashland. About a year before you left for your *lay-about* sabbatical at Duke. What'd you do there, anyway? Stretch out on a sofa and think deep thoughts?"

"I was buried most days in their Civil War archives, Bruce. I worked. Wrote several papers."

"Right," Robertson replied with a grin.

"Knock it off, Sheriff," Branden complained.

The sheriff's old intercom buzzed, and Del Markely, his dispatcher, spoke abruptly. "Sheriff, there's a problem. You need to hear this."

Just as abruptly, Del switched off. Robertson made a curt reply into his old intercom box, but Del did not answer. So, Robertson pushed out of his chair, advanced to his door, and turned left into the hallway, with the professor trailing

18

behind. At Del's front counter, Robertson asked, "What?" and Del Markely, up on her feet, held her microphone out, and pointed to her radio receiver on the consoles behind her counter.

"Say again, Ricky," she said into her microphone. "The sheriff's standing right here."

Over the radio speaker, they heard Ricky Niell's anxious voice. "We've got a body, Del. It's a young Mennonite woman in a lavender dress. North on County Road 77, then west on Township 606. On a Schwartzentruber farm."

Chapter 3

After Ricky Niell's call came in at the sheriff's office, Branden rode anxiously with Robertson in the sheriff's dark blue Crown Vic, north and east out of Millersburg through the rural countryside, on the winding black-topped, two-lane SR 241. The professor watched in a mournful daze as Robertson negotiated the slow, sharp left turn in the tiny livestock auction berg of Mt. Hope and then drove north on County 77, into Holmes County's northern nowhere-from-anywhere farmland. They proceeded west on black-topped Salt Creek 606, just as the sudden afternoon's storm had moved off to the east. Once they had turned onto 606, the professor's mind seemed to function rationally again. He knew what was coming, and he had managed, in at least a superficial way, to acknowledge it. This was Schwartzentruber country. This was the farm across the road from Lydia's parents. This was going to be Lydia Schwartz. 'Please,' the professor prayed silently. 'Let it not be Lydia.'

After a scant three-quarters of a mile, Robertson came up to Ricky Niell's cruiser at the top of a hill. The vehicle was still pulsing its red and blue flashers on its light bar. Ricky had parked at the edge of a weedy culvert that was running high with rainwater, beside a farmer's muddy lane.

The long and wide lane was fenced down each side with knarred post stumps and rusty wire, and it traced off through a field of tall green corn, toward a dense stand of trees, shot through with the white and gray trunks of tall-canopied Sycamores, three hundred yards to the back of the property. In the windy remnants of the storm, the tall Sycamore canopies were still bending and swaying erratically. Blue sky and large cotton-ball clouds had begun to replace the gray mantle that had blown over the county only a half-hour earlier. The professor took it all in mechanically. He saw, without really seeing. His emotions were a mixed flood of anxiety and worry. He was scratching nervously at his chin whiskers, and he had been shifting side-to-side on his seat, trying to dispel a mental numbness that had overtaken him.

As Robertson pulled his Crown Vic onto the lane, Branden spoke quietly. "This is the Yost farm, Bruce. John and Mary Yost. Ultra-conservative Amish. Schwartzentrubers. I'm afraid this will be my student Lydia. Mary Yost is her sister. Lydia is the only one out here who would be dressed in Mennonite attire."

Robertson proceeded slowly, steering carefully around mud puddles and negotiating high spots where he could manage it. But despite his best efforts, the Crown Vic dipped and slid into the ruts left by ancient iron wagon wheels. "How do you know these Yosts, Mike?" the sheriff asked, trying to distract the professor from his emotional turmoil.

"Mary Yost is the mother here," Branden said woodenly, as they approached the back of the lane. "She is Lydia's older sister, and Lydia has been trying to get in touch with a Mary. I think it's this Mary. Mary Yost, her sister on this farm. Sorry. I must not be making much sense. I don't want to believe this is Lydia."

"You're projecting, Mike," Robertson said as he inched along. "It might not be her. You don't know yet."

"I'm nervous. She was in a lavender dress this morning. Anyway, listen. This is the greeting on her phone. I first heard it when I called her this morning after class."

As the sheriff nudged and slipped his Crown Vic along the muddy lane, the professor tapped in a number and played out Lydia Schwartz's iPhone greeting on the speaker:

"Mary, if this is you, please, please, please come up to campus.
Call me, or just come see me before you do anything.
OK? Don't do anything until you talk to me.
Anyone else, just leave a message."

"She must have revised it since this morning," Branden said. "It sounds more urgent, now."

Robertson turned left around the bend in the farm lane, and Detective Ricky Niell came into view. His gray suit coat was hanging limp and wet from his shoulders. He was standing beside a small red Escort, where a narrow bridle path snaked through the woods and intersected the muddy lane. Two forensics technicians waited beside the ME's van, and on the path, ten yards into the timber, Missy Taggert, the Holmes County Medical Examiner and Sheriff Robertson's wife, stood with a rain-drenched English woman who was dressed in muddy jeans and a blue-checkered work shirt. In green hospital scrubs, Missy came away from the English woman and walked in her clear plastic rain slicker up to the Crown Vic as the sheriff and the professor were climbing out.

"She fell and hit her head on a rock," Missy said, brushing the hood of the slicker back from her head. "I have her phone. And a wallet from her purse in that red Escort. Lydia Schwartz. College student."

- - - - - - - - - - - - - - -

His first sight of the long lavender dress stopped the air from moving inside Professor Branden's lungs. He stood immobile, several paces back, and he realized that he wasn't breathing only when the autonomic reflex from his diaphragm dragged a sudden, hasty breath into him. 'Breathe,' his chest demanded, and as he filled his lungs, he shook his head for clarity. *How can this be?* he thought. *Is this real?* He was washed through with shock and denial, despite the fact that he had anticipated this on the long drive up from Millersburg. As prepared as he was to see it, the sight of Lydia sprawled in the mud put tears in his eyes and a woeful, "Oh no, no, no," whispering through his lips.

Lydia rested on her side, near the muddy creek that trickled across the bridle path, and her form, deflated and motionless, had the unmistakably flat aspects of death. Her face was as white as the whitest rice, and her body was draped over the rugged ground like a limp rope. Her lace prayer disk lay in the mud beside her head.

Branden stepped sorrowfully back along the bridal trail to the farm lane, and Missy followed him. The English woman in the blue checkered work shirt joined them beside the Crown Vic. "We were caught in the rain," she said plaintively. "Running down the hill. She slipped in the mud. Just fell right there. There wasn't anything I could do."

Robertson held out his hand and said, "Sheriff Bruce Robertson."

"Meredith Silver," the woman said, taking his hand. "I've known Lydia since she was a kid. Lydia Schwartzentruber. Schwartz. I can't believe this happened." Her eyes were wet and swollen. She looked as if she had cried a lifetime of sorrow in the span of the last single hour.

"Are you a neighbor?" the sheriff asked, holding out a bandana for her eyes.

Meredith Silver nodded, took the cloth and dabbed at her eyes. "I live just across the road. First house west of here."

Meredith gazed back toward Lydia's body for a long moment. Then, as if forgetting herself, she turned and started back along the farm lane. She stopped and turned back with an apology. "Sorry. Look, I need to get out of these clothes. Into something dry. If you don't think you need me here, anymore? I'll be at my house. Everybody out here knows me. Is that OK with you?"

"We'll have questions," Robertson cautioned.

"Just come over to the ranch house, Sheriff. Across the road."

Robertson gave a single nod of his head, and Meredith Silver left along the muddy lane.

Shaking his head, and not paying any attention to Silver, Professor Branden whispered to Missy, "I was talking to her just this morning. After class. I can't believe this is real."

Missy led Branden and her husband back to the body. She had rolled the body onto its side. She explained this and said, "She just fell forward, it seems."

The sight of her was a bleak contradiction to all the Professor's denials. The professor saw that she was in the same Mennonite clothes that he had seen her wearing after class. There was the long lavender dress, now muddy at the hem, and muddy in front where she had landed. There were the white string ties and a once-white apron. Her long brown hair was spilling out of a loose bun at the back of her head. One arm was spread wide, at right angles to the torso, with an appalling red gash in her temple. And all of her was splattered with mud.

"I turned her a bit," Missy said, "but she's lying right where she landed. Fell and didn't move. Didn't try to break her fall. Just sprawled out face-first on the ground and struck her head on that rock. It's like the rain pounded her deeper into the mud and rinsed all the blood away. Her clothes are soaked and muddy. Just like Meredith Silver's. They were running down the hill in the rain."

Robertson commented gently to the professor. "You seem to know her more than you would the average student, Mike. If you can, tell us about her. Tell us how you know her. I mean, I know she was your student, but there's clearly more than that. Who was she?"

Branden managed a weak nod. "I've been out here before," he said, and he heard his words as if there were a cavernous echo in his head. "She's the daughter of Mose and Ida Schwartzentruber, on the farm across the road. On the other side of 606."

"OK, but how do you know all of that?" the sheriff asked.

"When Lydia decided that she would leave her sect, Caroline and I offered her one of our scholarships. She passed her G.E.D. exam, and she started college right then."

"So, you know the families fairly well," Missy said.

"Yes," Branden said, "We know them all very well out here. But they blame us for Lydia. They blame us for making it too easy for her to turn away from their church. We gave her a place at the college when she wanted out of the sect. The Schwartzentrubers don't care for us these days."

Ricky Niell approached on the trail and said, "The ambulance is here."

The three followed him back out of the woods to the farm lane. Without lights and sirens, the ambulance was approaching slowly from their left.

To their right, a team of two roan Belgian draft horses pulled a ponderous farm wagon forward. The late-teens Yost lad who was driving the horses from the top rail of the wagon was known to Branden as John Junior. Junior pulled his horses to a stop, well back from the Crown Vic and the red Escort. There were five younger children riding in the back of the wagon, aged four to maybe twelve, the professor remembered. They scrambled down from the back of the wagon and clustered themselves beside the tall draft horses to watch the English folk, curiosity on all their faces.

All the youngsters were barefooted. The boys were dressed uniformly in dull-blue Amish denim, with black vests and long-sleeved dark-blue blouses. The girls all wore identical dark plum dresses and black bonnets.

After Junior had climbed down from his perch, stepping first on the iron rim of the wagon wheel and then jumping down to the ground, Branden pulled him several steps forward and away from his brothers and sisters, saying quietly, "There has been some trouble, Junior."

Junior nodded toward the ambulance, asking, "Somebody's hurt?"

"It's your Aunt Lydia, I'm afraid. She slipped on your bridle path. Running down the hill. She hit her head on a rock."

Stone faced and tense, Junior asked, "Bad?"

"I'm afraid she died," Branden said. "I'm sorry."

27

Junior's entire body shuddered with the shock of the news. He opened his mouth to say something automatic, but he closed his lips tightly instead, looking first back to his younger brothers and sisters, and then around again to Branden. He shook his head and drew a deep, ragged breath. "Are you sure it's our Aunt Lydia? I mean, are you sure?" He seemed to be fighting back tears.

Branden said, "Yes. I'm sorry, Junior. It is really her."

Junior turned around to face his brothers and sisters. He stepped back to them and gathered them close together. He knelt to take the two youngest children, a little boy and a little girl, into his embrace, and he spoke in Dietsche dialect. The youngest boy, three years old, blinked and looked confused. The youngest girl, four years old, stared back blankly at Junior. A middle girl of five filled suddenly with tears, and the two older children, a girl of seven years and a boy of twelve, obviously surprised and shaken, began asking questions of Junior. The questions came rapidly, and Junior stood and tried to embrace them. But one boy pulled away sternly, one girl stepped back from him, and the other boy wrapped his arms around Junior to take his embrace. Speaking to all of them, Junior said in English, "Back to the house now," and the children began to file toward the back of the wagon, while the oldest of the five continued with a flurry of questions. As they arranged themselves at the back of the wagon, Junior lifted them up onto the flat bed, saying each of their names as he did so. Ana. Rose. Dottie. Jonas. He reached out to take the hand of the fifth, but that boy refused his assistance, and climbed up himself into the wagon. Junior whispered, "Micah," as if completing the list of his siblings was a necessary formality in his sorrow. Then he climbed up to the reins and said to the professor, "We'll be back at the house with father."

Branden stepped up to the side of the wagon. "You didn't know we were out here?"

Junior shook his head. "Father told us to cut some more of the field corn. We were coming out to attend to that."

"He didn't come with you?" Branden asked. "You know, to help with the corn?"

Junior shook his head. "Father has his troubles. We can't get him to talk to us."

"Can we help?" Branden asked. He glanced back briefly at the approaching ambulance and turned around to Junior again. "Do you need us to come help?"

Junior shrugged his shoulders. He formed a tentative smile. "The bishop is coming. I sent Micah to fetch him earlier. Because of father."

Branden said, "Why don't you let me ride back with you?"

"It'll be fine," Junior said, slapping his reins to turn his team on the broad lane. "He's sad because Die Maemme left us. She took our little sister Esther with her when she left. So, he's having another bad spell, is all."

Surprised, Branden asked, "Can I visit with you and your father, when we're done here?"

"I suppose, Mr. Branden. It's up to you. We'll all be back at the house."

- - - - - - - - - - - - - - -

With labored back-and-forth maneuvers, the ambulance was turning around on the muddy lane. Once it was positioned backwards on the lane, Missy directed it to within fifteen yards of the body. The paramedics pulled the wheeled gurney out through the back doors of the ambulance, and they carried it up the bridle path with its legs tucked underneath the bed, to put it down flat on the muddy ground beside the body. With Missy's instructions, they lifted Lydia's body onto its back. As they were carrying Lydia back to the ambulance, the professor said to Missy and the sheriff, "I'm worried about this Yost family."

"Oh?" Missy said.

"The oldest son Junior said his father is having some trouble again. Or he's incommunicative. Something like that. So, he says. There's a history of depression. I'm not thinking too clearly. Sorry. Anyway, they can't get him to talk to them. I'm going to walk around the lane there, to see about them."

As the ambulance pulled away, Robertson's phone chirped. He checked the display and answered the call, saying, "Dan?"

Chief Deputy Dan Wilsher said, "You're still out on 606, Sheriff?"

"Yes."

"Well, I've got Baker and Johnson out there. Somebody called in a suicide. I gather it's near you, because Baker says he can see the lights on Niell's cruiser, down the road from his position."

"Got a name, Dan? Wait, I'm going to put you on speaker."

The sheriff made the switch to speaker phone and said to Wilsher, "OK, Dan. Who?"

"Meredith Silver, Sheriff. It's her sister who called it in. Louise Herbeck."

"We were just talking with Meredith Silver," Robertson said, looking at Missy and sounding perplexed.

"She's dead, Sheriff," Wilsher replied in the speaker phone. "Her sister says it's a suicide."

"How would she know, Dan?" Missy asked.

"Evidently there's a note. I sent Baker and Johnson out there. They've got the Herbeck woman out of the house. She was rather a problem. Refused to leave. Really shook up. They have orders that no one else is to go in, until you get there."

"My people just left in the ambulance with the Lydia Schwartz body," Missy replied.

"I'm sending Stan Armbruster out to Silver's place, for forensics, Missy. Plus, you've still got Niell and the sheriff, right? That ought to be enough for now, with Baker and Johnson already over there."

"We're going to need another transport, Dan. I need my ME's van to stay over here, while I process the scene of this accident."

"I know," Wilsher replied. "Stan Armbruster is driving the Medical Examiner's wagon. That should be enough for the Silver body."

Robertson said, "Just a minute," and he put his phone on mute. Addressing his wife, he said, "You about done, here?"

"Not really," Missy said, shaking her head. "I want my people to take some measurements. And photographs, while the light is still good."

Off-mute again, Robertson said to his Chief Deputy, "I'm taking Ricky Niell over to the Silver place, Dan. Missy isn't finished here at the Yost farm quite yet. And like I said, we were just talking with Meredith Silver. This is just too weird to be a coincidence."

Chapter 4

Robertson and Ricky Niell tried the Crown Vic, but
it was sunk too deep into the mud to be moved. So, they
walked out to 606 and took Niell's cruiser west for about
two hundred yards to a gravel driveway where Deputy Ryan
Baker was standing in uniform, out by the road to wave
them in.

"We're around back," Baker said, and he led the two
men past his cruiser, past a black Chevy Nova, and around
the side of a brick ranch house, to a picnic table on a small
back patio. A petite and frail woman of about fifty years, in
hand-me-down clothes, sat crying there. She was dabbing
fretfully at her eyes with an old handkerchief, and she was
muttering as she shook her head. She looked exhausted by
grief, and the haggard appearance of her clothes testified to
a difficult life.

"I can't believe this," she was saying, eyes cast
down. "There can't be that much blood in the whole world."

Baker said to Robertson, "Sheriff, this is Mrs.
Louise Herbeck. Meredith Silver's sister."

Louise Herbeck looked up at the big sheriff, and she
lamented. "Oh no. This can't be true. Are you really the
sheriff?"

"I'm Sheriff Bruce Robertson," he said. "Is it your
sister who is dead?"

"What?"

"Is your sister Meredith Silver?"

Herbeck nodded. "She's just lying in there on the linoleum. Why would she kill herself?" Suddenly excited and wide-eyed, Louise pleaded further, "Check, Sheriff. Please check. Maybe she's not really dead."

Robertson looked to Johnson. Dave Johnson shook his head and said, "Yes, I'm afraid she is dead, Sheriff. But you need to see this for yourself. There's a problem."

Robertson sat backwards on the end of the picnic table bench beside Herbeck, and sideways to her he said, "I'm sorry, Louise. My deputies tell me she is in fact deceased."

Herbeck moaned and shuddered in grief, and she cried out, "Please, no. This can't be happening."

"Are you the one who found her?" the sheriff asked.

"What?" Herbeck said. She began to breathe rapidly, jerking frantic breaths, and casting tormented eyes about as if searching for lost souls.

To Johnson, the sheriff said, "Hyper-ventilating," and Johnson immediately produced a bandana.

Robertson formed it into a cone-shaped cloth, and he held it in front of Herbeck's face. "Breathe into this," he said, "like you're blowing into a paper bag to pop it."

Herbeck grabbed the bandana, held it over her mouth, and blew in and out until her anxiety had passed. When she was breathing more normally, she dropped the bandana to her side, folded her forearms over the top of the picnic table, and laid her forehead down onto them. "She's just lying there," she moaned.

"I know," Robertson said. "Can you manage it, if we stand you up? I want you to walk around to your car with Deputy Johnson. I want you to try to walk around a little bit out front and try to calm down. We're going to go inside and check on Meredith."

Dave Johnson stepped forward, and he took Herbeck's arm to lift her gently to her feet. Robertson stood up beside them, and Herbeck reached out for the sheriff with trembling arms. She put her arms around him, and he embraced her carefully and briefly, he large and round, she thin and frail. When she released him, she took a step back to look up into Robertson's eyes.

"Please don't leave her lying there like that," she implored. "I can't stand to see her like that again."

"You won't have to," Robertson said, handing Herbeck over to Johnson. As Johnson started walking Herbeck to the front of the house, Robertson added, "I promise you, Louise, you won't have to see her like that again."

Then the sheriff turned directly to Baker and said, "Take me in, Ryan."

- - - - - - - - - - - - - -

Meredith Silver was lying out straight on her back, her head in a pool of shiny fresh blood. Her hiking boots were still muddy, and so were the cuffs of her jeans. Her blue checkered work shirt was still wet from the rain. Her left arm was flung out on the linoleum of the kitchen floor, and her right arm lay at her side. She had a single entry wound high on her right cheek, and she had a much larger, ragged exit wound at the crown of her head. Behind her and off somewhat to the side, there was a spray of blood against the kitchen wall and ceiling, and surrounding her head there was the red blood that her heart had pumped briefly until she had died.

Baker said, "There's a note, Sheriff, but do you notice the problem?"

Robertson studied the scene and arched a brow. "Have you searched for it, Ryan?"

"Yes. It's not here."

"Changes things a bit, doesn't it," Robertson said.

Baker nodded, frowned.

The sheriff then turned back to the kitchen table and leaned over to study the note that Baker had mentioned. "Anything on the back of it?" he asked Baker, and the deputy replied, "I haven't turned it over, Sheriff."

Robertson straightened up, looked sadly at his deputy and said, "I hate this kind of thing, Baker."

Ryan nodded wordlessly, and Robertson bent over again to read the short note. In hasty scrawl was written:

I'm sorry we were running in the rain
I was angry with her Lydia sweet Lydia I
am so very sorry
It was slippery in the rain I was upset, and I
shoved her in the back as we ran, and she fell
forward an accident
this should never have happened we should
never have started any of this
Mary forgive me for breaking our promises
to you
Lydia, please forgive me I'd take it all back
if I could

"What do you think that means, Sheriff?" Baker
asked as Robertson straightened up.

"I don't know, Ryan. If Lydia was shoved, Missy
should be able to tell us that. But 'never started any of this?'
I don't know what she means by that. And, take all of *what*
back? What does that mean?"

Baker shrugged his shoulders. "There are shoe
prints, Sheriff. Flat soles. Not the boots that Silver is
wearing."

Robertson walked a wide circle around Meredith
Silver's body, studying the faint blood prints of flat-
bottomed shoes leading across the hardwood floor of the
living room, toward the front door. "Photos, Ryan. Photos
of everything. But don't touch anything until Missy takes

charge of the scene. You can dust for prints after Missy has finished with the body."

At the screen of the back-kitchen door, Detective Stan Armbruster spoke. "I've got the forensics kits here, Sheriff."

Armbruster had his usual parted black hair, a ruddy complexion, and a sturdy build. He was dressed in jeans, a sport coat, white shirt and red tie. His detective's credentials case was looped into the pocket of his blue sport coat. Because his shoulder had not yet fully healed from the knife wound, he was assigned, much to his chagrin, to light forensics duty.

Robertson waved Armbruster into the kitchen. "Blood everywhere, Stan. Start by bagging her hands. First, boot your shoes outside."

Through the screen, Armbruster asked, "Missy isn't here, yet?"

Robertson frowned and shook his head. "She's still over at the Yost farm. It can't have been more than thirty minutes ago that we were talking with this woman."

Not pausing, the sheriff turned to Baker and said, "Ryan, bring Herbeck up to the front door. I want to ask her about our little problem here."

Baker exited through the back door. Soon he was ringing the front doorbell. Robertson was waiting at the door, and he opened it, but he did not open the screened door to admit Louise Herbeck. With the screen separating him from her, Robertson said, "Mrs. Herbeck. When you called our switchboard – I've just spoken to my dispatcher,

Del Markely, about this point – you said that your sister had committed suicide."

Still dabbing her handkerchief at her moist eyes, Herbeck said, "What? I mean, yes I suppose I did."

"Why did you call it a suicide, Mrs. Herbeck?"

Herbeck stammered with initial words, seeming to struggle for clarity of thought. Then she said, "Well, I suppose it was because of her note."

"Do you think your sister wrote that note?"

"Yes. Who else?"

"Anybody can write a note, Mrs. Herbeck."

"Well, can't you check the handwriting or something?" Herbeck said, frustrated. "It really looks like her handwriting to me."

"Of course, and we will. Depend on it, Mrs. Herbeck. But there's something else that troubles me."

"I don't understand."

"What did you do with the gun, Mrs. Herbeck?"

"Why, nothing. I didn't do anything with a gun."

"Did you see a gun? Take it away? Put it somewhere?"

"Why would I do that?"

"To conceal it, perhaps. You were in shock. You could have done almost anything by reflex. It's common enough. A citizen comes upon a tragedy and picks up a weapon by reflex. Without thinking. Did you do that, Mrs. Herbeck?"

"No. I wouldn't touch a gun. That was Meredith. She likes guns. I don't like guns at all. And I wouldn't touch one."

"That's the problem, Mrs. Herbeck. There is no gun in here. I've got a bullet wound in the head of your sister. I've got a suicide note. But I don't have a gun. Can you explain that?"

"No. You don't think?"

"I think you need to come in to clear this up. Maybe you'll remember something, once your thoughts are calmer. We'll just chat a bit, after you are calmer."

"I'd remember picking up a gun, Sheriff, I can promise you that."

"Still, I'd like you to come in with us to answer some questions."

"Oh, I couldn't, Sheriff. I've got calls to make. People need to know."

"They'll be time to make your calls, Mrs. Herbeck. I promise. But I'd like you to talk with us more about this, down at the jail."

Chapter 5

While Niell and Robertson were first arriving at the Silver residence, the professor had walked around the bend in the muddy Yost farm lane, to enter the barnyard from the rear of the property. He passed a tall milking barn on his right, a livestock shelter on his left, and he entered the barnyard at the back of the house.

The barnyard was covered with loose gravel, rutted by ancient iron wagon wheels and peppered with the hoofprints of the Yosts' massive Belgians. It was a space wide enough to allow a team and a long wagon to turn a complete circuit around a water well that sat in the center of the yard. The tall, long-handled iron pump on top of the water well was boxed around by a platform of rough-hewn boards, unpainted, and sitting on the platform was John Yost Junior. He was holding young Rose Yost on his lap. Junior's face was slack with sorrow, and Rose had been crying.

Branden approached slowly and bent over to address the girl. "Is this little Rose?"

Rose pulled herself in tight and pressed herself closer to Junior, hiding her face in her hands. Junior spoke a line of Dietsche to her, and she popped off his lap and ran up the back steps, into the mudroom of the house.

41

Branden took a quick moment to survey the barnyard and the buildings, reacquainting himself with the layout. Behind him and to his right stood the hay barn with its milking stalls. It had no doors. Inside, there was a wide avenue down the middle, with milking stalls to the left and antiquated iron farm implements to the right. Outside to his left sat the horse stables, with thick wood doors that rolled open and closed on wheels grooved to an overhead iron rail. Beside the stables stood an outhouse with a pit toilet.

Before him was the water well, and across the wide gravel patch, there was the back of the white clapboard house. It was two stories tall, with a basement. Long and heavy purple cloth curtains covered all the windows inside.

As little Rose disappeared into the house, Branden said to Junior, "I am sorry for your loss. I know Lydia was special to you."

Junior gave a sad nod of his head. "She was smarter than the rest of us," he said with a soft voice that was crackling with emotion. He scooped tears away from his eyes with the flats of his fingers and added, "Sometimes I wish I could have followed her, but Father says it's a sin. Our grandparents are really upset with her. The bishop has been trying to get her to come to her senses and come home."

"You know she couldn't have stayed Amish," Branden said, taking a seat beside Junior on the well's platform. He laid a hand softly on Junior's knee and then took it away before it became intrusive. "I am truly sorry for your loss, Junior. I wish there was something I could do."

42

Junior sighed. "Can you explain to five-year-old Rose what it means to be dead, Professor? Because that's what I was trying to do."

Branden shook his head ruefully. "It's a great sorrow, Junior. Does your father know?"

"I don't think so. We can't really talk to him right now."

"Then do your grandparents know? I could go across the street to them."

Junior shook his head and drew a ragged breath. "I sent Micah off again in his pony cart to tell the bishop about Aunt Lydia. Bishop Yost will take care of it. Probably before he comes here. He'll minister to Aunt Lydia's family, before he comes over here. He needs to be the one to tell her parents that she is dead."

Dottie Yost, a girl of seven years, came out of a wire hen house set off to the side of the farmhouse. Just as on the lane earlier, she was barefooted. She carried a wicker basket of brown eggs. Dressed in her long plum dress and her heavy black bonnet, she looked like a peasant maid from a bygone century. She could have been a weary orphan, a character in a Dickens novel.

Branden spoke gently to Junior. "Evening eggs? You don't collect them in the mornings?"

Junior shrugged. "The coyotes come at night."

"You have the children attending to their chores?"

"What else can they do, Professor? Sitting idle now would only make it hurt more."

The screened door slapped loudly behind Dottie, and she disappeared into the interior of the house. The professor judged that her countenance was downturned and that her eyes were dull and lifeless, as if all her memories of happiness had been washed out of her by the tragedy of her Aunt Lydia's death.

At the entrance to the milking barn, Ana, aged four and barefooted, carried out a rusty kerosene lantern that had apparently been cast aside as junk. She brought it up to Junior and asked what she should do with the kerosene that was left in the tank. Junior spoke a few instructions to her, and she carried the lantern to the side of the barn, to set it down beside another one that had a broken globe. Junior smiled at her and said, "That's right. I'll collect it later. You go inside and check on Jonas."

He rose to his feet, and said, "If you don't mind, Professor, I'd like to keep busy."

At the horse barn, a jumble of old and worn leather whips and tack lay outside on the ground, flattened and wet, suffering from long disuse. Junior scooped up the old leather and carried it to a barrel at the side of the house. On the side of the horse stables, a long exterior slat had blown off in the storm. The slat lay in the mud where it had landed. Junior picked up the slat and turned it over so that the nails that had held it in place were planted into the soil, making it safe for the moment for little feet.

At the back of the house, the edge of a double-bladed ax had been buried deep into a round chopping block. The upper blade stood up from the block like an accident waiting patiently for a victim. Junior dislodged the blade, and carried it into the milking barn, to hang it on wall pegs.

At the weedy garden beside the house, a garden rake lay in the weeds with its tines pointing up. The footprints of the children traced a path beside it, leading around the house to a trail that ran into a stand of trees. Junior took the simple precaution of turning the rake over, so that its tines were pointed downward.

With slow resolve, he came back to sit beside Branden, saying, "It doesn't really help to keep busy, Professor. I've always wished I could be like Aunt Lydia. That's what's going on with these whiskers. I haven't joined the church yet, and I can wear my beard any way I like. Aunt Lydia thought it was perfect. She is a nonconformist. She *was* a nonconformist. When I do join the church, I'll have to conform."

Junior Yost's blonde whiskers were a thin line, carefully trimmed to take a sharp bend at the base of his jaw. The fancy beard came forward on a narrow line and widened at the corners of his mouth into a mustache and a pointed chin patch. It made a statement. It was the Rumschpringe statement of a young man who had not yet taken his vows. He sighed and stroked his fingers over his rakish beard. "I'm to be married in the Fall, Professor. I'll have to wear a *proper* beard, then."

Little Dottie came out of the house again with a red plastic pail nearly as big as herself. She climbed up onto the boarded platform covering the water well, and she began to work the iron pump handle up and down. Branden stood up to give her room to work. Junior held to his place. Soon Dottie had water gushing out of the spigot into her pail, and once it was full, she bent her knees, took a firm grip on the metal loop, lifted it down off the platform with a grunt, and set it down on the gravel. Then she jumped down off the platform and struggled back toward the house with the full pail of water, spilling some water onto her plum dress and bare feet with each step that she took.

The professor walked over to her and asked, "Can I help with that?"

Dottie shook her head emphatically. "This is one of *my* chores."

Back at the well, Branden addressed Junior again. "I'm sorry, Junior. I've been a bit out of it. Did you say your father isn't well?"

Junior didn't answer. He couldn't. He was weeping, with his face buried in his hands. Branden lifted him to his feet and embraced him. The professor's own tears began to flow, and together they stood arm in arm beside the well, crying out sorrow for Junior's loss. For the professor's loss. For the loss of Lydia.

Junior shuddered in Branden's arms, then released the professor and dropped back onto the well's platform. Branden sat beside him, saying, "I'm sorry, Junior. I am truly sorry. What can I do? Tell me what I can do."

Junior tried for a brave smile, but he could not quite manage it. He shook his head. "Lydia was more like a sister to me, than an aunt."

"I know," Branden said. "I know. But can you tell me again about your father?"

"Die Maemme told us," Junior stammered, "not to bother him when he gets like this. We just do our chores. He's been so sad, lately."

"Is your mother really gone? What? Visiting relatives?"

Junior shrugged. "She left us. Three weeks ago, with little Esther."

"I don't understand."

"She ran off, Father says, but he's depressed. He's sad all the time, now. She couldn't take it anymore, I guess. Anyway, she's been gone for three weeks. I've been trying to hold the family together."

"What has your father been doing?"

"Sitting inside, in his corner. He always sits in his corner. But he's got his shotgun, today."

"What?" Branden said, popping up and taking a hasty step toward the back door. He turned back to Junior. "Where is he?"

"He's sitting in the corner. In the living room, with his shotgun again."

Branden spun and hurried to the back door. He climbed the steps, pulled the screened door open and crossed the mudroom into the kitchen. He passed the long pinewood kitchen table, and he hurried forward into the living room.

All the drapes were drawn. The room was dark. Branden advanced to the woodstove in the center of the room, and dimly in the corner, he saw John Yost in a wicker rocker. The butt plate of a double-barreled shotgun was planted on the floor, and Yost had his boney fingers wrapped around the barrels. The muzzles rested under his whiskers, up against his chin. Yost put his eyes slowly up to Branden, and Branden saw the unmistakable signs of anxiety and depression. Eyes half-closed, with drooping lids. A furled brow casting out the signs of a jumble of troubled thoughts. His mouth downturned with a seemingly unrelenting sadness. Fingers of his left-hand trembling on the barrels of the shotgun. Fingers of his right-hand fumbling inside the trigger guard.

"Go away," Yost said gruffly.

"Mr. Yost. John. What are you doing here?"

"Get out!" Yost shouted, rising half-way onto his feet and dropping back down onto the rocker.

"Let me just talk with you, John," Branden said, being careful not to move.

"She left me!"

"I know. I've just now realized that. I would have come sooner."

"You're too late, Professor. Yes. I remember you. I remember what you did to Lydia. Her parents have never gotten over it, and you're to blame. She left us for college, and you are to blame for it."

"Can you please take that shotgun out from under your chin?"

"Why? My wife's gone now, too. Esther's gone. Everything is darkness and sorrow. There's nothing left for me."

"Your family is here, Mr. Yost. Think of the children."

"They have no mother. I have no wife. No hope."

"Perhaps you are wrong," Branden said. "Think that you might be wrong."

Yost closed his eyes and sighed. He opened his eyes again and asked, "What do you want?"

"I want you to put your shotgun down."

"Can't."

"You just wait, John," Branden said, backing slowly away. "I'm going to use my phone."

In the kitchen, on the other side of the long table, while still watching Yost, the professor called the sheriff's cell phone. When Robertson answered, Branden said, "I need you urgently at the Yost farm."

"Mike?"

"At the Yost farm, Sheriff. Inside. I need you to get over here. John Yost is threatening to kill himself."

Chapter 6

Sheriff Robertson, sitting on a kitchen chair that he had set beside the Yosts' wood stove, in the center of the dim living room, got his first-ever look at John Yost Senior.

Yost's gray hair was long past his ears, and it was in a disheveled, fly-away condition. His long chin whiskers hung straight down onto his chest. To Robertson, they looked thinned out, rather than bushy, as if the man had been plucking nervously at his beard for the last several weeks. Above his lips, Yost had an unusual stubble, where typically an Amish man would have been diligent to shave himself smooth. His eyes carried a hollow aspect, showing a mind cast elsewhere. Or it was a mind turned too far inward, staring at a tumble of disconcerting thoughts. Yost's was a troubled mind, to be sure. Robertson saw obvious signs of depression and personal neglect. And under Yost's chin, the black muzzles of the double-barreled shotgun were still parked.

Yost's fingers on his left hand were clenched tightly, now, around the barrels. The fingers of his right hand were fidgeting with the two triggers. The stock was closed on the two breaches, the sheriff noticed, and the hammers were cocked back ready to fire.

Without turning around to Branden, Robertson spoke softly. "Mike, take the children out of the house, please."

Branden acknowledged that saying, "Sheriff," and he began to back out of the room, wondering how he'd be able to gather the children in time. But as he turned, behind him he saw that all the children, youngest to oldest, were clustered in the corner opposite to their father.

Branden stopped to address the sheriff. "Should I get Ricky Niell, Bruce?" he asked. "Maybe Pat Lance, too? I mean, who's at Silver's place, still? And who's available?"

"Call Lance and Niell," the sheriff said. "And Evie Carson. She'll know how to talk with Mr. Yost, here."

"Alice Shewmon, too." Branden said. "For the children, at least until the bishop arrives."

"OK, but don't bring her inside. She can make her arrangements outside. Is there still some light?"

"Some, Sheriff. A little."

"I've sort of lost track of the time."

"It's only maybe eight o'clock."

"Can you get them something to eat?" Robertson asked, and then abruptly he barked at Yost, "No! Don't do any more of that, Mr. Yost! Take your fingers off those triggers."

"I'll hurry," Branden said, and Robertson answered with a flip, "You think, Mike?"

Branden got the children turned and started back through the kitchen when he heard the Sheriff whispering his name again, "Professor?"

51

Branden turned back into the room and saw that Yost had his mouth stretched over the muzzles of his shotgun. For his part, the sheriff had his suit pulled back on his right side, with his hand parked on the grip of his small revolver.

Louder and rather sternly, the sheriff said to Yost, "If you are going to kill yourself, Mr. Yost, it would be pointless for me to shoot you. Right? I can't stop a suicide by using my gun."

Slowly Yost brought the barrels of his shotgun back below his chin. There was wretchedness in his eyes, as well as resignation. Tears began to flow down his cheeks.

"Just you wait," Robertson said to Yost. "You wait for my people. My best people. Evie Carson is a good talker. You can talk with her. I'm not really too good at this. It won't hurt any to wait, and then talk a little bit with Evie. And Alice Shewmon is good with children. She knows how to take care of children. You won't have to worry about them, Mr. Yost. And your bishop is coming. So, you just hold on a minute, here. You just wait, John."

A scratchy couple of words issued from Yost's thin lips. "Left me. Took little Esther. Three weeks. Pregnant again."

"OK," Robertson said, reaching out an open hand. "We can fix this. This is something we can help you to fix."

Yost shook his head with an emphatic 'No.'

Robertson eased forward on the seat of his kitchen chair. "We're going to find them, Mr. Yost. Your wife and

52

your little daughter. Then, don't you think little Esther is going to need her father?"

Tears spilled profusely out of Yost's eyes. Unrelenting sorrow seized his features. His face twisted like Edvard Munch's painting *The Scream*.

"The other children need their father, too," Robertson continued.

Yost shook his head 'no' again and said, "Need their mother."

"Their father, too, Mr. Yost. What does the bible say? Don't you remember? '*A man who will not provide for his family is worse than an infidel.*' They need you to stay here, to provide for them.*"*

Yost pulled his hand slowly off the triggers and raised a fist to rap his knuckles on his skull. "It's always so dark in here," he said, and he reached down again for the triggers. "I can't stand it any longer."

Softly, Robertson asked over his shoulder, "Mike? You still here?"

From the back of the kitchen, Branden said, "Kids are outside. I'm going to make those calls."

"Stay outside with the children."

"I'm fine right here, Sheriff."

"What good are you going to do from there, Professor? Really, what good? If he pulls those triggers, you won't have been able to stop anything."

Chapter 7

When Ricky Niell pulled his cruiser into the
barnyard, the professor had the Yost children gathered
beside the water pump. Niell, wearing high-topped leather
work boots, climbed out from behind the wheel and said to
Detective Pat Lance, "See what I mean about the mud?"

Pat Lance got out on the passenger's side. As she
stood up straight beside the sedan, she slipped a little in the
mud and remarked sincerely to Niell, "Thanks for the
warning, Ricky." She came forward in her own pair of
work boots, catching her balance against the front fender of
the cruiser.

Niell said to her, "The footing is better over here. On
the gravel."

From the back seat of the cruiser, Dr. Evelyn White
Carson stepped forward in a plain blouse with a modest
collar, and a pleated dress of conservative length. She, too,
was wearing leather boots. She approached the professor
and asked, "A Schwartzentruber father?" and Branden
answered, "Inside through the kitchen and back to the stove
room. The sheriff is still there. He's gonna be happy to see
you."

Dr. Carson nodded purposefully and turned for the
back door. She was a psychiatrist who had helped years ago
with the Martha Lehman case, and more recently with

Darba Winters. Her skill as an analyst had caused Robertson to trust her increasingly with delicate negotiations, such as one a month ago when she had talked an armed suspect out of his house without injury to his wife and daughter, who had been held captive for seven hours.

Carson paused in front of the screened door to look back at the professor. "A shotgun?" she asked, and Branden nodded.

"So, a vest really wouldn't help much," Carson said with a thin and anxious smile.

Ricky said, "Anyway, I have a vest in the trunk if you want it, Evie."

Carson shrugged and came back down the porch steps to the gravel. Ricky returned to his cruiser, brought back a vest, and he helped Carson strap herself into it.

Carson was a short woman with a round aspect to her build, and Niell adjusted the Velcro straps for her. It was a large and thick vest, with collars that wrapped up to surround Carson's neck. She looked like a member of a bomb disposal squad. She pulled her shoulder-length gray hair out from under the back collar of the vest, and she went inside the house. While she was still on the back porch, Branden came up to the door and called to her through the screen. "Make a right turn into a long kitchen, Evie. Go straight back from there, past a dining table, and into the sitting room. Robertson is at the wood stove, facing Mr. Yost, and Yost is seated in the far corner. It's a big room, so stay back at first. At least until you've assessed the danger."

Arching a brow, Carson nodded and turned into the kitchen.

Outside, Pat Lance and Ricky Niell got busy at the water pump, rinsing the caked mud from the feet of the five younger children. Once finished, they had each of them sit on the edge of the well's platform, with their feet hanging over to dry in the warm evening air. They were lined up as if for a photo shoot for something like *Ohio* Magazine, the boys in matching blue denim outfits and straw hats, and the girls in their plum dresses and black bonnets.

Junior stood back to watch with silent curiosity. He smiled sardonically and said, "It's just mud. Are they going to have to sit there all night? They have beds inside, you know. They're going to have to walk there, and their feet will just get muddy again."

The professor thought he heard a note of disdain in Junior's voice. It was an assertive note that was no longer just simply sad and mournful.

Detective Lance, with her hair quite blonde and grown out considerably longer than usual, turned to Junior with a smile on her round Germanic face, and she said, "A social worker is coming out, Mr. Yost. She's bringing a van. A small camper van. So, I just thought we'd clean them up for her."

With mild antipathy, mixed with a bit of wariness in his tone, Junior said, "We don't really need a social worker. The bishop is coming, and our grandparents live just across the road. We can take care of ourselves."

Lance didn't argue. Alice Shewmon would handle the assessment, once she had arrived. To Ricky, Lance said, "Any idea when you expect Alice?"

Ricky pointed down the long driveway, where a high-domed camper van was approaching. "She's here now," Ricky said. "She was supposed to bring a nurse, too."

Stepping forward briskly, Junior spoke with greater intensity. "We don't *need a nurse* here. We can take care of ourselves."

Detectives Lance and Niell gave him voiceless stares. Junior backed away and stood apart from his brothers and sisters, brooding. Despite his affected self-assurance, he looked conflicted. Confused. Unsure. The professor tried to engage him, but Junior would have nothing to say.

Still back somewhat on the lane, Alice Shewmon parked her camper van, climbed down from the driver's seat, and trudged forward in the mud. Once she had reached the gravel patch, she stopped and asked, "The father's still inside?"

Ricky answered, "With Robertson and Carson."

"Schwartzentrubers, right?" Shewmon said.

"Yes," said Niell.

"These all the kids?" Shewmon asked further, all business and rather too brusquely.

Lance said, "Yes, these five plus the older one here. John Junior."

Ricky Niell turned and addressed Junior. "Let us help here, Junior. You can see for yourself. We're here to help. I hope you'll let us help."

Junior tipped his head and shrugged his shoulders. "As long as we all stay right here," he said, acquiescing for the moment. "I have to take charge here. Father's in no condition, and I have to be strong for the family."

"Then I'll pull the camper up here," Shewmon said. "We can get them inside, before it gets too chilly. And I have chairs, beds and food. Do you kids like pizza?"

The five younger children sitting on the platform stared back at Shewmon as if she had spoken gibberish. Shewmon shrugged her shoulders, smiled and pulled reflexively at her long black ponytail. Again, she said to Pat and Ricky, "I'll just pull the van up here." To Ricky she protested, "You could have warned me that there was so much mud."

As Shewmon trudged back to her camper, Niell tried speaking to the children. "Ms. Shewmon is here to help you. Are you hungry?"

The smallest girl, about four years old, asked, "Is she a Maemme?"

Niell smiled. "No, but she likes children very much."

The older boy Micah asked, "Is she here to arrest us? Father says the sheriffs come to arrest people. And you can't do that. The bishop is coming. He'll tell you, sure enough."

Niell shook his head. "No, not at all. Ms. Shewmon is here to make sure you have a good place to stay, tonight. To make sure that you are all well, and maybe to fix you some supper."

Little Dottie said, "Die Maemme cooks for us. She's gone now."

"I know," Ricky said, sitting beside the girl on the platform. "Ms. Shewmon has a camper. You can go inside. She has a stove and a refrigerator. And a nice bathroom. Would you like to see inside it?"

The four-year-old Ana spoke with surprise. "A bathroom in a car?"

"Yes," Niell answered. "Ms. Shewmon wants to make sure that you are well. She brought a nurse from the hospital. You can just sit inside for a bit. You'll like it. Here it is, now."

As Shewmon pulled her Holmes County Social Services van up beside the well, a male nurse in a white waistcoat opened the side door of the van and dropped the folding steps down to the gravel. Niell lifted the smallest boy Jonas up to him.

Rose stood up on the water well's rough platform, and Lance took her under her little arms and lifted her inside, too. The other children followed, and even Junior came over to peer inside. To Niell, Junior seemed to have softened his attitude. He seemed, perhaps, to have become somewhat encouraged.

Junior stood outside to put his head inside the van and said to no one in particular, commenting as if he were agreeable, "They probably need a good meal. Die Maemme has been gone a long time, for children so young as these."

More sternly, though, Junior stepped back from the door of the van and said to Niell and Lance, "But there is no chance at all that your Social Services lady is going to take any of them away from our home. If my father causes trouble in there, we'll all go across the road to our grandparents. The bishop will never let you take us into your city."

"That's not our plan," Lance said to Junior.

Junior grumbled, shook his head, and made an argumentative frown. "I know what Social Services people do. Our preachers have told us all about it. How your government splits up families. How you put children into city homes with strangers. No matter what my father does, you are not going to do that to us."

The professor drew him aside and said, "They are here to help, Junior. We don't want to split up your family. But your father is in there with a shotgun, and we can't just leave you alone. Do you understand? Please, Junior. Try to understand. Whatever happens with your father, you'll all spend the night with your grandparents."

Junior nodded, lifted his straw hat and scratched at his head. "Father is not well. So, I have to be strong, here. That's all I am trying to do. Just be strong for my family."

A clatter of buggy wheels and hoof falls on gravel sounded from the barnyard behind Shewmon's Social Services van, and a black buggy came around the van and pulled to a stop beside the well's platform. A very large Amish man in black denim and a black felt hat climbed down from the seat, speaking authoritatively to Niell as he advanced. "I am Bishop Alva Yost. I want to see the children. I want to see John Yost. And I want to know what is going on here."

- - - - - - - - - - - - - -

Once he had satisfied himself that the children in the van were being cared for properly, the bishop followed Detective Lance into the house. Lance proceeded as far as the end of the dining table, and there she stopped. The bishop dropped his black hat on the dining table, walked directly into the sitting room, and knelt beside John Yost in the far corner.

John seemed not to notice the bishop's arrival. His eyes were closed. His cheeks were laced with tears. With his fingers still poised on the triggers, he had slumped a little, so that the barrels of his shotgun were pushing more firmly into his jaw line. The bishop tried speaking to Yost, using the sect's dialect, something near to the father-tongue German, but unique to Holmes County and unique as well to the people of his congregation. Another Amish person would have understood the majority of it, but it was a language unknown to both the sheriff and Evie Carson. The sheriff was still seated with his back to the wood stove, facing Yost in his corner. Carson had brought in a kitchen chair to sit a bit off to Robertson's right, closer to Yost. John Yost did not answer his bishop, and he did not open his eyes. He did however sit up a bit straighter, seeming at last to take note of the bishop's presence.

Alva Yost stood up beside John and turned back to address Robertson and Carson. "I am John's brother. I'm the Bishop in our congregation. I've told him that this is forbidden by the Word of God, but as you can see, he is stubborn."

Evelyn Carson said, "I am a psychiatrist, Bishop Yost. I think I was making some progress here. Please let me continue."

The bishop said, "We are not in the habit of using English doctors."

Carson responded. "I think he has been depressed for a very long time, Bishop Yost. Perhaps it is time you tried a new approach."

"I have been working with him for years," Alva said. "We pray. We counsel with the preachers and deacons. I've sat for hours with him, when he sinks into one of these spells. I have tried everything that I can think to try. We've had a long run of miserable years with this problem."

"Then let me have a little more time with him," Carson said. "I won't use anything but a little more time."

Bishop Yost took a step away from John, and he waved a 'go ahead' to Carson, saying, "If you can help, then, well, I hope you can. He has suffered long enough. His wife and children, too. The strain falls to them, too, you know. Of course you know. But if you can help? Well, I'd be grateful. We've tried everything we can think to try. He can't seem to break free from the sadness."

Evie nodded and spoke to John in the far corner. "Mr. Yost," she said. "John. Can you imagine anything worse than the torture you are in right now?"

Bishop Yost stepped suddenly forward, demanding, "What type of question is that?"

"Please, Mr. Yost. Bishop Yost. John and I have already been talking about this. I'm trying to take him to a place he can recognize. Right now, he doesn't register even to where he is. His mind can't process any way out of his depression. I need to reach him with something that he can relate to. I need him to catch just a glimpse of the kind of pain he will cause, if he kills himself here. Then maybe I can reach him. Please trust me with this. Can you do that?"

The bishop gave a hesitant nod, and Evie Carson said again to John, "Mr. Yost. John. Can you imagine anything worse than how you feel right now?"

Yost opened his eyes to stare down at his feet.

Carson sighed and glanced a hopeful but thin smile back to the sheriff. She appeared to consider that she had won a small victory. Then she said, "Mr. Yost. John. There is a pain and a sorrow that is worse than what you have now. It is worse than what you are suffering now, and it is a suffering that lasts a lifetime. Can you imagine what that is? Can you name it? We've already discussed this. Let your mind imagine it. Even in the middle of your sorrow, answer honestly. Let your mind answer that question. Can you imagine a sorrow worse than yours?"

Tears again appeared in John Yost's eyes. With a scarcely audible whisper, he said, "Children."

A wider smile appeared on Carson's face. "What about the children, John? You know it better than anyone. What will happen to your children if you kill yourself tonight?"

A stuttering breath pumped into Yost, and he screwed his shoulders back and forth as if writhing in pain.

Carson pressed forward. "You see it, don't you, John. If you kill yourself, your children will carry the sorrow of it for the rest of their lives. They will forever wonder what they could have done to have stopped you. They will carry the guilt of your suicide as if they had sinned themselves. As if they had pulled those triggers themselves. They will never escape it. Your sorrow, ten times worse, will pester them everywhere they go, for the rest of their lives. This will ruin their lives. It will invade everything that they should normally be able to enjoy. At their weddings. At the births of their children. They will always chastise themselves for your absence. They will carry guilt and sorrow into everything they do and think and say. Can you imagine it, John? This will be their lot, if you take yourself out of their lives tonight."

John's hands began to tremble. His shoulders hunched forward, and he pressed his chin down onto the muzzles. He looked directly at Evelyn Carson, and out of a deep and hopeless cavern, his eyes focused for the first time that evening on something other than the turmoil of his interior pain. "It is hopeless," he said to Carson.

"I can help you, John," Carson pleaded. "I know just what you need. I know how to fix this. You don't have to be

64

this way anymore. You don't have to carry the weight. It's heavy, right? It's a heavy burden to feel this way all the time. It's exhausting. But I know how to help you. Your life does not need to be so relentlessly sorrowful."

John Yost blinked his eyes. He drew a deep breath and sighed it out through pursed lips. He pulled his fingers away from the triggers, and he wiped tears from his cheeks with the flats of his fingers. Then he released the shotgun, and it bounced down onto the hardwood floor.

Alva Yost rushed immediately up to his brother, and he pulled him up from his chair. He wrapped his massive arms around his thin and frail brother, and he rocked on his feet, as if soothing a child.

Robertson picked up the shotgun and sprung the chambers open. He extracted the shells and placed them into the pocket of his suitcoat. The shotgun he stood in the corner, far away from John Yost. Then he crossed through the kitchen to stand on the back porch.

There he spoke out through the screens to Lance and Niell, "I need you inside, now. We're going to try to walk Mr. Yost out to your car. He's weak, and he's disoriented. He's depressed like you wouldn't believe. I don't expect any trouble, but I want each of you to take one of his arms and walk out beside him. He's not a heavy man, but he might resist or collapse to his knees with the strain of this. So, take firm grips on his arms, and let's walk him out to the cruiser. Let's try to get him into the village, to the hospital."

Chapter 8

On the farm lane, once he had his cruiser turned around, Ricky drove out to TR 606, heading back to the village of Millersburg. He had Evelyn Carson in the passenger's seat, and Pat Lance watching over John Yost in the back seat. Yost hadn't said anything intelligible after he had dropped his shotgun, but as Ricky drove, Yost was crying softly and muttering and groaning. He seemed to be engaged in a conversation with his mind, responding to a moiling of unhappy thoughts and emotions. His face was stretching into a variety of expressions, as if he were arguing and pleading with tormentors he could actually see.

As the cruiser rolled slowly out toward the road, Sheriff Robertson and Professor Branden stepped up into Alice Shewmon's camper van. The children were crowded onto the thin cushions of a U-shaped bench that embraced a small, rectangular dining table. They were silently and intently finishing the last of a thin-crusted pizza. To the side, Alice Shewmon stood in front of a microwave oven that was stacked on top of a small refrigerator, and she was watching the timer digits on the oven. After a glance back, she addressed the men, saying, "That's their second pizza, Sheriff."

The timer gave a soft ding, and Alice withdrew a third pizza from the oven. She used oven mitts to place it on a round tray on the table. "Careful," she said to the children. "It'll be hot."

The kids didn't wait. They each levered a slice out of the pie and started eating. It really did prove too hot for some of them, and two kids dropped their slices back onto the tray. The other three blew on their slices and then began to eat anyway.

"Hungry," Alice commented to Robertson and Branden. "Never had pizza before."

"Are they OK?" Robertson asked. "I mean physically."

Alice nodded and smiled. The nurse in the white waistcoat stood up from a small couch at the back of the camper and said, "They're fine, Sheriff. Maybe a little bit too hungry, but physically they are fine. They've been neglected, but they really are fine."

"Can you drive them over to their grandparents?" Robertson asked. "After they've had enough to eat?"

Shewmon said, "Certainly. But I'll want to stay there for a bit. I'll have to explain it all to them."

Robertson said, "Good. Thanks, Alice. Ricky has just left. They're taking John to Pomerene Hospital. Evie will probably ask that he be admitted for observation."

"I'll tell them," Alice said.

Robertson and Branden climbed down out of the camper. The bishop met them in the barnyard. He had his black hat on again, and he was standing beside his buggy. To the men he said, "Junior is going to stay here. I want him to start getting this place cleaned up. Everything has been neglected. I'm going to organize the congregation to help him with the crops and the livestock. The children will have to clean up around the house and barns. I heard your social services lady say that she's going to take them over to Mose and Ida's place. That's fine, but they'll have to come back here tomorrow to help with their chores."

"Thank you," Robertson said, walking up to the imposing Amish man.

Alva Yost was a surpassingly large man. He was larger and certainly taller even than the sheriff, who was widely regarded as the largest, gruffest man in Holmes County. But rather than being simply over-weight like the round sheriff, Alva Yost was built with ponderous strength. He was not only wide in the shoulders, but also unusually tall. If Robertson could hope, in a decent pair of shoes, to stand an even six feet tall, then he figured Alva rose easily to six-five. His chest and torso were so large that Robertson suspected he would be squeezed uncomfortably in even a 4x shirt. But with all of that, he wasn't fat or round or puffy. He was as solid as chiseled stone and as confident in his strength as a seasoned lumberjack. He had a powerful personal bearing in front of the sheriff, and he appeared to be supremely confident in his stature as a Bishop.

For the first time in years, the sheriff felt anxiously small in front of another man. He said to Alva, "Forgive me, Mr. Yost, but you are not built anything like your brother John."

Alva smiled. "We have different mothers. Our father was widowed when I was born. He married again, and a year later, John was born."

"Then it's no surprise, I guess," the sheriff said. "Are you headed into Millersburg?"

"No," Alva said. "I'm going over to Mose and Ida's. To see about getting the children settled there for the night. Three of them have school tomorrow. And Mose and Ida's family needs careful attention, now. They are devastated that their daughter Lydia has died, and they are still worried about Mary and little Esther."

"They'll all want to know about John," Branden said. "I'm sure they'll be surprised that he's been taken to a hospital."

"He's troubled," Alva said. "The children know that as well as anyone."

'No," Branden said. "Surprised, I mean, that you've sent him to the doctors in town. I gather that you don't usually make use of city doctors. I know how most Schwartzentrubers think about this. But you're the bishop, right? So, you can make that decision."

"Well, yes," Alva said, stroking his chin whiskers. "The whole congregation will be surprised by this. I'll have the deacons visit around, tonight and tomorrow, to explain this to the people. Then they will accept this as my choice. I'll have them tell everyone about Lydia's death, too."

"Then I think you made the right decision for John and his family," the professor said. "I think it's the right decision for the whole family. Especially since their mother has left. You haven't had much to say about that."

"It's a church matter," Alva said, standing a bit stiffer. "We have got to convince Mary to come home. This is her place, beside her husband and with her children. I think she has gotten herself talked into something that she will regret."

Before Branden could respond to that, Alice Shewmon called from the driver's window of the camper. "We're leaving now, Sheriff. Headed across the street."

Robertson gave a wave.

"Is that your Crown Vic out by the road?" Alice asked. "I can take you out to it."

Robertson nodded. "I had it towed out of the mud." He turned to Alva Yost. "Can you drive us out in your buggy, Bishop Yost?"

The bishop nodded, and Robertson turned back to Alice. "We'll get a ride with the bishop."

The engine started on the camper, and soon Shewmon had it pulled in a wide circle around the water well to head back out to the road. Bishop Yost watched it leave, and he said, "I understand those have stoves and refrigerators."

"They do," Branden said.

Robertson said, "They gave the children something to eat."

"I heard," Alva said. "Pizza. I was listening a bit at the side window."

"You are trusting a lot of English people, today," Branden said. "That's maybe a little bit out of the ordinary. Has it really been that bad here for your brother?"

Alva lifted a brow. "We've tried everything we can think of."

Branden took a step forward and held out his hand. "We haven't been introduced, Bishop Yost. I am Professor Michael Branden. I teach history at the college in Millersburg."

Yost took the professor's hand. "I assumed you were a sheriff, too. A deputy."

"A reserve deputy," Branden answered. "But I was also Lydia Schwartz's teacher at the college."

"Then you are the one who gave Lydia that scholarship."

"Yes."

"That wasn't very helpful, Professor. Really, I didn't appreciate that much at all. We had hoped that Lydia would join the church. Take her vows. Marry within the congregation. Raise an Amish family."

"I know," Branden said. "No disrespect, but that was never going to be enough for Lydia."

Alva answered somewhat resentfully. "We'll never know, will we. She was my responsibility, Professor. She fell away, and that is my responsibility. Now it's too late for her. She can never come home."

Branden said, "A lot has happened today, Bishop Yost. You can't take responsibility for all of it."

"I am their Bishop," Alva said forcefully. "It *is* my responsibility. They are all my responsibilities. The souls in my church. I am charged by God to safeguard the souls of my congregation, and for Lydia, I have failed. I may also have failed for Mary. We won't know until we have found her. *If* we find her. So please. Don't try to tell me what my responsibilities are. I know them well enough. They are a constant and terrifying burden for me. They would be for any Bishop – to safeguard the souls of so many people. It is the burden of a lifetime, and it is mine alone to bear. When one like Lydia falls away, it is my responsibility, and no one else's."

Alva studied the professor's eyes intently, and then as if he had exhausted himself, he turned to Robertson and spoke softly. "Sheriff, it's time I got across the street to the children. I can give you a ride out to your car, if you still want it."

- - - - - - - - - - - - - -

In Mt. Hope, the sheriff stopped behind the livestock auction barn, and Branden used a hose there to rinse mud off the tires and out of the brakes of the Crown Vic. They bought bottles of water from a machine in front of the new sporting goods store, and as Robertson was driving back to Millersburg along winding SR 241, he said to Branden, "My phone."

Branden answered, "What?" seeming distracted.

Robertson pulled his cell phone. "I've had it on mute. Check for messages. Calls."

Branden took the phone and clicked in. "What's your keycode?"

"Sherif, with one f."

"You're kidding."

"Just check the messages, Mike, OK?"

Branden chuckled, touched in the passcode and said, "Four messages. Three are from Del Markely at the jail. The fourth one is from a strange number."

"Play that one."

Branden used speaker phone mode. The message came from a woman, with the considerable background noise of a collection of chattering voices.

Sheriff Robertson? This is Mary Yost. I need to speak with you about my husband. I think he's dangerous. And Bishops can't be right about everything. I know that, now. I'm worried about the children, but I can't live there anymore. I'll call again. You have to understand. You know how John is. I just can't live there anymore.

The sheriff said, "Call that number back, Mike. Maybe you can still talk with her."

Branden took off the speaker phone mode and punched in the call. It rang twice, and a young-sounding girl said, "Applebees. Reservations?"

"No," Branden said. "I need to know if the woman who used this phone recently is still there. An Amish woman. I need to speak with her. She might have a little girl with her."

"My shift just started," the girl said. "I'm on the night crew. There are only a few customers here, and nobody looks Amish to me. But this is the bar phone. It's the one a customer might use, if they didn't have their own cell phone."

"Can you get your manager?" Branden asked.

"I *am* the manager. But I can tell you that there isn't an Amish woman still here."

"Does anyone know who made the call? Someone who might have been there earlier?"

"Wait. I'll ask the bartender."

Branden heard muffled voices and then a little thump as someone picked up the bar phone receiver. A man spoke. "When? About an hour ago?"

"Yes, an Amish woman placed a call to Sheriff Bruce Robertson, in Holmes County."

"Sheriff?"

"Yes," Branden said. "We need to speak with her. Did you see anyone like that make a call from there?"

"I didn't see any Amish people," the bartender said. "Sorry, but it gets busy here at the bar."

"Which Applebees is this?"

"Wooster."

"Well," Branden said, "at least that's not too far away."

When he handed the phone back to the sheriff, Branden said, "She called from the Applebees in Wooster. There's nobody there who remembers her."

"We need her to call us back," Robertson said.

"I hope she does," Branden said, and he slapped the beats of an anxious rhythm onto his knees.

"What?" Robertson asked.

"Something the bishop said about Mary Yost. It bothers me. *I think she has gotten herself talked into something that she will regret.*"

Chapter 9

In the observation room between Interview A and Interview B, at Millersburg's red brick jail, Sheriff Robertson and Detective Stan Armbruster stood watching in on Louise Herbeck, through the glass of a one-way mirror. She had eaten a couple slices of pizza, and she was nursing a cup of coffee. She sat alone in her stocking feet, because Armbruster had asked for her shoes for a luminol test. She had not protested.

Robertson asked, "The Luminol, Stan?"

"No blood."

"So, she didn't track that blood across Silver's floor."

"No, Sheriff."

"Where are her shoes?"

"Just out there, right in the hall. You can take them in to her."

"You look like your shoulder is still bothering you."

"It's not, Sheriff. I can get back to detective work. I'm ready."

Robertson shook his head with a consoling smile. "Not until the doctors and psychiatrists clear you, Stan. Until then, you're attached to Missy's forensics team."

Stan grew heated. "Sheriff, that's not fair. You were wounded in that hotel fight, too."

"Just my face, Armbruster. You've only just now started getting full range of motion out of your shoulder."

Armbruster snorted disrespectfully. "You've got to know that your beard doesn't really cover the scar, Sheriff."

"I'll let that pass."

"It's frustrating, hanging around the labs. The morgue. Pat thinks I'm ready. And she knows me better than anyone."

"I'm gonna wait, Stan. Maybe in a couple of months."

Armbruster grumbled deep in his throat, and he turned and stepped out of the room, saying, "Please don't start with Herbeck until I can get back here. I need a Pepsi."

Robertson nodded and turned to face the glass. He studied Herbeck and waited for Armbruster to return. When Armbruster entered the room again, Robertson took Herbeck's shoes from him, and then he crossed over to Herbeck's room, closing the door to Interview A behind him. He sat down across the table from Herbeck and set her shoes on the tabletop. She took them and slipped them on and held up her empty coffee cup. Robertson looked a glance over to the mirror, and soon Stan was coming through the door with another cup of coffee. After she had sipped at it, Robertson began his interview.

"You see the problem, don't you Louise?" Robertson said. "I've got a woman shot dead, and there is not a gun at the scene."

Calmly, Louise said, "I can't explain that, Sheriff. I don't know anything about guns."

"Did you bring a gun to her house?"

"I don't own a gun."

"Why did you go there at that specific time?"

"I was just dropping by. Meredith told me this morning that she had some clothes for me to sell."

"Do you have them?"

"Of course not," Louise protested. "I found her dead!"

"Take it easy, Mrs. Herbeck. We're just talking."

"You seem to think I had something to do with this, Sheriff. How am I supposed to *take it easy*?"

"I'm just trying to establish the facts, Mrs. Herbeck. Please, I have just a few questions."

Louise smiled thinly and gave a small nod of her head.

Robertson said, "Thanks, now where were you standing when you called 911?"

"In the kitchen."

"Next to the body?"

"Not really. Not close, really. I never got that far in. I was at the kitchen table, I think. I had read her note."

"Did you touch the note, Louise?" Robertson asked.

"No."

"Well, we know that there are two sets of prints on the note. If one of them is yours, we'll know soon enough."

Louise stammered. "Maybe I did touch it. How can you expect me to remember? Really, Sheriff, this is too much."

Robertson nodded to acknowledge her point, and to dispel some of the tension. Louise appeared to relax. She sipped again at her coffee, seeming to be satisfied with herself.

Next, Robertson asked, "How far into the house did you go, Louise?"

"Just to the kitchen table. That was far enough. I could see her lying there. I didn't go over to her."

"Well," Robertson said, "someone tracked blood into the living room."

"It wasn't me," Louise said. "I didn't get that close to her. I didn't go into the living room."

Robertson said, "As you know, we tested your shoes. There's no blood on the soles."

"Then why did you even ask me?" Louise complained.

"Mrs. Herbeck, I have to ask these questions. You'd want me to, if I were talking to your sister's murderer."

"Murder?"

"Yes. Otherwise the gun would still be there."

Louise puzzled over the implications of that and sighed heavily. "Are we almost done?"

"Not quite. What is your financial situation, Mrs. Herbeck?"

"I was a grade schoolteacher, Sheriff. I've always needed money."

"And did Meredith help you with that?"

"Yes. Like I said. She called me this morning and said she had some clothes for me to sell at a second-hand store. She would help me like that, from time to time."

"And that's why you went over to her house?"

"I've already told you that."

Robertson nodded again to acknowledge the fact. "I'm told you live in a rented trailer over on Harrison Road."

"So?"

"That can't be very pleasant. Your sister had a very nice ranch house."

"What? Like I'm jealous or something?"

"Are you?"

"No! It's insulting. She was my *sister*."

"Maybe you're rich, now, Louise. What do you know about Meredith's finances?"

"She had money. She had her husband's trucker's pension, and she owned her house."

"She was better off than you."

"Yes. It doesn't mean that I killed her."

"What do you know about her will?"

"What?"

"We found Meredith's will in a desk drawer at her house. She's left everything to you."

"What? I don't . . . . What are you saying? That I killed her for her *money*?"

"Or for her house."

Herbeck stared back at Robertson. Her face took a pink flush. Her fingernails started tapping on the wood of the tabletop. Her eyes narrowed with a thought, and she asked, "Am I a suspect?"

"Not really."

"Do I need a lawyer?"

"That's up to you, Mrs. Herbeck. But you're not a suspect at this time, and you are free to go."

After Herbeck left, Robertson said to Armbruster, "I want you to try for a warrant, Stan. To test her hands for gun-shot residue, and to search her car and house for a gun."

Chapter 10

"I can't believe she's dead," the professor said to Caroline. "Lydia. It was a stupid accident. I'm afraid I was a little bit *out of it*. At the farm, I mean. Can't remember everything I said. Just seeing her body was a shock. John Junior is torn up. Just completely torn up. She was like a sister to him. Lydia. Dead. And the neighbor out there, Meredith Silver? Shot in the face. It's surreal."

They had been sitting at the hand-crafted curly maple kitchen table that Bishop Eli Miller had given them almost twenty years ago. The professor had his hands pressed flat against the surface, as if he wanted the beautiful, swirling grain of the blonde wood to infuse his hands. To work its beauty into the hollow spaces in his mind. To comfort him.

He remembered old Bishop Eli, gone for several years now, once desperate to rescue his grandson Jeremiah, who was now raising his own family on the bishop's original farm in the Doughty Valley, out near Charm.

But the beautiful wood grain gave no comfort to the professor. He pulled his hands off the top of the table, and he reached over to take Caroline's hands into his. "Lydia was out at her sister's farm," he said, shaking his head. "North of Mt. Hope. Her car is still out there. It was just an accident. I'm having trouble believing this."

"What about this woman who left her husband?" Caroline asked.

"That's Lydia's sister. On the farm where Lydia died. Mary Yost. She left her husband and six of her seven children. Three weeks ago. Their youngest, Esther, is missing, too. I think she's about one and a half years old. Mary's pregnant with their eighth."

"Why would she do that?" Caroline asked, frowning. "Leave six children behind?"

Before the professor answered, the front doorbell rang. Woodenly and wearily, Branden pushed up from the table, plodded down the front hallway, and opened the door. Cal Troyer was standing on the stoop. Behind Cal, at the edge of the porch light, stood Reverend Ed Schell, a tall and slender man with combed black hair. He was holding the hand of a sleepy three-year old girl, who snuggled close to him with her arms wrapped around his leg.

Donna Schell was standing there too, a red-headed woman holding an infant in her arms. Donna had obviously been crying, and she was pressing a white hankie to her eyes. Her left hand was heavily bandaged, and the cotton gauze looked new and fresh to Branden.

"Your lights are on," Cal offered. "I know it's late. Do you mind? You remember Ed and Donna Schell. From Light-Path Ministries."

"Of course," Branden said, pulling the door open.

From behind Cal Troyer, Donna Schell spoke with a nervous tone. "We're worried about Mary Yost, Professor. And Meredith Silver. What is happening?"

"She left for Cleveland three days ago," Ed said, eyes cast downward.

"Mary Yost?" Branden asked, surprised.

"Yes," Ed said, looking up to Branden. "She was supposed to call. She was supposed to have called us by now."

- - - - - - - - - - - - - -

Caroline got them all seated in the living room with several of the lights turned on, and the professor brought glasses of water from the kitchen. Donna and Ed sat together on one sofa, and Mike and Caroline sat across the room, on the other sofa. Cal took an easy chair in the corner of the room. With her right hand, Donna held her sleeping infant against her shoulder. Her left hand, bandaged and apparently still painful to her, rested on the arm of the sofa. Ed let his older daughter lie curled up on the sofa, with her head resting in his lap.

Caroline asked, "What happened to your hand, Donna?"

"Oh," Donna said embarrassed. "I burned it on an oven rack, making cookies this afternoon."

"Sorry," Caroline said, and then of Ed she asked, "How old is Sophie, now?"

Ed said, "She's three."

"Three and a half," little Sophie said with a child's sleepy yawn, eyes closed.

"Yes, three and a half," Ed said, smiling. "Donna has Annie, there. Eight weeks old."

Donna laid Annie across her knees. She dried her tears with her crumpled hankie, and off-hand, she explained, "I've had a knee replacement, and the oven rack burned off some skin, I'm afraid. I'm not supposed to get an infection because of the metal parts of the knee, so I'm worried about this burn. Because of an infection."

Caroline said, "Just a minute," and she got up. Stepping into the guest bathroom in the hallway, she brought out a box of tissues, and she carried them to Donna.

Donna said, "Thank you," and she pulled four tissues. She used them right-handed on her eyes first, and then on her nose. She crumpled them into a pocket in her roomy, blue flowered dress, and she said, delicately, "Thanks so much. This is the worst day of our lives. Losing Lydia and Meredith, too. And now Mary is missing."

"When was Mary supposed to have called you?" the professor asked Ed.

"We took her up to the bus in Wooster. On Friday. We gave her a ticket for Cleveland. Round trip. She should have called us Friday. Or Saturday evening, at the latest."

"Why was she going to Cleveland?" Caroline asked.

Donna answered. "We recommended a family counseling program there. In Parma. She was going to try to get her husband to agree to some marriage counseling. She

85

was supposed to have called us by now, to tell us what bus she'd be on, coming back to Wooster."

"Donna?" Cal asked. "Had she been staying at your boarding house?"

Donna shook her head. "Just the one night. Just Thursday night."

Cal said to Donna and Ed, "Mike and Caroline need to understand how you operate at Light-Path Ministries."

Donna looked to her husband. Ed stroked the hair of his daughter Sophie, asleep by then with her head in his lap. "We have a special calling for Amish families," he said. "We minister to all people, but we try to help the Amish especially."

Cal asked, "You hand out tracts in towns?"

"We invite people to bible studies," Donna said. "Couples, if both are willing. But mostly it's unmarried Amish people. And then it's mostly people who come to us. You know, the ones who want to know more. If they come to us, we get them into a bible-study group at the church."

Caroline asked, "Did you do that with Mary?"

Ed nodded.

The professor asked, "Then how did you get started with her? I gather John Yost isn't the agreeable type?"

"John wasn't really involved," Ed said. "Donna went out to Meredith Silver's house, and Mary would walk over to meet them there. Mary never came into town. John wouldn't have permitted it."

"Lydia was out with Meredith Silver when she died," the professor said.

Donna nodded. "Meredith is who got us started with Mary. She said that Mary needed help. I just went out to talk with her. Just that first time, about six months ago. Then she asked me to come back. Mary did, I mean. She wanted to know more about what is in the Bible."

"I would think," Caroline said cautiously, "that Amish people know all about the Bible."

"Not always," Ed replied with a knowing tone. "The preachers and the bishops don't always preach from the entire Word of God. They are sometimes very selective. So, if they've never read it for themselves, some Amish people really don't learn that much about faith."

"They're the most faithful people I know," the professor argued.

"Mostly," Ed said. "Most of them, anyways. Not all, mind you, but most. But the Schwartzentrubers can be different."

"This seems improbable to me," Caroline objected. "You're talking about the most Godly people in the world."

Ed shook his head. He eased forward a bit on the sofa and said, "They are Christians. That is true. But the bishops don't always preach from the Bible. They mix in a lot of traditional lifestyle rules. They mix in the traditions of the *old country*. So, they're all stuck in the past to one extent or another. They won't accept modern ways."

"Like medicines," Donna said. "They won't use modern medicines. Or vaccines."

"Well, some of them do, certainly," Branden said.

"Not Schwartzentrubers," Ed argued. "Not the most conservative orders. Their children don't get any vaccinations. A lot of them die young."

Interrupting again, Donna said, "Tell them about the store in Mt. Hope."

Ed closed his eyes and drew a cleansing breath. "She's talking about their herbal remedies. They sell hundreds of them at the health food store in Mt. Hope. They've got herbals for everything. Even childbirth. But these are just the types of concoctions that they would have had in the sixteenth and seventeenth centuries. You know. From the old country. They'll accept those, because they are traditional. The bishops preach about holding true to traditional lifestyles, like it's straight out of the Bible. But it's not. They're just holding to their old-fashioned traditions."

The professor spoke up with a question. "This John Yost. If he's got a mental disorder – a psychiatric condition – he'll use only the herbal remedies that were available in the old countries?"

Ed Schell nodded grimly. "He's a Schwartzentruber. He could be manic-depressive, and the bishop would tell him that it is just his cross to bear. A child could have the mumps, and be at death's door, and they'd figure it was God's will. They're taught that they have to live right. To follow the scriptures and traditions and earn their way into heaven by being faithful to the rules."

"Surely not all of them," Caroline countered. "They can't be all like that. Cal?"

"Not all Amish," Cal said. "Not even most of them. But yes. If any are like that, it'll be the Schwartzentrubers."

"Ed," Cal offered next. "You sent Mary to see marriage counselors? Right?"

"Yes," Ed said, nodding. "It's a husband and wife team, actually. Paul and Nancy Culp. They specialize in family therapies for church people. You know. Pastors send them to the Culps. Sometimes they actually move into town, to be near a family, for more intensive interaction. It's very specialized, and we thought it would be just what the Yosts needed. If we could get John Yost to agree to it."

"But, have you heard from the Culps?" Cal asked, pressing his question again.

"We called them Saturday evening. Mary was supposed to see them on Saturday morning. Then she was supposed to come back to Wooster later, on one of the Saturday buses. Or Sunday, if it took longer. But she didn't, and she didn't call us."

"Did the Culps talk with her?" Caroline asked. "I think that's what Cal is getting at."

"No," Ed said, sounding defeated. "They never saw her. We don't know where she is. We've been calling hospitals, in case she went into labor, or something. I don't know. Maybe she's injured."

"Who took her to the bus in the first place?" Cal asked.

"I did," Donna said. "Me and Sophie. It was Friday, around noon. We had lined up a hotel room for her, for

Friday night. In Parma, right off I-71. It was for Saturday night, too, if she stayed to talk with the Culps more."

"Did she actually spend the night there?" the professor asked.

"The hotel never saw her," Ed said, shaking his head.

"Nobody knows where she is," Donna whispered.

"How would she have come back?" Caroline asked. "How would she have traveled back home?"

"We gave her cash," Donna said through broken sobs. "We gave her an open return ticket on the bus, and cash for the hotel, meals and such."

"So, what?" Cal asked. "She might have taken a bus back to Wooster and a cab home from there?"

"We don't know," Ed Schell said.

"We don't know where she is," Donna Schell cried. "Now Meredith is dead, too. We just don't know what's going on."

After a pause, the professor asked, "Donna, how did you learn about Lydia?"

"Oh," Donna said thinking. "Oh, it was Meredith. Meredith called me right then. On Monday night, just after the accident."

"From the Yost farm?" Branden asked.

"No. She was already walking home from there. I was in Mt. Hope with the children."

"Did you go to see her?"

"No. The kids were fussy. Sophie was hungry and starting to cry. Annie was screaming. Needed a new diaper and a bottle. I was parked at the hardware store, trying to take care of them. And Meredith said she'd be OK. We made a date for breakfast."

Softly, Ed said, "Donna, you can't blame yourself for any of this. You shouldn't be beating yourself up over this. We'll find Mary. You can't do anything about Lydia. And Meredith is not your fault.'

"I can't help it, Ed," Donna replied, standing up with Annie. "I can't help but feel that this is all my fault."

- - - - - - - - - - - - - - -

Cal walked the Schells out to their car, and once they had left, he went back to the professor, who was standing in the dark, out on the front stoop. "I know you, Mike," Cal said from the front walk. "What's troubling you?"

Stepping down to the walk, Branden said, "It doesn't add up, Cal."

"What?"

"The Thursday/Friday thing."

"Why?"

"Because Bishop Alva Yost told me that it was a full three weeks ago that Mary left her husband."

Cal scratched at an ear, frowned.

Branden held a pause and then added, "And Mary did make a call, but it was to the sheriff. She left a message on his phone, late this afternoon. She was just up in Wooster, at the Applebees."

Chapter 11

The professor arrived in the history building at Millersburg College only ten minutes before his Tuesday-Thursday seminar on The American Civil War. It wasn't so much a formal class on the subject, as it was a guided self-study discussion group for seniors. It carried full class credit for the students, but it gave Branden only half-a-course of teaching credit, because the students were supposed to take the lead in the discussions. Branden served more as an advisor and moderator, than a lecturer. Which suited him just fine that Tuesday morning. His mind wasn't especially well-focused on the Civil War. During the seminar, none of his students asked about Lydia Schwartz. News of her death was not yet common knowledge on campus.

When the seminar discussion finished at 9:30, Branden stopped briefly in his office. He told Lawrence Mallory what little he knew about the accident that killed Lydia, and the suicide of Meredith Silver soon after that, and he asked Lawrence to arrange a meeting with President Nora Benetti. He checked his day planner for appointments – a student to see at 3:45 and office hours at 4:00 that afternoon – and he walked directly home to retrieve his truck. He told Caroline that he'd be at the jail on courthouse square, and then he changed into his green and white

Millersburg College sweatshirt with blue jeans, and he drove down off the college heights in a morose mood.

In truth he was grumbling a bit. Lydia Schwartz – a tragic accident. Her sister Mary Yost – missing, along with her little daughter Esther. And the neighbor Meredith Silver? Shot dead in her own home. There were the troubles with John Yost, too. Troubles enough for a year, and all of it happening at the very start of a busy semester. It crossed the professor's mind that perhaps a move to Emeritus status might make good sense, after all.

In the sheriff's office, Branden found Robertson seated at his desk, talking on the phone. Robertson was in a gray suit with no tie, with his new bushy beard spilling out over his unbuttoned white collar.

"Nothing to suggest criminality in the Lydia Schwartz death?" Robertson was saying, scratching at the scar under his beard. "Just an accident? Because in her suicide note, Meredith says that she actually shoved Lydia in the back."

Branden stretched out in the low leather chair in front of Robertson's desk, and he listened to the sheriff's end of the conversation.

"Well, how long is it going to take, Missy?"

Robertson gave Branden a nod of his head, and he put his call on speaker phone mode. 'Missy,' he mouthed for Branden.

The professor heard Missy Taggert's response. "A couple of hours, Bruce. She does have a mild contusion over

94

her shoulder blade. So, she might have been shoved. But it wasn't done forcefully."

"OK," Robertson said, "then what about Silver?"

"Shot close range. The manner of death is homicide. The means of death is a gunshot wound to the head. Thirty-eight caliber. I've got bullet fragments out of the wall. But there are a lot of thirty-eight caliber bullets. Like three-eighties, thirty-eight specials, 9 millimeters, and three-fifty-seven magnums. So, without the gun? I don't know. I'll try to retrieve the other parts of the bullet from the body, but it'll take some time to get a composite image. One thing, though, we didn't find any ejected brass at the scene. So, somebody either knew to pick up the spent brass, or they used a revolver."

"Gun powder residue, Missy? What about that?"

"There's powder blast on Meredith Silver's face. Stippling. I estimate that she was shot from a distance of only three or four feet."

"What about her hands?" the sheriff asked.

"No gsr, Bruce. But I'm still testing."

"What about her phone?" the sheriff asked. "And Lydia's phone. You said you have them both."

"Haven't gotten to them," Missy said. "Lydia's phone is locked, so Stan will be unable to work with that one, unless we can get the key code from someone who knows it. She wasn't using fingerprint ID. We might need Meredith's fingerprint to get into her phone. Unless she used only a key code too, and then we'd have the same problem."

"When will you know?" Robertson asked.

"You can't rush this, Bruce. Let us do our jobs."

Robertson nodded. Frowned. "OK, Missy. Lunch today?"

"Can't. I'll just see you for dinner."

"OK," the sheriff said, and he hung up the call. To Branden, he said, "Missy's going to let us know."

Somewhat sourly, Branden said, "No surprise."

"You're having a bad day, Mike?"

Branden nodded. "Cal brought us some company last night. Ed and Donna Schell. And their two little kids. They say they put Mary Yost on a bus in Wooster, Friday afternoon. Now they say they don't know where she is."

"Yost muttered that she's been gone for three weeks," Robertson groused. "What's going on?"

"The Schells say that she spent Thursday night with them, and then got on a bus for Cleveland. Well, Parma actually. On Friday afternoon. Donna drove her up to meet the bus in Wooster."

Robertson leaned back in his swivel chair, with his fingers tented over his belly. "So where has she been in the meantime?" he asked the professor. "And where is the little girl?"

"They don't know. She's due to deliver her baby, and they don't know where they are. Neither do the Culps."

"Who?"

"Paul and Nancy Culp. They're marriage counselors in Parma. Mary Yost was supposed to see them on Saturday morning. She didn't show up. And she didn't show up at her hotel Friday night, either."

"Then what was that phone message yesterday afternoon from Applebees?"

"Don't know. This thing's a little cock-eyed if you ask me."

"We need to have a conversation with John Yost," Robertson said, standing.

"Is he still at Pomerene?"

"Yes."

"I'll drive," Branden offered, pushing up from his chair.

Robertson moved toward his office door. "You brought your little toy truck, Mike?"

"Yes."

Robertson shook his head. "Then we're taking my Crown Vic."

"You can just push the seat back, Sheriff. It's not that small of a truck."

Robertson harrumphed. "The Crown Vic, Mike. I know I can fit into that."

Out in the hallway, Robertson asked the professor, "Did the Schells mention the little Yost girl, Esther?"

"No."

"You didn't ask?"

Branden shook his head, skirting along in the narrow hallway beside the round sheriff. "I wanted to see if they would bring it up."

"And they didn't?"

"No."

Robertson stopped. "Why didn't you just ask them about her?"

"They didn't seem to know anything about Esther, and I let it stand that way. I think it's curious."

As the two men passed the squad's duty room, Detective Pat Lance came out into the hallway with her eyes locked on a printed page. Robertson cleared his throat, and she stopped and looked up.

"Lance," the sheriff said. "Talk to Ed and Donna Schell. Find out if they've heard anything more from this Mary Yost. She was supposed to travel up to Cleveland just this last Friday, but she was also supposed to have left her husband three weeks ago."

Lance nodded and said, "I got a call from Stan. They've dusted pretty much everything in the Silver residence. There are plenty of prints, and none of them is on record anywhere. Family, friends, neighbors, we can't tell. It'd be almost impossible to try to print everyone who might have gone to see her."

"OK, Lance, but once we have a suspect, the prints will help us."

Lance nodded and drew a burdened breath. "Are you going to let Stan go back on detective duty anytime soon, Sheriff?"

"When he's ready."

"He complains about it every night, Sheriff. It'd help me out a lot, if you could just clear him for duty."

"I'll talk to his therapist, Lance. That's all I can promise."

"I'd be grateful," Lance said. "I can't have him moping like this anymore, just lying around the house at night. His shoulder has mended. Getting back to detective work would do a lot to boost his spirits."

- - - - - - - - - - - - - -

In tiny Joel Pomerene Hospital, at the door to John Yost's room, Alice Shewmon was wearing a frown, leaning back with her shoulder blades pressed against the wall. Her arms were folded, and she was apparently embroiled in her thoughts. The professor came up to her ahead of Robertson, and he read the expression on the social worker's face. "What, Alice?" he asked. "What's wrong?"

As he spoke, the sheriff advanced farther down the hall, to speak with a nurse.

Shewmon said, "There's nothing really wrong, Mike. Well, actually, I'm working on the vaccine angle here. None of the Yost children has been vaccinated. Tetanus, measles, whooping cough. Nothing. Their grandparents say they don't believe in vaccines. And I'd like to talk with John Yost about it, to see if I can't make some progress on this. But Evie is in there with him. She's not allowing visitors, yet."

99

Branden said, "She has her own problems, I suppose. Getting John settled. Getting him some help. They're Schwartzentrubers, remember. They're not going to want to use medicine."

"Like anti-depressants?"

"And sedatives. Whatever."

"OK, how about this?" Shewmon said sounding hopeful. "I've got photos here of the types of parasites that enter through bare feet. I'll show that to the bishop. All their children go barefooted in summer. I'll bet he's never seen these types of microscopic parasites. I think it'll convince him to use pharmaceuticals, and that'll give me a lead-in to discuss vaccinations with him."

Branden said, shaking his head, "You got a good look inside Mose and Ida's home last night?"

Shewmon nodded. "The grandparents across the road."

"So, you've got to know that this will be an uphill battle."

Shewmon closed her eyes momentarily, and then she looked back to Branden. "It's primitive, Professor. The household furnishings are simple. Rudimentary, really. To the point of being archaic. I haven't seen much of that yet. That's the most primitive I've ever seen it, and I've worked with a lot of Amish people."

"But I guess you were content to leave the children there last night?"

"I couldn't find a reason not to. The house was clean, and there was plenty of food. The children seemed to know the place, like it was their second home."

"Probably it is," Branden said. "How did Mose and Ida take the news about Lydia?"

"The bishop had told them before I got there. They were crushed. First about Lydia. Then about John. Plus, they've been heartbroken about the disappearance of Mary and Esther. Really Mike, they were *just crushed* by it all."

Evie Carson came out into the hallway, and Sheriff Robertson came back to join the conversation. To Carson, Robertson said, "I need John to answer some questions, Evie. His wife is missing. His daughter, too."

Evie shook her head. "He's agitated, Bruce. And depressed. Manic with worry."

"Just a few questions, Evie."

"No, Sheriff," Evie said, almost in a whisper. "Not until he's stable, and not until I've counseled with him. I want him properly medicated. I want him mentally stabilized, before you question him."

"Why are you being so careful about this?" Robertson asked.

Evie asked, "Do you know anything about his younger brother?"

Robertson shook his head, and he leaned in a bit. "What?"

"I've had a talk with Bishop Yost this morning. Didn't you see his buggy in the lot?"

"No."

"Then you just missed him."

"OK, what about this brother?"

"A younger brother. He used to have a family and a farm. In Indiana. Now he's in a psychiatric facility. He suffers from this kind of clinical depression, too, and he has been refusing antidepressant medications. He says his church doesn't believe in them."

Chapter 12

Driving his white pickup under a bright noonish sun, Professor Branden followed the sheriff's Crown Vic northwest out of Millersburg, through sleepy Mt. Hope, and then north to TR 606. There Robertson turned in at the Yost farm, intending to check on John Yost Junior and then head off to find Bishop Yost, if he wasn't with Junior. Branden however continued west on 606 to the next property across the road, the home of Meredith Silver.

He turned into the graveled drive and saw a long tan-brick ranch house with a covered front porch. Farther down the drive, fifty yards past the house, a Freightliner tractor truck was parked with its wide, flat nose facing out. The sleeping compartment behind the cab rose up taller than the cab, and on top of that there was a wind deflector of rounded silver metal arching backward to shield a trailer in tow from the wind. But there was no trailer attached to the back of the parked cab. With a tangle of weeds growing up around it, the truck looked like it had been parked in retirement for quite some time.

In the driveway, there was a black Chevy Nova, and as he shut his engine off behind it, Branden saw a short, thin woman backing out through the front screened door with a black garbage bag brimming over with clothes. He came forward on the walkway, and he introduced himself to

Louise Herbeck. Once she had shaken his hand and explained who she was, Branden insisted that she drop the clothes on the floorboards of the front porch.

"They've got it roped off out here," she complained with sorrowful eyes, pointing to the yellow crime scene ribbon that had barred the steps leading up onto the front porch. "But her clothes are all back in her bedroom, and I can't see how this'll hurt anything."

Branden eyed the cut yellow crime scene ribbon, and he proceeded up the porch steps. "You're not supposed to cross the barrier, Mrs. Herbeck."

"It's just for the clothes," Herbeck argued. She dapped at a sheen of tears with the corner of a bathroom towel.

Branden decided to let it drop. "She was your size?" he asked. "Meredith?"

"Oh, no. Not really. She was an exercise nut. And much taller. No, I'm taking these to a resale shop. I need the money. When they release the house, I'm going to wipe up all of that fingerprint dust and move in here." Shaking her head sadly, she added, "Meredith left it to me."

Although he had introduced himself to Louise by name, Branden figured it was appropriate to explain his status to her as a reserve deputy in the sheriff's department. He took out his badge case and showed it to her. She seemed surprised and said, "I thought you were just a friend," Herbeck said with a nervous glance at the yellow ribbon that she had cut.

"No, I never really met her. I mean I did speak with her briefly last night at the Yost farm, but that was because Lydia Schwartz had died. Did you know Lydia?"

"Sure. But how do *you* know her?"

"I was her professor at the college."

"A deputy and a professor? How do you manage all of that?"

"Sometimes I'm not sure that I do. Anyway, I'd like you to tell me about Meredith. And her neighbors out here, if you know them."

"I know them all, Professor. Like what?"

"Can we sit here on the porch?" Branden asked, pointing to the wicker chairs that sat to his left. "You really shouldn't go back inside."

Herbeck shrugged. She gave the appearance of not caring what she did next. "I suppose," she answered tentatively. "I can't offer you anything to drink. They've got the entire kitchen all roped off. Bathroom, too."

"We could just talk a bit," Branden offered, and he led Louise across the porch.

They took seats, and Branden said, "It's about Mary Yost, actually. Meredith was hosting bible studies with her and a Donna Schell from Millersburg."

"What about her?" Louise said. "I haven't seen her lately. Really, she was Meredith's friend." Herbeck's eyes were moist again, and she pulled a handkerchief and blew her nose. "I should have paid more attention to Meredith's friends. I should have paid more attention to her."

"Were you expecting to see Mary? I mean did you run into her regularly over here?"

Louise nodded and smiled. "I was over here from time to time. Visiting. Mary came over here once a week or so. When she could get away."

Louise gave thought for a moment, and then she popped up onto her feet and said, "Wait right there." She stepped off the porch and went down to the Nova on the driveway.

Branden took the opportunity to survey the property. The Silver's front lawn was wide and green, recently mowed. A stretch of blacktopped TR 606 was visible past the Silver's culvert fence, and a car sped by, passing a black buggy. Branden waved at the family in the buggy – a mother in a black bonnet, with a father in a black vest and four young children, also dressed entirely in black – but they didn't see him.

He felt isolated on the open farmland, with corn, soybeans, green beans, and all the crops spreading wide, out over the hills and beyond, surrounding him like a testament to a slower, simpler life than the one he knew at the college. Life in the *big city*, as someone had called it. As if the quaint and tiny village of Millersburg could ever qualify as a big city. As if the pace at the insular college could be considered too hectic.

After searching through her garbage bags of clothes in the trunk of her Nova, Herbeck came back with a knitted black sweater. She sat back down next to Branden, handed him the sweater and said, "This is Mary's I believe. You can return it to her."

"I can't," Branden said. "She's missing. She's evidently been gone for a while."

"Then she finally did it."

"Did what?" Branden asked, leading her.

"Left him, of course."

"John? He's that bad?"

"Swings good and bad. You never know which John you're gonna get. Normal John or sad John. It gets pretty bad over there. Worse than ever, lately, Meredith said."

"Did you study scripture with them, Mrs. Herbeck? Or was it just Mary who did that?"

"Just Mary. Whenever she could get away. Which wasn't that often, with her kids and all."

"Do you know the children?"

"Not really. But Meredith knew them all. All the children, on all the farms. Should I call you Professor or Deputy?"

"Why not just Mike? You don't think John Yost is a stable person?"

"No more than his brother, Mike."

"Alva?"

"No. Alva is fine. As far as Schwartzentrubers go. I'm talking about Daniel. The younger brother. He's like John. Always so serious. Stern. Can't seem to keep himself happy."

"Daniel's the one in the hospital? I gather it's a psychiatric facility."

Louise nodded. "He's the youngest of nine Yost boys. Mary has good reason to have left John."

"Why?"

"He's always so moody. Demanding. Most of the time he just sulks."

"No. Why is Daniel in prison?"

"You really don't know anything," Louise commented, smiling briefly.

"No, I guess not."

Louise frowned. "Daniel got into one of his spells. He had a wife and a young son. But he gets into bad spells of depression. One day he walked out into the road in front of his house. He was almost catatonic, and he tried to kill himself by getting hit by a car. Now he's in the psych ward of an Indiana state hospital. And John Yost is a lot like him. He's a troublesome man."

Branden nursed a moment of silence. He ran his fingers through his combed brown/gray hair, and he blew out a cleansing breath. "I guess I understand that," he said after the pause. "But my question is about the children, Louise. Why would Mary be willing to leave six of her children over there, on the farm with John?"

Herbeck shook her head sadly. "It was Meredith," she said, suddenly sad again, and seeming to remember her sister. "She said it to Mary Yost more than once. 'You have to save yourself, before you can save anyone else.' If Mary really has left, you can bet she has a plan to rescue her other children, too."

- - - - - - - - - - - - - -

"I can't imagine why she would leave them, Michael," Caroline said at lunch. "OK, you have troubles with a mentally unstable husband, or even with an abusive one? That's not a reason to leave the kids. No, Michael. Something else must have happened."

They were seated at the glass table on the screened back porch, eating chicken salad sandwiches, with sliced fruit from a bowl. All the tall porch windows were open, and the breezes of the day were blowing gently through the screens. Cotton ball clouds drifted over the Amish valley beyond the drop-off cliffs at the edge of their property. The rains that had raced through the county yesterday were only a memory. Summer heat had not yet bled out of August. It seemed to promise a hot September.

"Louise Herbeck made it sound like Mary needed to be rescued," the professor said. "Maybe she was going to get away first, and then arrange to take the children off the farm later. Isn't that how she would do it? Get herself out first, and then file a complaint to bring the other children out legally?"

"I don't know, Michael. Why couldn't she have put them all in a buggy and driven them into town? To Social Services. Or to the Family Assistance Agency. They have an F.A.A. up in Wooster, too, and if she had gone up there, she would have put some distance between her and her husband.

Those are safe places where troubled families can get some help. Wouldn't someone like Donna Schell know how to work with a program like that?"

"I'll ask Alice Shewmon," the professor said. "To see what programs we have in Holmes County. But even if Mary knew about one of them, she'd be reluctant to trust them."

Caroline considered that for a moment. "And why would she take only Esther with her? Because she's the youngest?"

"Maybe she figured the older ones could manage for a couple of days," the professor said.

They heard loud knocking at their front door, and then they heard Bruce Robertson's voice calling through the screened door. "Are you home, Mike? Anybody home?"

Branden walked out to the front and brought the sheriff back to the porch. Caroline laid a third plate on the glass table, and she put out half a sandwich for the sheriff. While Branden and Robertson got themselves seated there, she went into the kitchen and brought back iced water for Robertson.

"We've found Lydia Schwartz's diaries in her dorm room," the sheriff said as Caroline sat down. "Pat and Ricky are going through them now. I brought this one for you to see."

The sheriff handed a steno pad to Branden. It was flipped open to one of the very last pages. The professor read aloud from the journal.

Need to talk with Dithy. Maybe she knows where Mary is. Can't believe she's been gone this long. Pray she's OK - Please Lord, let them be OK. Dithy must know something. Talk with Donna too. This is a BAD IDEA. Check on babies and midwives. See who would know about private births. Check with the midwives. She must have delivered by now. She would use a midwife. Mary must have a new baby by now.

"There are several more of these diaries," the sheriff said. "Lance and Niell are going through them now, plus other things in Lydia's dorm room. If the diaries are right, she had been worried about Mary for months. She was trying to find her last week. And the most recent entries in her diaries? *BAD IDEA*. All caps. *BAD IDEA*."

Chapter 13

When the professor approached in the second-floor dormitory hallway, there was a college girl standing off to the side, outside Lydia's room, leaning sideways against the wall. She looked distraught, Branden thought, and perhaps also a little impatient. She had cropped blonde hair – with a streak of red dye on the side – and she was fidgeting with a gold eyebrow stud. She nodded curtly to the professor, and he returned her slight greeting, saying, "Hello, I'm Professor Branden," as he held out his hand.

She took his hand lightly, briefly, and she pushed away from the wall to stand up straight. Some of the emotion bled out of her expression. She still fiddled with her eyebrow stud. "I know who you are," she replied. "Professor Branden. History."

"Are you Susan?" he inquired. "Susan Randall?"

"Yes, Professor."

"You must be pretty upset about Lydia."

Susan shrugged, and her fingers came away from her eyebrow stud. "She was nice. I didn't know her too well. Really, I just moved in with her at the start of the semester."

"Didn't you know her last year? While you were sophomores?"

"I'm a senior, actually," Susan said. "But yes, I've known her for a couple of years. We didn't hang out too much. She's been in this room since May. Took summer classes. The Dean of Students told my parents that I needed a 'quiet and reserved' roommate. So, here I am. She's Mennonite. *Was* Mennonite. But she was OK."

Branden studied the closed door to Susan and Lydia's room. "Are you locked out, or something?"

"Or something. The cops are here. They're going through all Lydia's stuff. They said that I have to wait out here. But I have a class, and I need my backpack."

Branden smiled with a sympathetic nod of his head. It registered with him that her *cops* had come out a little too flippantly. He knocked on the door and opened it. Pat Lance and Ricky Niell were in the room. Lance was paging through some documents at one of the student desks, and Niell was standing beside one of the twin beds that were raised up on lifters, with boxes and laundry baskets stacked beneath them. At the door, Branden asked, "Can Susan have her backpack?"

Pat Lance looked up from a term paper she had been reading. "Ricky?" she said over her shoulder, and Ricky, with two backpacks opened on the bed, asked, "Red or black?"

Susan Randall said, "The red one," and Detective Niell zipped it closed.

He carried the backpack out to Susan and said, "We've been through it, Ms. Randall. We're done."

Seeming to Branden to be anxious, Susan Randall took her backpack and swung it over a shoulder. Her nervous fingers went back up to her eyebrow stud. "Did you take any of my stuff?" she inquired of Niell.

Ricky smiled. "No, it's all there."

Susan gave out a sigh. "I'll know if you took anything," she scolded, and she turned to walk down the hallway.

"Mike," Pat Lance called out from inside the dorm room. "Is this one of your course books?"

Branden stepped into the room. Lance was holding up a thick, paperback tome by Tyndall. The professor shook his head and recited the title as he remembered it. "*Slave and Owner Mentalities, with Emphasis on Slave Cultures in the Americas.*"

"One of yours?" Lance inquired again.

Branden took the heavy book from her. He noticed that it was a library copy. "No," he answered thoughtfully. "This is a graduate level text. It's the kind of book I use for background reference, when I'm teaching my class on *Slavery in the Americas*. Was Lydia reading it?"

"I think so," said Lance. "She had been taking notes." She held up a blue spiral notebook. "Very extensive notes."

"Well, it's at the graduate level," Branden replied.

"Are you surprised, Professor?"

"A little. Lydia was asking me about something related to this, the last time I spoke with her. It was yesterday morning, actually, after class. She asked about births of slave babies."

114

"There are some entries here about that kind of thing," Ricky said. "In her diaries."

"How many diaries did she have?" Branden asked.

"Maybe fifteen," Ricky said.

"Was she using email?"

Lance answered. "Not very extensively. A few friends on campus. Some emails to Light-Path Ministries."

"That's Ed and Donna Schell," the professor mused aloud. "How about Facebook? Twitter? Instagram? Pinterest?"

"Nothing that I could find," Lance said.

Ricky said, "She had several notebooks in her backpack." He held up three, in different colors, with frayed edges and spiral-wire bindings that were sprung and pulled out a few inches, straight at their ends. He wrangled them all into a black backpack, and he folded the loose wire strands in after them. Finished, he came away from the bed and offered his hand to Branden.

The professor shook it and said, "How's the family?"

"I think Ellie misses the job," Ricky said. "She stays at home all the time, with the twins, I mean."

"Twins OK?" Branden asked.

From her seat at the desk, Lance quipped. "Don't get him started, Professor."

Ricky's face took a blush, and he said, simply, "They're all fine. Great, really."

Lance stood up and offered her hand, too. "There's nothing here of interest, Professor. Everything is here, like you'd expect it to be. Clothes, books, toiletries, music on her CD player."

"What did she listen to?" Branden asked.

Ricky reached in front of Pat Lance to push down the play button on Lydia's CD player. Branden heard a wild run of guitar cacophony.

"That's Pearl Jam," Ricky said, switching it off. "It's hard-driving grunge rock for the most part. It's not what you'd expect from a Mennonite girl, with the guitars grinding out like that. Plus, it's quite a bit dated. But it certainly isn't Mennonite."

"I suppose not," said Branden. "Really? I'm surprised."

"It's in her diaries," Ricky said. "She loved college. She loved music, and she really loved the old songs. Rock and Roll. Country. R&B. She embraced it all. More than the average student, I think. She called it freedom. Liberation. Her class notes are detailed. Her diaries are extensive. It's like she was soaking it all up, here at college. Soaking up freedom."

"Every teacher's dream student," Branden said softly, mournfully.

Lance asked, "You talked with Bruce? He said he was going to show you one of her diaries."

"He did," Branden said. "Where is he now?"

Niell shrugged. "He was going to talk with you."

"He did that."

"Then he was going out to TR 606," Lance said. "To find the bishop."

Branden stroked a thought across his chin. "He'll stop off at the Yost farm, again." He glanced to Lydia's desk. "Is that Lydia's computer? The laptop?"

"Yes," said Lance. "She was searching the internet. She has several dozen bookmarks on Firefox/Bing."

"Like what?" Branden asked.

Lance sat back down at the desk and clicked with the mouse.

"No password?" Branden observed.

"No," Lance said, as she turned the screen so that Branden could read it. "Like here. She bookmarked an internet document about slave populations in South Carolina."

Branden leaned in and read a few lines on the screen. "That's an old census," he said. "A census of slaves and their owners in Clarendon County. It's an historic document. Someone will have scanned it from an original. They probably found it in the basement of an old courthouse."

"She has a couple dozen of these bookmarks," Lance observed. "They're all about slavery."

"That's what she wanted to know about," Branden said. "Births to slave women. Census records of new births, I think."

"Why?" Niell asked.

Branden made a wrinkled smile, showing a measure of consternation. "I'm not sure."

Softly, Lance said, "The way I understand it, Mary Yost is due."

Branden nodded. "Did you talk at all with the roommate, here?"

"She wasn't very talkative," Niell answered. "But she was clearly upset about Lydia. And she was probably nervous about the weed she had in her backpack."

"A joint?" Branden laughed.

"Yes."

"Did you take it?"

"No," Ricky said, smiling. "I figured it wasn't worth the paperwork."

Branden smiled. "OK, what about the phones? Lydia's and Meredith's. Any luck yet with one of those?"

"No," Pat Lance said, standing up. "They are each key-code protected. Six digits for each of them."

"OK, what about Meredith Silver's suicide note?" Branden asked.

"Missy sent it to the BCI labs for handwriting analysis," Ricky said. "We sent samples of her handwriting from her house, for comparison."

"It looks like a match to me," Lance said, "for what that's worth. I think it's her handwriting."

"But there are definitely two different fingerprints on the paper," Ricky offered. "Someone other than Silver did handle the note."

Branden stroked his whiskers. "That'll be the someone who took the gun away," he said.

Lance said, "Missy does have something on the bullet fragments. They add up to something just short of a

110-grain bullet. So that's likely a .38 Special. A 110-grain lead wad cutter."

Ricky spoke up. "Missy has something going on with her gun-shot residue tests on Meredith Silver. She's calling it a radial differential test for gsr. She's testing Silver's face around the entry wound."

Branden shook his head. "That's a bad way to go – shot in the face like that."

Ricky Niell said, "Missy is trying to determine if Meredith really did shoot herself. She thinks the gsr pattern around the entry wound will tell how far away the gun was held when she was shot."

"Seems reasonable," Branden commented. "There'll be gsr on her hands, too, if she shot herself."

"Well, there isn't," Lance said. "But you know Missy. She's going to test everything. From every angle. Before she's done, we'll probably know how long Silver had been home, before she was shot."

Chapter 14

Branden had an appointment with a student at 3:45, and office hours from 4:00 until 5:00, so it was late in the afternoon before he arrived at the Schells' Light-Path Ministries church building and boarding house. Still August, it had been hot and humid, but afternoon shadows were starting to reach out under the trees and taller buildings, and the evening promised a quiet and peaceful end to the day. What little rush-hour traffic there was in the village had dissipated. Most folks were already home from work.

Professor Branden sat in his truck with the air conditioner running, and he rehearsed in his mind the list of questions he had for Pastor Ed Schell. There were several questions, to be sure, but one question. One particularly vexing question. A telling question. He doubted that he would be satisfied with the answer.

The professor entered the double doors of the church – a square and squat metal pole building – and then traversed the back of a small sanctuary with gray industrial-grade carpet and folding chairs with padded red seats. The chairs were set into arching rows, with an aisle down the middle that led to the front of the sanctuary. Behind a small wooden lectern, Branden could see the deep immersion baptistry, with overhead lights making bright sparkles on the pool of baptismal water.

After passing down the center aisle, he turned left at the lectern. A wooden door in the corner was labeled OFFICE, and the professor knocked on the door. A voice called out in a throaty tone, "Come on in," and Branden recognized it as Ed Schell's voice. The professor entered as the tall Schell was standing up behind a black metal desk. "Come right in," Schell said with his hand stretched forward over his desk.

In no time at all, Schell had them seated in upholstered armchairs in the corner of the office. A pedestal table sat between the chairs, holding up a gilt-edged, leather-bound Bible, with black finger indents marking the Books inside. On the wall behind his desk, Schell had pinned up a map of Holmes County, with small areas marked by patches of yellow high-lighter. Beside each yellow patch, he had written in a man's name.

Branden started directly, as he was settling into his chair. "Pastor, have you heard from Mary Yost?"

"Nothing," Schell said. He fluffed the top of his parted black hair and smiled, first amiably and then with some concern. "We've been making phone calls, to hospitals all over northern Ohio."

Branden nodded and held his focus on Schell's eyes. "Do you know anything about her daughter Esther? She's supposed to be about a year-and-a-half old."

"No," Schell said, with hesitation drawing out the word. "What about Esther?"

"She's Mary's youngest child."

"Oh, I know. What about her?"

"She's not at home with the other children," Branden said.

A deep sigh came forth from Schell. His eyes shifted right, as if he were composing an answer. "Well, she was with Mary," he said eventually. "Thursday and Friday. Donna said they both got on the bus in Wooster."

"Can you tell me again how that worked?" Branden asked.

"Well, like we told you last night, Mary showed up here Thursday afternoon. She was worried, but otherwise she seemed fine to me. As I remember it, she did have Esther with her. We put them on a bus Friday afternoon. Well, Donna put them on a bus."

Branden asked again about Mary. "How close to her delivery do you think she is?"

"I'm not really sure. Donna would know."

"And, you've learned nothing from any of the hospitals?"

"No, but I've been thinking," Ed said, shrugging his shoulders. "Mary would probably ask a midwife for help in her delivery. If not a relative, then she would surely use one of the Amish midwives."

"There are dozens of those," Branden observed.

"In Holmes County, alone," Schell agreed.

"But Mary has been gone from home for over three weeks," Branden said. "Why was it only last Thursday that she showed up here?"

"Don't know, Professor."

Branden pressed more questions forward. "If Mary gives birth to her child at a midwife's house, who would know about it?"

"That's a strange question, Professor."

"Not really. Lydia was asking about something like this. Who would be obliged to report private deliveries by Amish women? If she uses a midwife, I mean."

While Ed Schell considered that, Branden pressed on to another issue. "You helped Lydia negotiate her first year at college?"

"Quite a lot. You were on sabbatical."

"Did she talk with you about Amish birth records? Or slave birth records?"

Branden could see Schell making the connection behind his eyes.

The pastor cleared his throat before asking, "Like, *who would know*, you mean? Slave babies and Amish babies?"

"Precisely."

"We teach about the repression of Amish women and children, Professor. It's an extremely Patriarchal society. Amish life is hard on the women and children. But we've never suggested that they were slaves."

"I'm sure," Branden said. "But for some reason, Lydia was asking about this yesterday, after my morning class. She asked about records of births to slave women."

"We never got anything like that from her," Schell said, struggling a bit nervously in his chair. He scratched above an ear, and his sight turned inward with a thought.

Eventually, he said, "No, Lydia seemed fine to us. For her first year, and last year too, when she was a sophomore. She was adjusting slowly to English life, but getting along fine. She didn't mention her family really much at all."

"Maybe that was a little strange, Ed."

"Not really. Once they're out of the cults, they need to turn completely away from that. For a while, anyways. It's like a relief for them. It's liberating, to see the truth, and then to act successfully, to get themselves out of it. It's something of a victory, to get themselves out, and then to stay out."

"I guess that's what you do here? Help them get out? Is that what Mary is doing?"

"We don't push, Professor. We wait until they are really ready."

"Is Mary Yost ready?"

"Yes."

"Is John Yost abusive? Physically abusive?"

"That would very much surprise me, Professor. But if he was, she probably wouldn't have told anyone. She said he was more like just depressed. Sad all the time. It was a burden for her. An extreme emotional burden. And there was some danger. She told us that his shotgun fell out of his hand, hit the floor, and shot off one of the shells. It was just birdshot, but still. Someone could have been hurt. Or killed."

"OK, that makes this even more important," Branden said. "Here's my question. Why didn't you send Mary to a family services organization, like the Family Assistance

Agency? There's an F.A.A. office in Holmes County, and one in Wooster, too. That's Wayne County, if you thought she needed to get away for a while, maybe to hide from her husband. They're in the business of helping troubled families. Even Amish families. They know about dangerous husbands. They know how to protect families."

"But they don't address the spiritual side of things," Ed Schell said directly. "They can't, really. That's why we're here. For spiritual guidance."

"But did you send her to one of those? Or even to the county's Children Services? To someone like Alice Shewmon."

"I don't know her."

"She's a psychologist and counselor at Holmes County Social Services."

"I mean I don't know *her* in particular. She must be new."

"She is. She came here from Akron University. She's working on their case, now, while John Yost is in the hospital."

"Well, good. They need someone like that. Good."

At that, Ed Schell rose from his chair and took a seat behind his desk. Branden stood, too.

Writing on a notepad, Schell said, "I'll get an appointment with Alice Shewmon. How do you spell it?"

Branden spelled it out for him. Then he asked his question again, more directly this time, and more insistently. "OK Ed, really, why didn't you refer Mary Yost to Social Services? Or to the F.A.A. program? Or to any organization like that? I mean, any outfit where a wife could get some help for herself? Or get some help for her children? Because you had to know that the Yosts were living in a difficult environment. John Yost does not seem like a stable man. We had to take his shotgun away from him. And he's certainly not a happy man. He's in the hospital, with acute depression."

Standing again, Schell answered with somewhat of a defensive tone. "It's simple, Professor. We focus on the spiritual side of the equation. We think that's where the help is really needed. We think that is what is most important. Those other agencies are completely secular. They don't address the spiritual side. Social Services is a government agency. So, they can't. And F.A.A. doesn't, either. Nothing spiritual."

The professor's eyes moved to the map on the wall behind Schell. He studied the numerous yellow highlights. He nodded at them and asked, "You're keeping a record of those locations, Pastor? Those yellow dots?"

Schell smiled. "Those are the Schwartzentruber settlements."

"And the names?"

"Bishops. Schwartzentruber bishops."

"Why is that special to you? There are Amish people all throughout Holmes County."

"Schwartzentrubers are especially important to our ministry."

"Do you mind telling me why?"

Ed Schell smiled apologetically. "That's easy, Professor. I used to be a Schwartzentruber. I know very well how old-fashioned they are."

- - - - - - - - - - - - - -

Outside beside his small white truck, with longer evening shadows reaching across the gravel parking lot, Professor Branden considered the timeline. Mary Yost - missing for over three weeks. Except for Thursday and Friday last week. Pregnant, and now due to deliver her baby. Esther Yost, the youngest Yost daughter? Also missing. And Monday morning after class? Lydia had been asking about births to slave women. And by Monday evening? Well, by Monday evening, Lydia Schwartz was already dead.

And the professor wasn't sure that he admired the Schells' practice of dealing only with the "spiritual side of the equation," especially when there was such obvious psychiatric trouble in the family. That had been the real question. Surely, Branden thought, the Schells should have known how difficult John Yost could be. They must have known how depressed he was. They must have known that he had a severe and untreated psychiatric condition.

So, had they tried to help only Mary, or had they tried to help John, too? Had they taught the Scriptures to only Mary, or had they ministered also to John? And if only to Mary? Well then, why not also to John? That's where the real trouble lay in the Yost family. Why not try to help John?

Chapter 15

When Caroline and the professor had just finished the dinner dishes, the bell rang at their front door.

"Are you expecting anyone?" Caroline asked as she moved down the front hallway toward the door.

Branden called after her, "It could be Bruce," as he finished wiping the counter.

He heard the front door open, and then he heard Caroline's curious, "Michael, I think this is for you."

He turned out of the kitchen and into the hallway, and he saw Junior Yost standing on the front stoop. Junior was dressed in dull black denim from head to toe, and he was wearing his summer straw hat. Behind him stood his hobbled buggy horse at the curb, drinking from a plastic pail of water. Caroline stepped back as the professor advanced, and once they had Junior inside, the professor introduced him to Caroline.

Junior spoke a shy, "How do you do," and Caroline said, "Please come in," indicating the living room to Junior.

But Junior saw the carpet there, and he looked down to his boots. They were crusted with mud and manure, with bits of pale straw packed into the mix, and Junior seemed embarrassed. So, Caroline suggested the kitchen table instead, and Junior relaxed when he saw that the floors in the hallway and kitchen were tiled. He thought more about it, and then he bent over to remove his boots.

Caroline led him into the kitchen, with the professor following. With a glum and haggard expression, and a slumping and weary posture, Junior eased himself onto a kitchen chair at the table, commenting that, "Somebody knows how to handle curly maple woodworking," as he traced the grain of the wood in the tabletop with his fingertips. "Somebody really knows what they're doing, here."

Branden sat opposite him, at the side of the table, and Caroline took a seat to Junior's left, at the head of the table. "I'm sorry about your Aunt Lydia," she said. "Truly Junior, I am very sorry."

Junior sighed heavily and nodded with a simple 'what can I do?' acknowledgement. "I haven't been able to get any sleep," he said. "And I haven't been able to eat anything, either. My grandparents are very sad, but other people are kinda stiff about Lydia. You know, not liking how she left us all and went English, to go to college. They're being kinda judgmental, so I don't have anyone I can talk to. I understand, really, but people are a little too stiff to talk much about Aunt Lydia with me. I can't believe she's really dead."

The professor said, "I've wondered how folks would take it. That she died, I mean. But it's not like she had joined the church and then walked out on her vows."

"No," Junior said, contemplating the elaborate wood grain of the table. "It's not like that at all. That would have been worse. She would have been shunned, if she had forsaken her vows. She just never joined the church, so there's that, at least."

Branden saw Junior's interest in the tabletop and said, "Jonah Miller made it, over in the Doughty Valley. His father gave it to us after his grandson Jeremiah was rescued."

"That must have been a while ago," Junior commented.

"Almost twenty years," the professor said, smiling at the memory.

"He's a Diener, now," Junior said. "Jeremiah. He has a family. He's respected. I'd have to give that up, if I went English like Aunt Lydia. I'd give up a position in the church."

"Have you thought about that?" Caroline asked.

"All the time," Junior said, turning his eyes to her briefly. Then as if shy, he turned back to study the tabletop and added, "Aunt Lydia talked to me about this sort of thing. I told her I wanted to live in town, and she told me about all the things I'd give up, if I did that. But she also told me about how much she liked college. She said that I'd never really know myself, until I got an education. She said it like I was thwarted, somehow. Blocked from truly knowing myself. She said that knowledge was light. She said she felt like she had escaped to the light of freedom, by coming here to your college. I mean, that's actually how she used to talk about it."

"You must have talked with her a lot," the professor remarked. "You've decided that you'll stay with the Amish church?"

Junior nodded. "I'm to be married in the Fall," he said solemnly. "Besides, I'm not nearly as smart as Aunt Lydia. Modern life is not for me."

Caroline said, "It's all the modern things that Lydia liked so much, Junior."

"I know," Junior said. "I'm not sure what that means, but I know she liked it better than living Amish. I admired her. She was courageous. It wasn't easy for her. I'm just not that smart. But I don't really know what her life here was like. I was raised on the farm. I was raised in the church. All of my friends and family are Amish. I couldn't leave all of that, and I'm not smart enough, anyways."

"It's not so much a matter of being smart, Junior," the professor said. "Lydia found all the church rules to be oppressive. She just couldn't live Amish anymore."

"I know," Junior said sadly. "I just miss her, that's all. I mean, I've missed her since the day she left, but especially now that she has died. And I never really found out what her life here was like. She'd come out to see me, but I never came into town. I know she had a car. And a phone. And I know she tried her best to see Die Maemme as much as she could, but Mother didn't think it was such a good idea, having Lydia visiting all the time. But she did take a phone that Aunt Lydia bought for her. That was a surprise. Father didn't know. They talked on their phones, and Father didn't know."

Branden asked, "Why did your Aunt Lydia advise you to stay Amish, Junior? I mean, what did she tell you?"

"She explained how much I'd give up by leaving for the city," Junior said, misting a bit in his eyes. He pulled a crumpled bandana and wiped tears away. Then he became even more sorrowful. He sniffled some and wiped his eyes again. "Grohs-mammi wanted her to come back. To come back and be sensible again. I knew she'd never do that, so I just kept my mouth shut around people."

"Your Grandmother?" Caroline asked.

"Yes. Grohs-mammi Schwartzentruber. Ida. Grohs-daett Mose, too. They wanted her to come home and live Amish, like she was always supposed to do."

"I don't think she could have done that, Junior," the professor said.

"I know. She was too smart to live Amish like us."

"Again, Junior," Branden said, "I don't think it's a matter of smart or not smart."

Junior shook his head. "I know what I'm saying. Aunt Lydia could see it, too. If I lived English, I'd end up a common laborer. That's all. Nothing more. But if I live Amish, I'll be a landowner. A father. A husband. Maybe one day a Deacon. I'd be a leader in the church, just like Jeremiah Miller and his grandfather. Eli, right? Old Eli Miller, the Bishop. Aunt Lydia says that those are much more important things than being an English laborer, and I believe her. I mean she *said* that."

Eyes spilling out suddenly with tears, Junior whispered, "Oh, Oh, Oh no. She's really dead, isn't she."

"Yes," the professor said, standing. He lifted Junior to his feet and embraced him. He felt Junior shudder in his arms and begin to weep. Junior sagged into the professor's arms, and Branden took the weight of him, supporting him as Junior drained out his grief over the professor's shoulder. Eventually Junior eased himself away and dried his eyes again. "Sorry," he said, taking his seat.

Drying her own eyes, Caroline stood up and said, "I'm going to fix us something to eat, Junior. What would you like to have?"

Junior cleared his throat, smiled bravely and shook his head. "Really, Mrs. Branden, I don't think that would make any sense right now."

"I'll make whatever you want, Junior," Caroline said. "You just tell me what it is."

Junior smiled as if he had framed a mischievous thought.

"What?" Caroline pressed. "Be honest, now."

"OK," Junior said, hesitating. "I guess. I mean, well. Pizza?"

- - - - - - - - - - - - - - -

Pizza was delivered, the three of them ate it at the kitchen table, and Junior finished the last slice, his fifth. He smiled at his audacity, and he seemed to have relaxed, as if his sorrows had faded into the background, in his momentary brush with modernity. He leaned back from the table and wiped his lips with a napkin, saying, "Die Maemme would never have cooked anything like that."

"It's easy enough," Caroline said. "Or you can just order it, like we did."

Junior's smile faded a little as he thought about that. Eventually, he said, "I'm not sure Father would approve. I mean, we don't exactly have pepperoni on the farm."

"Maybe if you took some home to him?" Caroline suggested.

Junior shook his head, and his happy smile changed to something that was mixed heavily with resignation. "Father is difficult to deal with these days. I mean, maybe he'd like pizza. If he wasn't so depressed. You can never tell what he's going to say. Mother has had some tough times with him. No, I don't think I'd even try bringing him pizza. Not with him this way."

Taking the opportunity to speak on this topic, the professor asked, "Was it too much for your mother, then, to deal with him? Was it because of his depression?"

Junior nodded. He fumbled nervously with his napkin. "She tried, Professor. She tried everything. It was so hard. She couldn't get anywhere with him. She was beaten down by it. He was closed off. Like you couldn't talk to him about anything. The chores went wanting. The little children couldn't understand. I tried to do his work and mine, too. Mother tried to cheer him up. But he pulled back. He pulled inside somewhere. I don't know. The bishop told her it was her duty to stand by him. To help him. To take the weight,

135

as a wife should do, until he had mended. Oh, we had the deacons and the preachers. But when they left, we were alone again with Father's sorrows. And by then, Die Maemme was showing him scripture verses. You know, like, 'here it is John. You can read it for yourself. We don't have to live this way.' Those kinds of things. She had been studying across the road with Dithy Silver, and some lady from town. So, she had all these pestering questions for Father, and he couldn't handle it. I think it just made him worse. Then the bishop would tell her it was her duty to tend to him. To wait for him to heal. But she didn't think he would. I saw her giving up on him. She tried so hard. She was trapped. She was hopeless about it. She was telling me that there was more in the Bible than what the preachers were telling us. So, I got to the point where I wanted to leave, too. But Aunt Lydia talked me out of it. If Die Maemme had been willing to trust Aunt Lydia, I think she would have talked Mother out of leaving. It's funny that way. English life was right for Aunt Lydia, but she knew it would not be right for Die Maemme."

The professor asked, "Do you think that's why your mother left? Taking Esther with her?"

"Yes. The day before she left, she was carrying little Esther around and grumbling. Stuff like 'I can't do this anymore. I can't take this anymore.' So, yes. She wanted out. It never seemed to me that she'd just *leave*, though. I never thought she'd do that."

"I'm sorry, Junior," the professor said. "I'm sorry that you're having this trouble."

Junior sighed. "Anyways," he started. He stared at the grain in the maple tabletop and eventually said, "Well, there was actually a reason that I came here."

Earnestly, Caroline said, "Tell us."

"She was a modern, right? Aunt Lydia? Could you show me some of the campus? Maybe her apartment? Room? I don't know what you call it. But I thought that if I saw her places, maybe it'd help me be happier about my memories of her."

"Her dormitory room," Branden said, smiling. "I can show you that this evening."

"And her things? I'd like to see her music player. She talked about that a lot. Or even just where she slept. That'd be nice. To see where she slept."

"Junior," Branden said, "I'll show you anything you want. I've got one of the grand master keys on campus. I can show you everything."

"Classrooms?" Junior asked. "Could we see one of those?"

"Whatever you want, Junior. The campus is right here, and we can walk. I'll show it all to you."

As they left, Junior's eyes were misting over again.

Chapter 16

Missy Taggert parked her car at the curb in front of the Brandens' brick colonial, and her husband the sheriff got out on the passenger's side in the dark, as she climbed out from behind the wheel. She waited for him as he rounded the front of the car, and she saw him sidestepping something on the pavement. Grumbling under his breath, the sheriff came up to her and said, "Road apples."

While Robertson was scraping the soles of his shoes on the curb, Missy rang the front doorbell, and by the time the professor had pulled the door open, Robertson was coming up the short front walk saying, "Mike, a horse left you a present out here on the pavement."

Lumbering as usual, Robertson came up to the stoop, kicked off both of his loafers and stepped inside after Missy, in his stocking feet.

All the while, the professor had been laughing at the sheriff. It provoked a defeated growl from Robertson.

"Caroline's in the kitchen," Branden said, still chuckling.

"It isn't really that funny, Mike," said Robertson.

Missy preceded them into the kitchen, and Branden brought the sheriff along in his stocking feet, saying, "Junior Yost was parked out front. He just left ten minutes ago."

138

"I ought to write him up," Robertson griped. "Did he have any lights or reflectors on his rig, Mike? Because it's dark out, now."

"I didn't notice," the professor answered judiciously. "But he's a Schwartzentruber, right? So, you know he's not going to use a reflector."

"So, I'll go out and catch up to him," Robertson said, smiling at last. "Write him a ticket."

Caroline spoke up amiably. "You'll do no such thing, Sheriff."

Robertson snorted, and Missy, standing beside Caroline, held up her car keys and jangled them for the sheriff. "I drove," she said and laughed.

Robertson sighed and surrendered, with his wrists crossed in front as if waiting for a pair of handcuffs.

With a laugh, the professor said, "Don't tempt us, Bruce. Really. Don't tempt us."

Robertson shook his head and smiled. "You people," he mumbled, exasperated.

"Just what people would that be?" Caroline challenged.

"Oh, you know," Robertson started to say. "Oh, just forget it."

Airily, Caroline piped out, "Coffee, Sheriff? Missy?"

In unison, each answered, "No thanks," and Caroline asked, "Then maybe lemonade?"

The sheriff nodded agreeably, and Branden helped Caroline pull four glasses down out of the cabinet. They took their glasses out onto the back porch, and the professor switched on only a single corner lamp, so that they sat on a mostly darkened porch, the professor remarking, "You can hear the crickets if you don't turn on all the lights."

"Wonderful," Robertson commented sarcastically.

"It'll be fine," Missy said. "I've got preliminary results from the two crime scenes. Lydia's death is obviously manslaughter, if you believe Meredith Silver's suicide note."

"Do you have reason not to believe it?" Branden asked.

"Perhaps. We're comparing handwriting samples from documents recovered from her home, but the note was scrawled out hastily, so I'm not willing to conclude that Meredith Silver actually wrote it herself. The BCI labs will sort it out for us."

"She didn't kill herself?" Caroline asked.

"No," Missy said, hesitating.

"No gun," the sheriff explained.

"Right," Missy said. "Right, and she couldn't have shot herself from four feet away."

"Louise Herbeck?" the professor asked.

"She insists not," Robertson said. "And there wasn't blood on her shoes. So, she didn't track those prints across the floor."

"So that's a homicide of one kind or another," Caroline said. "What about Lydia?"

Missy said, "She has a slight contusion over her shoulder blade. And Meredith admits in her note that she did shove her, causing her to fall. We can't know if she did that on purpose."

"What do you make," Branden asked, "of Louise Herbeck's carting clothes out of her sister's house?"

Robertson answered. "She claims that she's strapped for cash."

"Could be," Branden said. "But it's a little bit suspicious. I'd expect her to be more bereaved by her sister's death. At the very least, it seemed callous to me."

Robertson said, "So I've got Lydia's death as a tragic accident – involuntary manslaughter, if you believe Silver's suicide note – and Silver's death as a murder. Even if she wrote her own suicide note, it'll be someone else who shot her."

The professor asked, "What did you get from the scene at the Yost farm?"

"Just what you'd expect," Missy said. "Two sets of footprints, overlapping one another, going up the hill before the storm, and coming down in the middle of it. There are a lot of Silver's boot prints in the mud around the body, as if she tried to check for a pulse or something."

"OK, but Missy," Robertson said. "It's the two fingerprints that are interesting."

"Right," Missy said. "Getting to that. There are two sets of fingerprints on the suicide note. One set from Silver, and another one that's not in the system. So, we can't identify it."

"Except," Robertson said, "we've gotten a warrant for Louise Herbeck's fingerprints, and a search warrant for her trailer and car. We'll be looking for the gun."

"You going to wait until morning?" the professor asked.

"Oh no," Robertson said. "Pat and Ricky are over there now, searching her place on Harrison Road. I'll have her prints tonight, and I'll also know if she's got a gun hidden in her car or trailer."

"Could she really have killed her sister?" Caroline asked.

"That's the thing," Missy said. "The muzzle of the gun was back about four feet from Silver's cheek when she was shot. There's gunpowder stippling on her face, but it's a widely scattered spray, so she can't have shot herself. It's centered on her cheek, but it spreads radially out across her entire face and diminishes at every angle, with distance from the entry wound. I call it a radial differential. It gives me the approximate distance to the muzzle."

"So that's a wide spray," Branden said. "Four feet to the muzzle?"

"Yes," Missy said, smiling.

"Was there any gsr on Silver's hands?" Branden asked.

"None," Missy said. "Nothing on her hands. It was all on her face and neck."

"And you can't dust the gun for prints," Branden commented.

"We can dust it when we find it," the sheriff said confidently. "And we are going to find it someday. You can all count on that."

Chapter 17

Wednesday, August 30
10:05 AM

Professor Branden's meeting with President Benetti was to take place Wednesday morning, in the Millersburg College Trustee's board room, on the third floor of Jadet Hall, just down the corridor from Benetti's office. It was on their schedules for the quarter-hour right after his 9:00 class on slavery.

Branden climbed the worn marble steps inside Jadet Hall, and twice on the way up in the cool and shadowed stairwell, he paused with his thoughts. He hadn't slept well Tuesday night. He hadn't been able to set aside his questions about the Schells, and his questions about what it was that they really did with their ministry. And as he had laid awake, he also ruminated over the crime scene evidence, the visit by Junior Yost, and the sorrowful response by Junior, while they had traveled around the campus that night, seeing the places and things that his Aunt Lydia had loved so much. Plus, all through the night, concerns about Mary and her little Esther had pestered him. How troublesome had it been for her, married to John? Where could she have gone for help, if the bishop was unwilling to step in? What must she be thinking, now that she was out in the English world?

Then there was Lydia, who had obviously been searching for Mary. Had Lydia known something more than just that Mary had reached her limit with John? Who had convinced Mary that leaving her husband, her family and her church was a good solution to her problems? All through the night, Caroline's most fundamental question had found its way into the forefront of his consciousness. Why would a mother leave her older children behind?

When Branden arrived inside the board room, Benetti was already seated and working on documents at the long, polished boardroom table. She was a slight woman with short black hair, and she had a tendency to smile in almost any circumstance. She had tried to devote herself to academic issues, but her main responsibility was always to raise money for the college's endowment. For the meeting that morning, she had placed herself at the head of the table, and a chair on the corner beside her had been pulled out for Branden.

Benetti held her peace while Branden took his seat, and then without preamble, she looked up from her paperwork with an apologetic smile. "Look Mike," she said softly. "Your firearms museum is causing some speculation. You know we've talked about this before. It's prime real estate on campus."

"It's a unique museum, Nora," Branden said. "There isn't a duplicate anywhere in the country."

Benetti took her glasses off and smiled solicitously. She relaxed her posture, and she leaned forward to rest her elbows on the table in front of her. "Mike," she said, "it doesn't bother me, particularly, but we're dealing with a complicated science. It's *neuro*science. It does necessarily involve neurotoxin research, and the environmental impact studies tell us that the only place on campus where we can locate the isolation labs is your museum's location. The issues are air handling and scrubbing and water decontamination. For that, we need the space that your museum occupies."

"Nora, this couldn't come at a worse time."

"I know. I am truly sorry about your student. Everyone is shocked. Everyone is sad. But I want to move forward with this new major, and I want to recruit the best senior faculty to the college. So, it's more complicated than you realize."

"OK, I hear you, Nora. I hear you, but I need some time with this."

Benetti nodded. "What about Lydia Schwartz, Mike? Was it just an accident?"

"I've still got to run some things down, Nora."

"But it was an accident, right?"

"It's more complicated than that."

"How?"

"Lydia's sister seems to have left her husband. She's been missing for three weeks."

"Which is it, Mike? She's left, or she's been missing? There's a difference."

"I know," Branden said, frowning.

"Your best guess?"

"I'm not sure, Nora. I'm really not sure."

"Isn't it possible that she's been harmed?"

"I'm not sure, Nora," Branden said. "I hadn't wanted to think in those terms, but yes. It's possible."

- - - - - - - - - - - - - -

"How did it go with President Benetti?" Caroline asked.

She was driving her blue Miata with the top down after lunch, out past Mt. Hope to TR 606, to see Mose and Ida Schwartzentruber, and to check on the Yost children.

In the passenger's seat, Branden laughed at Caroline's question. "It went as well as we could have expected. The location of my museum is the problem. It's where they want to place the neuroscience labs."

"Really then, Michael. Should you be out here like this? Off campus, I mean. If your museum is in play?"

"I'll be back in time for my afternoon class. I'll talk to some of the professors."

"That's not my point."

"I know that. Should we turn around?"

"Don't be silly, Michael. I need to check on the children. I need to meet their grandparents."

"So, do I. Check on the children, I mean."

"Eggshells, Michael. You need to be walking on eggshells for your museum problem."

"First the Schwartzentrubers," Branden said. "I'll call Lawrence. He can help us while we're out here."

- - - - - - - - - - - - - -

"Mallory," Lawrence answered the professor's call. "Professor Branden's office."

"It's Mike. I need you to make a couple of calls."

"Okay who?"

"Second call, to Kathryn Rausch. Trustee. I need an appointment with her."

"Okay when do you want the meeting, Mike?"

"I'll fit into her schedule. At her earliest."

"What about?"

"Money, Lawrence. It's always about money, when you're talking to the trustees."

"Can this wait until the council of the Board? She'll be here for that."

"Not really. I'll go up to Cleveland if her schedule is tight, but ask politely if she can come down here instead. This week or next."

"And the first call?"

"Pam Stone. Find out if she's willing to tell us anything quietly about Benetti's moving forward with construction. I need to know how much time we have."

"And if Pam knows something?"

"When you call Rausch, Lawrence, spend a little time telling her what you and Pam know about all of this."

148

Chapter 18

When the Brandens pulled in at Mose and Ida Schwartzentruber's drive, Alice Shewmon was sitting in a wicker rocker, out on the front porch at the farmhouse. Her black ponytail was pulled around in front, and as she scribbled notes rapidly on a pad, she was fiddling with the strands of her hair. The Brandens climbed the wooden steps together, and Alice turned her head up to smile at them, looking like a woman whose intensity was matched only by her determination.

Caroline spoke a greeting and brought a straight-backed porch chair around so that she could sit beside Shewmon. "You look like you've been out here for a while," she said to Alice.

"Since 9:00," Alice laughed. "I don't think I've made any progress here. I've been trying to teach them about vaccinations. They say it's for the bishop to decide."

"OK," Caroline said, chuckling. "Good luck with the bishop."

Upon hearing that, the professor left Caroline with Alice on the front porch, and he rapped loudly on the porch door. A woman answered with a call from the far back reaches of the house, "It's still open, Miss Shewmon."

Branden entered the farmhouse through the front screened door. Inside, on the bare living room floor, two of

149

the Yost girls were down on their hands and knees, playing a game of marbles. They had the circle surrounding the marbles laid out with a length of brown yarn, with its ends tied together. They looked up warily when Branden approached.

"Where is your grandmother?" he asked the girls, and one of them pointed woodenly to the back of the house, saying only, "Laundry." As Branden moved past the girls, they tracked him with their suspicious eyes.

Branden sorted his way through to the back porch, and there a wrinkled Amish woman in a black dress and a black bonnet was stirring a galvanized tub of sudsy water with a canoe paddle, turning the clothes over and around to immerse them. She was a slight woman, and thin. The hem of her full-length black dress brushed the floorboards of the porch. She was Ida Schwartzentruber, Lydia and Mary's mother, and she was not a fan of the professor.

She said tersely, without more than a glance to Branden, "You caused this, Mr. Branden. You are the reason that she's dead."

"No, Ida," Branden said, trying for a smile. "Lydia made her own choices."

Ida frowned, and she didn't speak. She didn't look up from her washtub.

"Are all the Yost children over here, now?" he asked.

"Two are still at school," Ida said, continuing to stir her wash with the paddle. The bonnet so completely covered the side of her face, that Branden could not see her expression. "Except little Esther," she added. "They say she is with her mother, but I don't know that for certain. The other young one, Jonas, is napping. Frankly, I don't know why you'd care, after all the trouble you English have caused. Dithy Silver was a decent enough woman, but she didn't know what was right for our Mary."

"Please, Mrs. Schwartzentruber. My wife and I came here to see about the children. And to see about you and Mose. Are you all going to be OK out here? Is there anything we can do to help? We know how sad you must be."

Ida stood her canoe paddle against the house and turned to face the professor. "We are fine. And what would you know about sadness? Has anyone you loved ever died?"

Branden stepped back a little bit. He bowed his head and said, "We lost three children to miscarriages, Mrs. Schwartzentruber. Like I said, we know how very sad you must be."

Ida softened and said, "I am sorry, Mr. Branden. Sorry for your loss, but our Lydia got that scholarship from you. That's when she left us to go *English*. That's when all the sorrows began for us. When Lydia left. You'll have to forgive me if I remind myself every day that you are the ones who did that to her."

"I'm sorry," Branden said. "I'm here with my wife Caroline. I was across the road last night, after they found your daughter. After they found Lydia's body. I am sorry for your loss, too. I am brokenhearted about it."

Ida rubbed her fingers nervously on her work apron, and she pulled open the back screened door to her house. As she went stiffly inside, she said, without looking at Branden, "We have no use for your English *Social Services*, here, Professor. We can take care of our own."

Branden followed her inside to a large kitchen. He waited while she leaned over to add small slats of wood into the belly of her cooking stove. "Mose is out in the fields," she said, standing upright and facing Branden directly. "You'll need to talk with Mose," she said as if dismissing him.

"Please tell me, Mrs. Schwartzentruber. Where has Mary Yost been for the last three weeks?"

"You'll need to speak with my husband," Ida said sternly. She turned and left the room abruptly.

- - - - - - - - - - - - - - -

Out on the front porch again, Branden found Caroline and Alice Shewmon standing together at the end of the porch. They were talking quietly, side by side, and Alice looked to Branden to be considerably more perplexed than before. She was listening intently to what Caroline was saying, and she was shaking her head as Caroline spoke to her. The professor thought better of interrupting, so he took a seat in a wicker rocker, and he listened to Caroline.

"Faith, yes," Caroline was saying. "But they have rules based on how they interpret the Bible. And they have rules based on what their bishops and preachers tell them about traditions. Their peasant lifestyle is as important to them as your career is to you. They'll never abandon their traditions. It is what makes them Amish."

Shaking her head, Alice said, "The children? They don't have a choice. They're the most in danger here. Really, I think I can help them. I think I can convince them."

Caroline led Shewmon to a rocker beside the professor, and the two women sat down together, Caroline beside Alice as before.

"What can we do?" Alice asked. "There's so much I could do to help, here. I thought I'd be able to reason with them. But they're all so reserved. Unapproachable. Even the children. I can barely get a word out of them. It's like they don't trust English people at all."

Branden nodded. "They *are* reserved, Alice. They really do not trust us. They won't accept your help. They'll never abandon their lifestyle. And Schwartzentruber kids are taught not to talk to us English. They're taught to be suspicious of us."

Alice scoffed. "They need to let me help them, at least with vaccinations."

Caroline stood with her. "We're trying to tell you something important, Alice, about their traditions."

Shewmon took up her bag, clipped down the steps and turned back on the driveway to look up at the Brandens, saying, "I'm going to find a way around these traditions. I've got some things to show the bishop. I'm hopeful, and I'm not giving up."

- - - - - - - - - - - - - -

Mose Schwartzentruber came into his house through the back-porch door. He seemed surprised to see Caroline in his kitchen. She was helping Ida there, cutting thin slices from a loaf of warm bread. Without speaking to her, Mose came up to the cutting board and gently moved Caroline's hand over so that her next slice of bread would be doubly thick.

The professor joined them in the kitchen. In his fingers, he was rolling three glass marbles around. "It has been a long time since I played a game of marbles," he remarked.

He held his hand forward and said, "I am Michael Branden. I am a reserve deputy with the sheriff's department. Lydia was my student at the college. This is my wife Caroline. I am hoping that you remember us." He handed the three marbles to Mose.

Mose nodded and took the marbles. He did not offer to take Branden's hand. He gave an appraising look to his wife Ida, and then looking to Branden but not to Caroline, he said, "I know who you are, of course. We can talk on the front porch."

Once they were all seated outside, Mose said, "That Social Services lady is not welcome here anymore. We'll never let her take our grandchildren away."

"I understand that," Branden said. "It'll never come to that."

"Have you actually *talked* with this woman?" Mose asked.

"Yes," Caroline said. "We're trying to get her to understand."

Mose did not turn to Caroline when she spoke. Addressing only the professor, he ignored her rather purposefully. "Do you know where Mary is, Mr. Branden?" he asked. "She's our daughter, too."

Caroline smiled knowingly at his rebuff and held silence.

"No," Branden answered. "But we are looking for her."

"And Esther?"

"We are looking for her, too."

"Our whole congregation has already been doing that," Mose said pausing to look down. When he looked up, he asked, "When can we have Lydia's body for burial?"

"I don't know."

Mose took a moment inside his thoughts. Then he said, "The Yost children need their mother to come home. Every family needs a mother. I don't care what she's been hearing, she still has to know that."

Branden drew a breath and wrinkled a stitch between his brows. He looked into Mose's eyes. "We think Mary left a voice message on the sheriff's phone. She didn't say she wanted to come home, Mose. She said rather the opposite, really."

"She has to come home," Mose pronounced like a judgement. "She belongs with her family. She is needed at home."

"What if John just got to be too much for her to handle, Mr. Schwartzentruber?" Branden asked.

Still speaking only to the professor, Mose said, "God does not lay on us more than we can bear."

Branden studied his eyes. He noted his upright and challenging posture. "Mr. Schwartzentruber," he began, "Mose. Are you going to accept the help of the county's Social Services office?"

"No."

Branden rose. "We'll let you know if we find your daughter. And Esther, too."

Caroline stood, too. She turned to descend the steps, but changed her mind. Turning back to Schwartzentruber, she spoke gently and softly. "I'm sorry, Mr. Schwartzentruber. I was trying to explain some things to Ms. Shewmon. She really doesn't understand yet. Sometimes, neither do I. Please try to understand how she feels about this. How I feel about this. Vaccines can really help you. You should listen to her."

Mose replied sternly. "It is for the bishop to decide."

- - - - - - - - - - - - - - -

In the Miata driving home, Caroline said, "I had to say it to him, Michael. I had to give it a try. More and more I find that I agree with Alice Shewmon. It's the children who suffer the most. It doesn't seem fair to me anymore."

"You know Amish folk as well as anyone," the professor commented.

"Yes, but not so much the Schwartzentrubers. Their sect isn't much like the others. They're the most insular people we know. And Alice is right. You just can't talk to the kids. They don't respond. Except someone like Junior, who is curious about English life. He's a smart kid. I think he'd be happy, getting out of the Amish church. But I don't think Alice has much of a chance, here with Mose and Ida, convincing them to get vaccinations."

"She's been working here only a year?" Branden asked. "In Holmes County?"

"Maybe that, why?"

"I don't know, Caroline. I can't fault her for her enthusiasm, but she's clearly seeing how stand-offish they are. I don't think she was prepared for that."

"No."

"So, she's going to have to learn some things, Caroline."

"Like what?"

"Like the Schwartzentrubers don't really want her kind of help at all."

157

Chapter 19

Rather woodenly, the professor taught his 3:00 class on American History, the sorrow of Lydia's death hanging over him like a pall. He worked in his office during the weary afternoon, but the article he was preparing for the journal *Civil War History* failed to hold his interest. He had tried to scribble out notes for his history department's staff meeting coming up on Thursday afternoon, but he was not able to concentrate. And several times during the afternoon, students and faculty stopped by to hear news about Lydia. How had she died? Was it really an accident? What can we do to honor her? When news spread that Branden was talking with students in his office about Lydia, people had begun to arrive.

One student was especially sad, remembering that, "Everybody knew Lydia, Professor Branden. If you missed a class, it was Lydia's notes that you wanted to copy. She always took the best class notes."

"I appreciate that," Branden said, "but Monday in class, she was distracted. I don't think she took any notes at all. Does anyone know what was troubling her?"

Two students answered in the negative. Two more stood shaking their heads, looking down at their feet.

"Was she active on campus?" Branden asked. "Was she popular?"

A student who had arrived later than the others said, "She did everything, Professor. All the concerts, all the lectures, seminars, discussion groups. She was always busy. And if she wasn't doing anything else, she was writing in one of her diaries. So, she was popular, but she was also too busy to hang with any one crowd."

An economics professor wandered into Branden's office and asked, "Mike, are we going to have a memorial service?"

"I don't know at this point," Branden answered.

"Well, she was a good student, Mike. The best. We should do something to remember her."

The gathering of students and professors eventually filtered out of Branden's office, and he was left alone to stare with a deep melancholy out through the windows of his office, down into the Oak Grove. Time passed without his noticing it, and when he eventually stirred from his thoughts, it was already early evening.

Then walking home on the brick walkway through the oak grove for dinner, Branden was approached by a student in the white and green-striped uniform of the Millersburg College baseball team. He approached Branden with his head down, slapping his mitt fiercely against his thigh, his eyes shadowed by a pair of dark sunglasses.

"Professor Branden?" he said. "Do you have a moment? Lydia was my friend. We were dating. Can you talk for a minute? I've got training, so it'll just take a minute."

The professor stopped and turned back to the fellow.

He was tall and wiry, fit and trim, handsome in his uniform. He pushed a finger up under his sunglasses and rubbed anxiously at his eye. His finger came away wet with tears, and he seemed distraught as he settled his glasses squarely back over his eyes. "We were dating," he said again, this time in a broken whisper.

"I do have time," Branden said. "We should talk. Here on this bench?"

"Oh, I couldn't sit down, Professor. I can't stop moving. I haven't slept in two days. I can't get a minute's peace. I love her. I *loved* her. I feel like this is going to crush me. I find myself walking into her dorm room, and then I remember. She's like a habit that I can't break. I don't know anything, anymore. It feels like it should have been me who died. I think I'd prefer that. I don't know what to do. Professor, I've never felt so alone."

"Try to sit here a minute," Branden said, and he got the fellow seated on the bench beside the walkway. They were shaded by one of the broad oaks. The grove was mostly deserted, with just one couple throwing a Frisbee on the far side of the lawn. Branden faced the boy and reached over to press his hand down on the ball glove, saying, "You shouldn't keep bouncing that against your thigh."

"It's nerves," the ball player said. "I can't seem to stop. I've got a bruise there, but it helps. Does that make any sense at all? Am I losing my mind?"

"Tell me your name," Branden said. "Tell me about Lydia."

"I don't think I can."

"Then just your name."

"Audi Kanuff," he said, removing his sunglasses. He pulled a bandana from his hip pocket and pressed it to his eyes. "I'm sorry, Professor. I was angry, yesterday. Now I'm just so sad. I don't know what to do."

"It's OK, Audi," Branden said. He put a hand on Kanuff's knee. "If you haven't been sleeping, have you at least been eating?"

"No," Audi said, shaking his head. "I'm not hungry."

"Funny," Audi continued after a pause, "I am James Audent Kanuff III, my parents are benefactors of the college, I've got a place in the family business when I graduate, a fortune if I want it, and I'd trade it all right now for just another ten minutes with Lydia."

"Yes," Branden said gently. "Time is the only asset of any significant value. Ten minutes with her now, and you'd gladly give all the rest of it away."

Audi broke with a strangled laugh, and tears appeared again, lacing his cheeks. He buried his face in his mitt, and his shoulders shuddered, as he drew a deep breath and released it as a ragged cry. He wrapped an arm across his gut as if he were afraid he would spill all of himself out onto the walkway and die. The professor took his shoulders and pulled him into his embrace. Another baseball player hurried over from one of the dorms, but Branden waved for him to stop and stand back to give Audi some privacy.

The other baseball player stepped back and sat on the grass with his arms wrapping around his knees. He waited there, thirty yards away, while Audi spent himself in the professor's arms. Then he came up to Audi when Branden waved for him, and he lifted Audi to his feet and walked him back to the dorm. Branden stood to watch them go, and he stayed there until they had entered the building.

Then Branden resumed his walk home, drying his own eyes and making a call to Detective Ricky Niell.

"Ricky," he said when Niell answered, "How many diary notebooks did you and Pat find in Lydia Schwartz's dorm room?"

"Probably fifteen," Niell said. "Why?"

"I need to get started reading them, Ricky."

"I can bring some over after dinner. Then maybe tomorrow, you could make a little trip with me? The sheriff was going to have me ask you about it, anyway."

"I have an 8:00 seminar and a staff meeting at 4:00."

"If I picked you up at 10:30 Mike, we'd probably be home by 2:00. Would that work?"

"OK, but where?"

"Parma," Ricky said. "The marriage counselors. Because the voicemail greeting for Mary on Lydia's phone is too urgent to be just an ordinary greeting. So, I'm making this trip to Parma, tomorrow. These are the counselors Mary was supposed to see last Saturday. Can you drive up there with me?"

"Yes. Sure. But I want to start reading Lydia's diaries tonight."

"After dinner, Mike. I'll bring them over."

- - - - - - - - - - - - - -

Lydia's diaries were a revelation to the professor. He read them late into the night. She had written about everything. Her classes, her friends, her love affair with Audi Kanuff. She had written about her professors and her favorite subjects. Literature, history, economics, biology. She had embraced the liberal arts experience like the earnest students the professor remembered from his earliest years as a teacher. But most importantly, she had written about her family, and about her struggle to break away from the Schwartzentruber sect and find her way in the English world. There were entries about her parents and her brothers and sisters, plus all her dozens of nieces and nephews, cousins and aunts and uncles. Even entries about her preachers and the bishop. The church. The congregation. The life she had forsaken when they had all grown cold toward her, because she had left her family behind. Well maybe not all were cold to her. Mary her sister, it seemed, had stayed close.

Mary had been Lydia's tether to her old life. If the diary entries were trustworthy indications, Mary had been Lydia's pipeline to news of family and friends who would no longer be pleased to have her visit. It had been a burden that almost broke Lydia, but not quite. Her relationship with Mary had preserved enough of a connection with her family that she could embrace the English world and the life at

163

college, just as she needed to do. Just as she needed to do in order to be free. To be herself. To be the real and complete Lydia Schwartz. Or so it appeared in the diary entries that Branden read that night.

Then also, there were the entries about Mary. These were the saddest. The most conflicted. These were the ones that most convinced Branden that the trip to see the Culps tomorrow in Parma would not be wasted. Mary, Lydia had written, was also struggling with her own life's choices and options.

On a Thursday last May, Lydia had written:

> *Mary is so sad. She has it the hardest. She gets no relief from John. He's never going to understand. I'm not sure the Schells are really helping. They're telling her the right things, but they can't really know what they are asking of her. So sad. I just have got to talk with Dithy. Have to talk with Donna, too. Maybe they're pushing Mary too hard?*

In early June, she had written:

> *Mary There's so much she doesn't know. She's too isolated. Bishops can't always be right. Family? Self? What is more*

164

*important? Where is the freedom? Am I
really free? I miss them all so very much.
But I can't go back. I wouldn't want to
anyway. Audi is right. I just can't go back.
It's such a waste, to make them all live like
that. If the bishop shows up here again, I'm
going to tell him just that. I'm going to
explain to him about the light. Knowledge
brings light, and light brings freedom. But
what about Mary? How can Amish life be
right for her, under her circumstances? Is
John really that bad? But no, Lydia, think.
There are the children! This might be a
mistake. Schells? What have they promised
her? Will they really be there for her in the
rough times ahead?*

In late July:

*The phone! Brilliant! She can call me. I
can call her. It's a lifeline for her. Call me,
Mary. You can call every day now. Nothing
yet. Gonna call tonight. No, can't do that.
John will hear the phone ring. So she has to
call me. Maybe when she's over at Dithy's?*

165

Two days later, the entry was:

I simply must call Mary. I have to risk it. John? It's worse than ever. Is she really in danger there? Dithy says so. I need to call Donna. Oh really, Lydia? What are you thinking? Just go out there with Donna for the studies, to hear what they are telling her. Tell Donna/tell Mary/call me! Please, please, please just call me Mary!

Later in August:

It's all foolishness. Of course she has to stay with her family. She really has no choice. The children are so very important. Mary can't leave them. She just can't leave them all behind like that. She can't stay either. Impossible situation. I need some time with the babies. Up on the hill. Quiet, cemetery quiet. Talk to the babies. I just can't think straight any more. Dithy and Donna? They don't really understand. They talk, but they haven't been through it. It's too easy to give advice. Mary, what will you do? Impossible No answer will ever be good enough. Can

166

you really be safe there? OK, Lydia, what about you? You made it out just fine. Really? Did I? Oh, so much do I miss the light of home lanterns.

- - - - - - - - - - - - - -

Caroline found him on the sofa, with one of Lydia's diaries laid across his chest. She nudged him softly. "Michael," she whispered. "Michael, you've got a class." "What?" he stirred slowly awake. "Mary?"

"What about her, Michael?"

"Mary wasn't sure. Neither was Lydia. She wanted out, but she couldn't figure a way. She couldn't leave the children behind."

"I told you, Michael. This never made any sense to me. To leave her children behind? It never made any sense to me at all."

The professor pulled himself off the sofa and stood in his bare feet on the carpet. He displayed the last diary he had been reading and said, "Lydia writes about 'Dithy' a lot. That's gotta be Meredith Silver. Mere*dith*. Dithy. Also, Donna Schell. I don't think Lydia thought they were giving Mary such good advice. But she wavered. She wasn't certain about any of this, herself."

"Certain about any of what?" Caroline asked, leading him into the kitchen.

"Certain about leaving. About Mary's leaving the church. That's what they were talking about. I think Donna and Meredith were having more than simple bible studies with Mary. And I think Lydia was really quite troubled by that."

"Michael, it's not reasonable to leave your children behind."

"You've said that before," the professor complained.

"You don't have to be cross with me, Michael. I'm just telling you. It's too extreme. There'd have to be something drastic to make her do that."

"Perhaps her life there with John was really horrible. Remember what Junior said."

"Or someone got her talked into it. Somebody got her talked into leaving."

"What do you mean?"

"I read one of those diaries myself, Michael. Lydia didn't know what Donna was telling Mary. Also, I don't think she was sure about 'Dithy' anymore. She was worried that maybe there was something more than just Bible study going on out there."

"Caroline, it was Donna who was so much help for Lydia when she was getting out herself. Right? When she was starting college. It was Donna Schell who helped her get through it."

"Yes, well maybe Donna has been helping Mary too much. It's like I told you, Michael."

"I know. You don't think she'd do it."

"I think it would be very hard for her. I think she'd doubt herself forever. I think she'd go back for the other children. That's what gets me. The older children. If she really has left, she must have a plan to go back for the other children."

"Louise Herbeck said something like, 'you have to save yourself first,' as if they were advising her to get herself out, and then go back for the other kids."

"Then that's the only way any of this makes any sense to me, Michael. It's either that, or Mary is dead, too. Just like Lydia."

Chapter 20

At the Culp's counseling offices in Parma, in the south-central section of the Cleveland metropolis, after they had parked in front of the steel and glass building, Ricky displayed his detective's badge for the receptionist.

"Police?" she asked. "Do you have an appointment?"

"Sheriff's Office," Ricky said. "From Holmes County."

"With all those Amish people?"

"Right. And yes, we do have an appointment."

The two men waited for half an hour in padded reception room chairs, and when Paul Culp came out to greet them, Ricky displayed his badge again. Culp showed them into a small front office with a desk and two chairs placed in front of it, and as they sat down, the professor said, "We are here about Mary Yost. She was supposed to see you last Saturday."

Culp sat behind his desk and pulled his chair in. He flipped a few pages in his desk calendar and said, "We never saw her."

"Did she have an appointment?" Ricky asked. "What can you tell us about her?"

"An Amish lady from Holmes County?" Culp asked. "It was the Schells who arranged the appointment. Honestly,

170

the way my wife explained it to me, we were supposed to go down to Millersburg, eventually. Sometime this week. To speak with Mary Yost's husband."

"Did you intend to stay?" Branden asked.

"I couldn't say. It would have depended on what we found there. Nancy is more familiar with this. She spoke with the Schells."

"Can we talk with Nancy?" Ricky asked.

"She's in a session. Won't be finished for another thirty minutes. You'd have to wait."

"We can do that," Ricky said. "Back out in the lobby?"

Culp shook his head with a smile. "No. We've got a more comfortable place than that," and he showed Branden and Niell into a counseling room, with two soft lounging chairs and a straight-backed armchair. A small desk was angled into the corner.

When Nancy Culp appeared, Ricky was leaning back in one of the loungers, and Branden was seated in the armchair. Paul Culp followed into the room behind his wife.

The Culps were genteel people. Round and delicate. Soft and placid. Careful by practice, the professor suspected, not to aggravate or to startle.

Nancy took the lounger next to Niell, and Paul sat at the corner desk. Looking to each of Branden and Niell, Nancy said gently and softly, "We got a call from Donna Schell. That's about all we know. We cleared our weekend schedule, because Donna said it was somewhat of an emergency, and we waited here at the office. Nobody showed up. Neither Saturday nor Sunday. We were ready, too, but she didn't show up, or call."

"Is Donna Schell the excitable type?" the professor asked. "Maybe too quick to call for help?"

"Anything but," Paul Culp said. His voice was deep and melodious. But it was hard to hear. Branden turned to face him, to watch his lips as he spoke. This was his calm counselor's voice, the professor surmised, practiced to put his patients at ease.

"Donna's about as levelheaded as you can get," Paul Culp continued. "Devoted to her ministry. Sober. This time, though, she might have reacted too soon. Clients aren't always ready to talk. At least not when their friends want them to. Maybe Donna got a little bit ahead of herself."

Nancy voiced disagreement. "She wouldn't have called if it weren't a critical situation, Paul. She said Mary Yost needed immediate help. She said the husband there was depressed. That he was troublesome. Hard to live with. Stern with the children. She hinted that he was dangerous, but she wouldn't explain."

Ricky asked, "Do you think he's capable of violence?"

Paul shook his head. "We don't know him. We don't know anything about him, other than what Donna said last Thursday on the phone."

The door to the counseling room opened, and the receptionist from the front desk put her head inside. "We might have some trouble," she said. "Jimmy Matt."

172

Nancy got out of her chair quickly. "Is he coming here?"

"I don't know," the receptionist said. "He was angry on the phone."

"Call the police, please," Paul Culp said. "Tell them what's going on. Maybe we should get them over here."

Nancy Culp sat back in her chair. "We sometimes have a dangerous situation."

Branden asked, "You weren't worried that you were walking into a dangerous situation in Holmes County?"

"With an Amish family?" Nancy said nervously. "No, not really. We were just going to talk to Mary Yost on Saturday, counsel her, and maybe travel down there later, to meet this John and assess the situation. If he was agreeable, one of us would have taken a room at a nearby hotel. We have patients during the week, and normally we're very busy. One of us would have had to come back here for that."

"Is this Jimmy Matt a dangerous man?" Ricky asked. "Because, I mean, you've asked for the police. Is he going to be a problem?"

"You never know," Paul said. "Families present a complicated dynamic."

"You don't actually move in, to stay with troubled families?" Branden asked. "I would think that is dangerous. At least potentially."

"Well," Paul Culp said, "we do that only when it's necessary. That'd be an extreme situation."

"Donna called you Thursday?" Ricky asked. "This last Thursday?"

173

"Yes," both Culps said.

"I've been wondering," the professor said. "Why wouldn't Donna have referred Mary to a program in Holmes County? Like our Family Assistance Agency. They are in the business of helping troubled families."

Nancy smiled. "It's all about the ministry for Donna. Programs like F.A.A. don't address spiritual issues. Donna said she doesn't really trust them."

Suddenly, from out in the lobby entrance, there was the crashing of steel and the shattering of glass. A diesel truck engine growled once, was shut off, and sputtered on fumes. Shouting ensued, and the Culps, followed closely by Branden and Niell, darted out into the lobby.

A large pickup had smashed its way through the glass at the front doors of the building, and the receptionist was backed up against the wall, wild-eyed, watching a disheveled man in front of her desk. He was leaning forward with a drunken sway, and he was shouting aggressively at her. "Where's my wife? You have no right! I want my wife back, and I mean right now!"

He had one fist planted on the desktop, and he had his other hand cocked back near his ear. He looked angry enough to swing a fist at her. The muscles along his jaw were rippling with tension.

Ricky parked his hand on the butt of his gun and flipped that strap that covered the hammer. He advanced immediately to the angry man. "Back up!" he shouted. "Back up and calm down."

Jimmy Matt drew back his fist, and Ricky hit him in the face. Matt stumbled backward, almost losing his balance. He righted himself, but shattered glass gave way beneath his boots, and Matt slipped on the shards and fell over forward, onto his hands and knees.

Niell pointed at Matt. "Sheriff's Department," he barked out. "Stay down."

Matt cranked his neck to glare up at Ricky. "My knees!" he shouted. "My knees are cut." He held out his palms, and splinters of glass were protruding from bloody wounds there.

By now, the receptionist was on the phone. Paul and Nancy Culp were standing back in a corner. The professor stepped up to Matt, being careful not to slip on the glass himself, and he helped the man to his feet.

"I just want my wife back," Jimmy said, sounding wretched and defeated.

Branden could smell beer on Matt's breath. He felt the man waver on his feet, despite the fact that Branden had a firm grasp on his arm. "He's drunk," Branden said, and he spun Matt around to help Ricky buckle his wrists into handcuffs.

At the desk, which was covered with broken glass and bent metal strips that had broken away from the door jam, the receptionist spoke on the phone. "There's a deputy here, but I need police."

Her face was bleeding at the cheek, where there was a sliver of glass sticking out from a wound. She laid the handset of the phone down on the desk, and using her

175

fingertips, she put a hand to her cheek. She winced when she felt the glass that was imbedded there, and she stumbled over to a lobby chair in the far corner. Paul and Nancy Culp rushed forward to attend to her.

With the angry Jimmy Matt, Niell started asking questions. "What are you doing? Are you crazy?"

"I just want my wife," Matt said, struggling against his handcuffs.

Ricky pressed in. "You've hurt people, here," he declared.

"I'm sorry about that. I didn't mean to. I've been drinking. She left me. They told her to leave me! The crooks! They took all our money for their stupid *counseling*, and then they just told her to leave me anyway!"

"You're gonna to have to calm down," Ricky said, backing Matt against an interior wall. "The police are coming. You've done a lot of damage, here."

"I'll pay for the damages," Matt sputtered nervously. "I just want my wife back."

An ambulance arrived, and medics moved Matt to a seat, away from the Culps' receptionist. One medic stayed with Matt – cutting off his jeans at the knees – and the other went to the receptionist. A police car pulled up out front, and officers came in to stand over Jimmy Matt, while the paramedic tended to Matt's knees. A white sedan came into the parking lot, and a police captain, with a badge case hooked over his suit pocket, came inside, stepping over broken glass and metal. To the officers, the captain said, "You have this?" and both officers answered, "Yes."

176

The captain turned next to question the Culps and their receptionist. "This is your third angry husband," he said with a trace of ire to Nancy Culp. "In what? Something like four months?"

"Five months, actually," Nancy Culp said evenly. "The third in *five* months. It didn't used to be like this."

- - - - - - - - - - - - - -

Ricky drove on the trip home, and the professor remained silent, with his right elbow parked up on the window ledge, and his head resting sideways against the palm of his hand. Ricky let him have privacy with his thoughts.

As they were traveling back into Millersburg on SR 39, the professor's contemplations were disturbed by a call from President Nora Benetti's Executive Secretary Pamela Stone. He checked the display, answered the call and said, "Hi Pam. You ready to come back to the history department?"

"You wish, Mike. Actually, I'd almost be tempted. There's more going on here than I really wanted to know about. You know, it's all campus intrigue up here in the tower."

"Something that involves me?"

"Your museum, Mike. There's been some movement on your museum."

"I talked with Nora about this yesterday. I thought we'd have some time, yet."

"It's gone a little bit above Nora, Mike. Some of the trustees are looking at your museum space, too. They're talking about moving forward by the first of the year."

Branden sighed. "Is Nora just out of the loop on this, or has she been hiding this from me? Because like I said, I just spoke with her yesterday."

"She's playing the angles, Mike. You know how it is. She's protecting the endowment. Anyway, I thought you should know. Maybe you can work something out to save your museum. Benetti is concerned about the college's endowment more than anything else, so maybe you could use that information, somehow."

- - - - - - - - - - - - - -

By 2:00 PM, the professor was back in his office, preparing for his 4:00 staff meeting with department of history faculty. As he was keying the last line into his agenda document, Louise Herbeck appeared at his door.

Once she was seated in front of the professor's desk, Herbeck asked, "Have you learned anything about Mary Yost? Do you know where she is? And little Esther, too. I'm worried."

178

"Nothing yet," Branden replied. "She was supposed to see the Culps on Saturday. I gather you know who they are?"

"Yes, but my sister would have known them better," Herbeck said. "There's really no word?"

"No."

Louise shrugged. "Well, I'm worried about her. About Mary. And Esther."

"I think we *should* be worried," the professor said. "I know I am."

Herbeck showed a deep frown and shook her head, troubled. "I never believed John would actually hurt her," she said without much conviction. "Well, I really can't get myself to believe he would, even if I think I have to. Meredith was complaining about this sort of thing, but she might have over reacted."

"Is there really any chance of that?" Branden asked.

Herbeck shook her head. "Not really. It's unthinkable. Amish? No. But Donna Schell is worried, and I guess I am, too, since Mary didn't show up at the Culps."

"You seem to know a lot about what's going on. I gather you know Donna quite well."

Herbeck said, "Since over a year ago. I got to know her because they studied together at Meredith's house. You've met her? Donna, I mean?"

"Yes," said Branden.

"She does have a mission for the Amish," Herbeck said. "She's devoted to it."

"And her husband Ed?" the professor asked. "Do you know him well? Did you know he was raised Amish?"

"Ed," Louise pronounced, nodding her head to punctuate her tone. She drew a heavy breath and sighed.

"What?" Branden asked.

"Ed Schell is a puzzle," Herbeck said. "Raised Amish like that, and a Schwartzentruber, too. You've gotta wonder how he got out of the Amish church."

The professor asked, "Do they focus on Schwartzentruber Amish? Does he 'have a calling' for Schwartzentrubers? You know, a special ministerial 'calling'?"

"Something like that," Herbeck said.

"He has a map on his office wall."

Herbeck nodded, looking somewhat perplexed. "Meredith told me about it. It's supposed to be all the Schwartzentruber settlements in Holmes County?"

"Yes. How did he map them out?" Branden asked.

"The way I understand it," Herbeck said, "he used the wagons. They bring those old European wagons into town, you know. Big green wooden wagons, with two draft horses. Massive iron wagon wheels. He watches for them, and he follows them back to their farms. He hands out religious tracts when he follows them home, and when he finds them in town."

"Exclusively for Schwartzentrubers?" Branden asked.

"Well," Herbeck said, "mostly. Yes. That's the focus. For Ed, anyways."

180

"Is he successful?" the professor asked.

"Sometimes," Herbeck said, hesitating. "A few times, I guess. Donna has the better approach. Careful and subdued. Like with her bible studies. She brings them along slowly, prayerfully. To teach them. But Ed? He's too nervous. Too earnest, if you know what I mean."

"Too pushy?" the professor asked.

Herbeck considered the question. She turned her eyes to the carpet and then looked back up to Branden. "Meredith didn't like him that much. He was too much in a rush, I guess. And not always insightful. He's ready to give up a lot of the times. And he's shallow. Something. I don't know. He's not willing to go deep into the issues with them. Meredith complained about this. She said he wants a quick conversion, and he's impatient when he doesn't get one."

"The superficial evangelist?" the professor asked. "Won't take the time to teach and persuade?"

"I guess."

"You're not sure?"

Louise paused with her thoughts. Eventually, she said, "I'm not making a generalization, mind you. Not everyone fits, here. But sometimes the ones with the strongest opinions are the ones who have done the weakest thinking."

Branden laughed nervously. "It doesn't sound like you care for him all that much."

"He's OK," Herbeck said. "But Meredith did consider him to be – what'd you call it – superficial."

The professor shrugged. "You don't have any idea where Mary is?"

"None at all."

"Do you think Donna has good thinking? Good opinions?"

"She's committed, Professor. As committed to her ministry as anyone I know. But she's not as intense as Ed. She's inclined to sit and pray, whereas he's more the type to stomp around behind his lectern for his Sunday sermons."

Branden gazed across his desk at Herbeck, and he considered a gamble. Maybe, he thought, it might be too raw a nerve. But he pressed forward, anyway, saying, "Can you really get that much money for used clothing, Louise?"

Herbeck smiled nervously. "You're thinking it was callous of me to sell her clothes for spending money?"

"Perhaps a bit. You know you can't go back inside Meredith's house just yet."

"I talked to her lawyer this morning," Herbeck said. "About her will. I'm to get the house and some cash. It'll be enough. But I can't get any of it until it clears probate. So, I'm glad I took those clothes."

"What clothes did you take?" Branden asked, coming forward onto the edge of his seat.

"The ones that I had already loaded into my trunk, Professor. You didn't check there, so you also didn't tell me that I had to put them back. I'm going to need the little money that I got for them."

Smiling with chagrin, Branden asked, "How much was that?"

"Four-hundred and eighty dollars, cash."

Branden didn't reply, hoping that Herbeck would feel the need to explain further.

"Meredith was a widow," she said with a sigh. "Her husband was a truck driver, and she was set up pretty sweetly with her share of his pension. My husband? He was a farmer. I taught grade school, and he worked the land. But he died four years ago, I got behind on the taxes, and they sold the land out from under me for back taxes, fines and penalties. That's why I'm living in a rented trailer. Because the government can take your house. Land. Anything they want, really. That's why I need used clothes to sell. The four-hundred and eighty dollars? That's more money than I've had at any one time since my husband died. So, yes it was a little callous of me, to be over there yesterday taking out her clothes. My guess is, Meredith doesn't too much mind."

- - - - - - - - - - - - - -

As soon as Herbeck left his office, the professor called the sheriff.

"Bruce," he asked, "Did you match Louise Herbeck's prints to the second set that was found on Meredith Silver's suicide note?"

"No," Robertson said. "They don't match. It wasn't Herbeck who handled that note."

"OK, did you find a gun at Herbeck's house. Or in her car?"

"Why, Mike? What's going on?"

"Well, either I just witnessed an amazing display of bravado, or Louise Herbeck is completely innocent."

"No gun, Mike. She didn't have one."

"That gun could be anywhere, Bruce."

"Yes, but none of the prints on the suicide note match any of her prints. So Herbeck's a dead end for that issue."

"OK. Thanks. It's just that Herbeck seems a bit too forthright to me. Like she's bluffing it through."

"I don't think so," the sheriff said. "Now tell me, what did you think of the Culps?"

"Decent folk, I guess. They wanted to help, but Mary just never showed up."

"That's pretty much what Ricky told me."

"So, where is she?" Branden asked, perplexed. "Why is there no trace of her?"

"Don't know, Mike. Maybe she's not *with us* anymore."

Chapter 21

The professor parked his truck that evening on TR 606, at the head of John Yost's farm lane. He was beside the culvert where Ricky Niell had left his cruiser Monday afternoon, with its lights flashing.

Here, Bishop Yost was working a team of draft horses near the road, cutting the outermost stalks of corn around the perimeter, to open the field for harvesting. Once opened like that, the feed corn would stand under the autumn sky until the harvest, when the families of the church would join to bring in one family's crop and then another's, until the corn of the entire congregation had been loaded into the wood and wire corn cribs that stood on every Schwartzentruber farm.

Branden climbed out of his truck and called out to the bishop. They spoke together there at the edge of the field, and Branden secured permission to walk the farm. As he explained it to Bishop Yost, he wanted to see again where Lydia had died on the bridle path, and he wanted to see the farmhouse where the family lived. The bishop pronounced it a strange request, but Branden said in pleading his case that, "I want to help find Mary and Esther. I want to know why Mary left, and I want to talk with her about bringing Esther home."

The bishop nodded his appreciation and said, "We have nothing to hide, Professor. Just do not bother the people who are working here. There's been a lot of neglect here, and we're trying to get the place straightened up. Everyone is helping, but they have their own farms to tend, and I want them finished here, in time to do that."

"I'll stay out of the way," Branden promised. "I just want to walk the farm. It'll help clear my head. I hope we can still find Mary and Esther."

Pointedly the bishop asked, "Are you also hoping that John can come home from the hospital, to his children?"

"Of course. Why not?"

"That Social Services lady – your Miss Shewmon – has been a bother to us. She is not sympathetic."

"I have no desire to break apart the family, Bishop Yost."

Yost frowned with obvious skepticism. "Are you not the one who gave Lydia that scholarship?"

"I think you know that I am."

Yost considered that for a moment and shook his head. Then sternly he said, "Just see that you keep yourself out of the way. We have work to finish this evening. If all you want to do is look around, then I can't see any harm in it. But don't interfere with the people who are working here."

Branden asked, "Why didn't you want Lydia to go to college, Bishop Yost?"

The bishop's reply was quick and stern. "She left her church, her family, and her brothers and sisters of the congregation. She'll never have a chance to join the Amish church. You pretty much saw to that with your scholarship. But the failure is mine. She's a lost soul, and it is my fault."

Branden considered that for a moment, and then he said to the bishop, "Lydia can't be your only loss in the church. Surely other people have gone out into the world."

"None, Professor. None since I have been Bishop. I am charged by God to safeguard the souls in my church. Lydia has been my only failure."

"Do you really think that she . . . "

"Professor!" the bishop cut in. "I can see that you don't understand. Now you can walk the property, if you still wish, but please leave us all alone. We have work to do, and we are all burdened by our loss. So please do not bother any of my people tonight."

- - - - - - - - - - - - - -

Branden realized that he had been dismissed, so he tipped a curt nod, locked the doors on his truck and started north on foot, walking along the wagon lane. The bishop returned to his labors.

Branden found that most of the high spots in the dirt lane had dried since Monday. But in the deep cuts of the wagon wheels, brown water still stood. Even in the

187

shallower hoofprints and tracks of car and truck wheels, the soil was still somewhat pasty with mud. Branden negotiated the irregular ground of the lane toward the woods at back, and he discerned the wider tracks of the ambulance and then the knobby tracks of the tow truck that Robertson had sent to retrieve both his Crown Vic and Lydia's red Escort.

As he progressed down the lane, on Branden's left, the corn stood tall, with its tassels fluttering in a warm evening breeze. On his right, there was open pasture, where cows were grazing under a westerly sun. Most of the cows were facing homeward, forming something of a line, and behind the line, two Amish men were walking with long sticks to encourage the animals forward. It was nearly time for milking, and the cows were heading slowly and ponderously back to the far corner of the pasture, grazing continuously along the way. There must be other Schwartzentrubers coming, the professor thought. To milk so many cows.

The sky overhead was pale blue, but clear. The temperature was up, well over eighty degrees, the professor judged. The sun was baking the muddy soil into hard, rigid forms. It would be easy to find the prints in the bridle path where everyone had stood around Lydia's body on Monday night.

The far bend in the lane took Branden left, to head west. Soon he had reached the spot where Lydia Schwartz had died. He found the ruts where the ambulance had turned around and backed in to retrieve her body. He found the depression in the mud where Lydia's body had fallen. He also found the rock on which Lydia had struck her head.

Without any particular intent, Branden started pacing along the lane toward the farmhouse. John Yost? he thought. Dangerous? Or was he just depressed? Was that the extent of it? Untreated depression? Well, unmedicated depression, anyway. Just like his brother, Daniel. There were bound to be other brothers and sisters from that Yost clan, born to the same Yost parents. Make a note, the professor told himself. Find out about the other Yost siblings of John, and Alva and Daniel. And ask Evelyn Carson. Is a susceptibility to depression an inherited disorder? Can John Yost be quickly stabilized with medicine? If Daniel Yost had been willing to take modern medicine, or to use modern doctors, would he still have his family in Indiana?

Branden followed the curve in the lane, south toward the barnyard with its hand-pump well standing in the center of the graveled yard. At the pump, a lady in a black dress and bonnet was working the pump handle vigorously, to bring water up into a pail. Another lady stood aside, waiting to take her own turn at the pump.

On the screened back porch, a young girl was working with a broom and dustpan to sweep the floorboards. Beside her, two women were bent over galvanized tubs, washing clothes by hand in sudsy water. Clothes that had already been washed were being pinned to a clothesline that ran on a pulley system, slanting from the front corner of the house, up to the peak of the milking barn's roof, on the other side of the barnyard.

Branden stood with the horse barn to his left and the milking barn to his right. Men were working in each of them to fork manure into heavy iron manure spreaders, and other men were hitching horses to the tongues of the boxy red machines. In the loft of the hay barn, a boy with a long-tined fork was casting fresh straw down to replace that which was being taken up with the manure.

Then beside the house in the family garden, two ladies in black were bent over to pull weeds. They had worked nearly half of the garden at that point, and a little girl was walking the rows to take up the weeds into a basket. A boy of a similar age was carrying another basket of weeds out of the garden rows, to dump them in a heap at the far edge of the garden.

A swing set stood beside the house, and two small children were playing there on the swings. A clanking windmill towered over it. Branden crossed the graveled ground of the barnyard, and he stood back at the corner of the house to watch the people work. One of the women at the wash tubs took note of him, and she stepped inside the house. Soon a man in charcoal denim came out to challenge him, saying, "What do you want here?"

Branden replied, "I have permission from your bishop to have a look around." He displayed his badge. "I was here Monday evening to help with Lydia, and I thought if I could just walk the grounds? Well, maybe I could help find Mary and Esther."

That brought a belligerent stare from the Amish man. "We don't have much use," he said, "for English visitors. You should be moving along. Unless you want to help with the chores. Otherwise, I don't think you should stay. I think it was time you were leaving."

The professor knew it was. He walked to the side of the house and turned the corner to leave along the lane that ran out to the road. It would put him out on TR 606, some hundred yards west of his truck.

They are peasants, he mused as he reached the front corner of the house. He paused there, thinking. Peasants yes, but peasants for a purpose. For an ideology. For religion, to be sure, but also just for the sake of tradition. For the simple-minded task of 'keeping the old ways.' And here were all the old ways on display. Families of the church, helping another one with a need. Community. Belonging. The bonding of families under the leadership of the bishop and the commonality of the scriptures. The actions of faith on clear display. These were the peasants of faith. They were peasant farmers to be sure, but they were not unsophisticated. They were simple, but not simpleminded.

As he took a seat on the front steps of the house, a team of Standardbreds came down the lane with a livestock wagon clattering along behind it. As it passed by the professor, the driver gave a stern and wary look at Branden. In the wagon there was a caged pig. The driver passed by Branden without making comment.

Behind him, the front screened door opened on creaky hinges, and Junior Yost came out of the house to sit beside Branden on the steps. Junior took off his hat, and he wiped out the inside of the brim with his handkerchief. He didn't speak at first, but seemed content just to sit beside Branden in the warm evening air. Eventually, though, he spoke.

"The bishop isn't happy with us, Professor. He thinks father has let the place run down, and so it's my fault for not stepping in as the oldest son."

Branden put a hand briefly on Junior's bent knee. "You're getting help now, Junior. If fault is to be found, we can ask your bishop why he hadn't been keeping a closer watch on the condition of your family."

Junior snorted. "Fat chance. He's been trying to find our mother."

"He could have stopped in here from time to time."

"No, it really is my fault. I should have kept after the other kids to help."

"They're young, Junior. They're just too young."

"Anyways, Professor, why are you out here? People inside are grumbling a bit about you."

"Oh, really? I don't mean anything by it."

"They don't see it that way."

"No, I suppose not. I don't know, Junior. I thought if I had a look around, it'd help me understand why your Aunt Lydia had to die. Why Meredith Silver died. Why your father is so depressed. I guess I just needed a place to walk and to think, and this seemed like as good a place as any."

"So," Junior led. "Why did Aunt Lydia have to die?"

"I'm afraid it was more than an accident. Meredith Silver wrote in her note that she gave Lydia a shove while they were running down the hill in the rain."

"Note?"

"Apparently Mrs. Silver left a suicide note."

"She shoved her?"

"Yes, Junior. There is a faint bruise over Lydia's shoulder blade. Where she was shoved. That's what made her fall."

Junior shook his head sadly. "An argument? They had some kind of stupid argument?"

"That's what it seems like."

Junior laid his head over into his hands. He made a lamenting growl and seeming embarrassed by it, he straightened up and made a show of clearing his throat. "This is about my mother, again. This was an argument about die Maemme."

"Probably."

"The bishop tells me I can't, but I'm starting to get quite angry with Die Maemme. I know it was bad here. I know it was bad for her. But this bad? And why was she citing scriptures to my father? What did they tell her at those bible studies in Dithy's house?"

"I don't know, Junior. It's a good question."

Junior rose to his feet and stepped up onto the porch. "If you ever find out, Professor, please don't tell me. Right now, I really don't think I want to know."

Branden reached up to catch Junior's hand, and he said, "Sit back down a bit, Junior. Please. Let's just take a minute more to talk."

Junior sat again on the porch steps beside the professor, and Branden asked, "What did you think of the college, Junior?"

"It was nice enough," Junior answered.

Branden asked, "Do you know why she had to get out? Do you understand why Amish life was never going to be enough to satisfy her?"

Junior held a long pause, thinking with his eyes closed. Then he said, "Starlight," and he opened his eyes to turn to look at the professor.

"Starlight?" Branden asked.

Junior nodded and smiled with a memory. "We used to lay ourselves out on the grass at night, to look up at the stars. You can't see them so good in your cities, because you all burn so many electric bulbs. But out here, we can see them all. And Aunt Lydia used to ask me – all the time she'd ask me – "Junior, don't you want to know what they are? Haven't you ever wondered what starlight really is?"

Branden held a respectful silence and let Junior continue.

"Well, Professor, I answered her 'no.' I really don't need to know about it that much. I know they are there, and I know they are beautiful. That's always been enough for me. But I also know that that'd never have been enough for my Aunt Lydia. Professor, I've known that since I was a child."

Simply and softly, the professor said, "I understand."

Junior rose to his feet. "As for college," he said, "and about her going to college? She called it her Starlight Quest. She said she was going off to chase the starlight."

- - - - - - - - - - - - - - -

After a spell of thought and a period of remorse, the professor got himself up on his feet, and he began a circuit around the front of the house, intending to circle around on the far side and walk back down the lane the way he had come. But at the side, just beyond the grass of the yard, he saw a path leading into the woods, and with idle despair, he entered the woods.

The path took him straight into the timber, heading west and a little south. Oaks, walnuts, maples. Locust trees and sycamores. Tangles of underbrush and vines beneath the forest canopy. It was cooler in the deep shade as he walked along the path.

When he came to a clearing, he saw that it had access from TR 606 beyond the trees. Here were other wagon ruts in the mud. These were the ruts of heavy wagons with wide iron wheels. There was a rustle in the brush behind him, and he turned to see a bushy blonde tail bouncing off toward the north, deeper into the woods. A dog? He started in that direction, and he stumbled. He almost fell.

At his feet, there was the rounded edge of a massive shoulder bone, buried just beneath the surface of the dirt in the clearing. He studied the ground where he was standing, and more bones were laying there. A femur, the size of a cow. Rib bones as large as a horse. The ground at the center of the clearing had been pawed loose, and more bones had been unearthed, some with small fragments of red flesh and white tendon still adhering to the bone.

Coyotes, he realized. Coyotes had been digging at the dirt. Deep in the woods, he had found a slaughter pit. He had found the carcasses of farm animals that had been slaughtered for the meat. At the far edge of the clearing, he saw a deep hole, with dirt mounded beside it and a shovel stuck into the mound, handle up. So, another slaughter was scheduled for the evening. The hole had been dug for the bones of a pig.

Branden walked a wide circle around the perimeter of the clearing where the bones of the animals had been buried, and he came back to the path he had followed from the house. Opposite that position, the path continued into the woods. He crossed over the boneyard, and he continued west and south along the trail. After about a hundred yards, the trail took a turn toward the south, and fifty yards later, it let out onto TR 606, at a position opposite Meredith Silver's ranch house.

The professor surmised that he had walked the path that Mary must have used to leave home for her clandestine scripture lessons at Silver's house. Here is where she would have crossed the road. Here is where she would have crossed from the seventeenth century into the twenty-first.

He stepped over the narrow culvert and out onto the blacktop. He turned east toward his truck at the other end of the Yost property, and as he walked, his phone toned in his pocket with a call from Robertson. He answered the call saying simply, "Sheriff?"

"Where are you, Mike?" Robertson asked. "I'd like to come over."

"At the Yost farm, on 606."

"I've gotten a couple of hang-up calls from a burner phone. But she did speak once, rather briefly, and she said she was Mary Yost. She sounded nervous, Mike. She said she'd call back tonight. She clicked off before I could say anything."

"OK, why do you want to come over? It'll take me a least half an hour to get back home."

"This is huge, Mike," the sheriff said. "Rachel is setting up to trap Mary's call. If I can get her to talk, I want you to listen. And maybe Caroline can speak with her. We've got a real chance here, Mike. A really good chance. If she calls again. And I think Caroline would be the best person to speak with her."

Chapter 22

As late as it was, the evening was still warm on the Brandens' back porch. A steady and humid night breeze was washing through the screens. The back yard was swaddled in darkness.

Robertson was there with Rachel Ramsayer, his IT Chief. She was the daughter of Pastor Cal Troyer. Rachel was a dwarf woman in her forties. She had found her father after her mother in Atlanta had finally told her about him. It had been a broken marriage that ended while Cal had been serving as a medic in Vietnam. Rachel had been born without Cal's knowing it. Then once her mother had died, Rachel had come to Millersburg to find her father. Tonight, Rachel was waiting with the others, to see if Mary Yost would make another call to the sheriff's phone.

Cal was there, too. Caroline and the professor had served a light snack. Robertson was standing at the far end of the porch with his phone out, hoping for another call. The Brandens were seated in wicker chairs with Cal and Rachel. To the professor, Cal seemed nervous - fidgety and maybe also frustrated by something. Rachel cleared her throat, and looking anxiously to her father, she said, "Dad has some news, I'm afraid."

Cal tried to shrug it away, but Rachel pushed him for a response. "Tell them, Dad. You do, or I will. It's not some awful *secret* kind of thing."

Cal shrugged again. He tangled his fingers in his beard and hesitated. He stood up on his short legs, but he seemed uncertain of himself there, and he dropped heavily back down onto his chair.

"What?" Caroline asked. "What news?"

"Well," Cal said hesitantly, "I guess I'll be up at the Cleveland Clinic next week."

"What for?" the professor asked.

Cal gave a rueful glance at the professor. "I guess it's not that big of a problem, really."

"He's got colon cancer," Rachel declared. "Really, Dad, this is getting frustrating. You haven't told anyone. Not even your congregation. What were you going to do? Mix it in with Sunday's sermon?"

"Something like that," Cal replied weakly. "It is what it is, Rachel. Can't be that bad."

Caroline asked, "You've had tests? They're sure about this?"

"Yes," Cal said. "I'm to go in for surgery next week. Wednesday morning."

At the far end of the long porch, the sheriff's phone rang. He answered the call, speaking a careful, "This is Sheriff Robertson." He listened for three seconds or so, and he pulled his phone down from his ear. Holding it out to the room, he switched to speaker-phone mode. Then he tapped two of Rachel's new icons on his screen, and they all heard a woman in mid-sentence, ".... fine. We're fine, Sheriff."

"Where are you, Mary?" Robertson said into the base of his phone. To the room, he silently mouthed, *"Mary Yost."*

"That doesn't matter," Mary said. "We're both fine. I'm having some labor now, so I can't talk. But, we're fine. It's just that, well, it's not as easy as Donna said it would be. Living English, I mean."

"You need help?" Robertson asked. "Let us help you."

"I have a woman with me."

"A midwife, Mary?"

"A nurse. I'm fine. I can't talk."

Then as if speaking to someone in the room beside her, Mary asked, "What?" and said, "OK."

Back to Robertson she said, "I need to hang up, now," and the call switched off.

Immediately on her feet, Rachel asked the sheriff, "Did you get it?"

Robertson checked his display. He tapped one of Rachel's icons and smiled. "Fort Wayne."

"And recorded?" Rachel asked further.

Again, Robertson tapped an icon, and a recording of his short conversation with Mary Yost played out into the room.

Rachel advanced to him. "Call the Sheriff there?"

Robertson nodded. "We have her gps location, now. Call Ricky and Pat. They're going to have to drive over there tonight."

Rachel was already passing through the sliding door, headed back into the house. "I need to get down to my systems," she said. "Dad?"

Cal rose to his feet, but Caroline stood, took his shoulder and directed him back into his chair. "Oh no," she intoned. "I'll give you a ride home later."

Robertson called after Rachel. "If she leaves that location, can you track her cell phone? And what kind of place is she at right now?" He was already redialing Mary's number for a second time. Muttering, he said, "At least we know she's not dead."

Back over her shoulder, Rachel said, "That's what I'm doing. Tracking the call." She stopped to study the screen on her phone. "I've got it mapped. It's a motel in Fort Wayne." She came back out onto the porch. "I'm calling the motel's office now." She handed her phone to the sheriff.

Robertson closed his phone and spoke when the motel desk attendant answered Rachel's call. "I am Sheriff Bruce Robertson, Holmes County, Ohio. Do you have an Amish woman staying there?"

Branden, Caroline, Rachel and Cal heard the sheriff's side of the ensuing conversation:

- "OK, maybe not Amish then. A pregnant woman and her little daughter?"
- "No, look, this is urgent."
- "Good. Check that room, please. Hurry."
- "I don't care. Get over there and knock on her door."
- "Then give me the direct number to the phone in that room."
- "Cell phone! She called me on a cell phone! I've got that, already. I want the *land line* into that room.
- No, because she's not answering her cell phone."
- "You just check that room!"

Then pacing back and forth on the long porch, Robertson kept the phone to his ear. Eventually, with sarcasm permeating his tone, he growled back into Rachel's phone, "Great! That's just Great!" and he switched abruptly out of the call, saying to Rachel, "She's already gone. We missed her."

Looking at her phone's map display, Rachel countered, "Sheriff, her phone is still there."

Immediately Robertson called the motel back. Once he had the man on the line, he said, "Please go back and look for a cell phone in the room."

Presently the sheriff said, "Good. Thanks. I'm going to need that phone. I'll send someone for it. You make sure you hang on to it."

After switching out of the call, the sheriff said to Rachel, "She left her phone in her room. It's a burner phone, like from Walmart."

- - - - - - - - - - - - - -

After Rachel and the sheriff had left for the jail, Cal said to Mike and Caroline, "I'm going to need a ride back home, you know."

"Not like that," Caroline scolded him. "You're not going to skirt it like that, Cal."

"I'll have the surgery," Cal said, lifting his palms. "They'll cut it out."

"Just as easy as that?" Caroline pressed anxiously.

"Sort of, I guess."

"Who's going to be up there with you?" the professor asked.

"Rachel," Cal said. "Maybe some church people."

"When did all this start?" Branden asked.

Cal shrugged his shoulders. "There was some blood," he said. "I got a colonoscopy. They say I have cancer, and they want me to have this operation."

"You don't want to?" Caroline cried with obvious anguish.

203

"I don't know," Cal said evenly. "We're old, right? We're all older, now, and I've had a good life. I'm not afraid to die."

Caroline got up on her feet slowly. She could not control her emotions any longer. Tears began to line her cheeks. She took a step toward Cal, and her fingers clenched nervously at her sides. The professor saw her sorrow, and he realized that she wanted to chastise Cal for his stoicism.

She took another step toward Cal, and she forced her fingers to open out straight. But they closed again, and she fixed her sight on her husband, on the other side of Cal. She couldn't speak past her tears, so she waved a hand toward her husband and reclaimed her seat.

Branden took up her cause. "You haven't thought this through, Cal. You need help with this. If you need surgery, then you have friends who will help you recover from it."

"I'm not afraid to die," Cal whispered.

Popping up onto her feet, Caroline tried to speak again. But her voice cracked out only a loud and frustrated, "Aaah!" Then softly she said, with her voice stuttering with emotion, "Who   told you that you're going to die?"

"Nobody," Cal said, smiling enigmatically. He turned his head toward Caroline with an expression of apology and admission. "But they say I might have waited a bit too long to have that colonoscopy."

Caroline again took a step toward Cal. Her palms lifted at her sides and slapped back against her legs. Her cheeks flowed with tears, and she wept. She brushed a knuckle under each eye, and still she wept.

"It's not really so much about any of you," Cal said. "It's my decision to make."

"This isn't fair to Rachel," Caroline insisted. "She's just found you. She's just getting to know you as her father. How do you think she feels?"

To acknowledge her point, Cal laid his head sideways and tried for a convincing smile. He stood up and said, "Wednesday, next week. I'd be glad if one of you could come along to sit with Rachel."

"Yes," the professor said. "Good. You needed to tell us this. And you're going to need a ride."

"Rachel," Cal said. "Rachel will drive me up."

"We're going, too," Caroline said fiercely. She moved to Cal and embraced him. He turned to her and took her embrace, and he put his short arms around her.

"You're not going to do this alone," Caroline said. "You have too many friends for that."

"I am not afraid," Cal asserted again.

He released Caroline, but she held on to him longer. He put his arms back around her, gave a squeeze, and released her again. Still she held him, saying, "What were you thinking?"

Cal gently took her arms down from around his neck, and he stepped back a little. He turned around to the professor, and then he turned back to Caroline. "I've preached the Gospel of peace and hope for nearly forty years," he said to them. "Lots of people get sick. Lots of people die. It's my turn, now, and I will not lose hope. It's just not going to happen. I am not dismayed, and I am not afraid."

"Then we're going to be afraid for you," Caroline said. "We can't lose you."

Cal's eyes acquired a moist aspect. Branden saw something like perplexity pass across his eyes.

Cal shook his head. Then he sat again and bowed his head. "I'm not afraid," he whispered, and looked up. "But I am disconcerted. I am very disconcerted. There is only one thing that frightens me. It frightens me to face death finally, only to crumble because I couldn't handle the truth."

"What truth?" Caroline demanded. "The truth that you're going to have surgery? The truth that your friends will be there with you? The truth that you can't avoid this, now? What, Cal? What truth?"

"No," Cal said. "That's not what I mean. This is just life. We've always known it was like this. Long or short, life is the process of dying. It's not avoidable. And when I do die, it will not be premature. Like I said, we are all old, now. I've had a good life."

"So, what?" the professor asked. "You're just going to accept it?"

"Not at all. No. That's not what I'm saying."

"What, then?" Caroline asked, wiping tears from her cheeks with the flats of her fingers. "Tell us what, Cal!"

"Like I said. I've preached the Gospel for forty years. And what? I haven't believed any of it? No, I can't accept that. I couldn't face that. To lose faith now? If that were to happen, I couldn't live with myself. I wouldn't *want* to live with myself. No, it is simple, even if it is frightening. Living *by* faith means that you must face everything in life, even death – especially death – *with* your faith. For me, it can't be any other way."

Chapter 23

Friday, September 1
5:30 PM

After all his classes, appointments, office hours and commitments, the professor took his truck into town, Friday at dinner time. The matter had bothered him all day. It had nickeled away at his background thoughts during all his college duties, and finally at the end of the day he had found that he could pursue it. Pursue the Schells, that is. Ed and Donna Schell, and their church and boarding house. Because Mary Yost had said on the phone:

> *"It's just that, well, it's not as easy as Donna said it would be. Living English, I mean."*

Donna. Donna Schell, who had conducted bible studies with Mary Yost. Surely Donna had talked with Mary about very much more than just the Scriptures. And so that little statement of Mary's had pestered the professor all day.

In the village, he turned onto Perkins Street, and after a second pass, he parked a block away from the Light-Path Ministries church building and boarding house. It was the closest parking spot he could find.

After he had switched off the engine, and before he had opened his door, the Schells stepped onto the side porch of the boarding house, Donna pushing out hurriedly on the screened door, so that it banged against the side of the house and then slapped back into place behind her. A moment later, Ed Schell pushed out backward, carrying two large and battered suitcases. He was obviously struggling with the weight of them, and when he dropped them onto the porch boards, Donna started talking with her eyes pointed away from her husband. They seemed to be in a conversation that had started inside the boarding house. And Donna seemed to be upset about something. Ed started talking, too, and Donna turned to face him, nodding agreement with him and talking over Ed's words. Ed didn't seem to mind. They were five paces apart, and they were facing each other, with Donna folding her hands, and Ed nodding his own agreement as they both spoke, with their words running over each other's, as if their thoughts were so aligned that they could anticipate each other's statements.

Branden rolled down the window of his truck and tipped an ear in the Schells' direction. He managed to hear only a few snatches of Donna's words, and he wasn't certain that he had gotten all of it right, but she seemed to be saying, " . . . never again!" And " . . . haven't worked this hard to let . . ."

Branden decided to sit in his truck and watch the proceedings. He decided to sit, and if he could manage it, to listen.

Ed turned his head, and Donna leaned in to address his ear. She was so close to him that her lips must have been brushing against him. Ed wore the somewhat militant expression of a determined evangelist.

Eventually, Ed Schell seemed to have mellowed a bit. He bent down to pick up the two heavy suitcases. He went backwards down the porch steps, resting the suitcases with each step, and at the bottom, on the side walkway to the drive, he stood to catch his breath and ease his muscles. He shook both of his hands at his sides, and then he picked up the suitcases again. Donna Schell pulled the porch door open, and she stepped back inside the boarding house.

By the time Ed had wrestled the suitcases over to the back of a blue passenger van in the driveway, Donna was coming out again, this time holding the door for a young couple in Old Order Amish dress, followed by a young Amish girl, who was holding the hand of a three-year old boy in a black vest and black straw hat. The Amish couple wore doubtful expressions, and the little Amish boy watched forward warily.

Donna gathered the family close to her, and they all bowed their heads. Donna closed her eyes, and the others did, too. As Donna spoke a prayer, the mother and father nodded their agreements with her supplications, and when she looked up again, they all said, "Amen."

Donna took the porch steps one at a time on uncertain legs, holding tightly to an iron hand railing. When she had made it down to the side walkway, she turned back to offer a hand of assistance to the woman of the Amish couple. Then she helped the girl and the little boy on the steps, too. She took a moment to rub at her sore knees, and then she escorted them all to the side door of the passenger van, where she helped them climb up to bench seats, directing the couple to the second of three benches, and the girl and little boy to the first of the three, where a child seat was waiting for the boy. The girl buckled the boy into his seat.

At the back of the van, Ed Schell had stowed the suitcases and closed the double doors. He rushed around to Donna, opened the passenger's door for her, and helped her step up to her seat. He waited for her to arrange herself on the seat, and then he gently swung the door closed and pushed on it, to latch it in place. Again, Donna had been rubbing at her knees. She still wore a large cotton bandage on her left hand.

By now the professor had his phone out, ringing through with a call to Sheriff Robertson. He said, "It's Mike. I'm going to follow a light blue passenger van away from the Light-Path boarding house. The Schells are driving it, with four Amish passengers."

"To where?" Robertson asked.

"Don't know. But I don't like something about this. The Schells are anxious, and they have an Amish family in the van with them. They have two large suitcases. There's also an older white van still sitting in their driveway. They are both Amish-hauler vans, for maybe a dozen passengers each."

"You want help?"

"No, but I don't know where they're going. I'm going to follow them. I've just got a weird impression from what Donna was saying. I mean, from the little bit that I could hear."

"Saying what, Mike?"

"I didn't hear much of it. They were concerned. They seemed to be upset about something. I'm just going to follow them."

"Does Caroline know where you are?"

"She's my next call."

- - - - - - - - - - - - - - -

The professor had his wife on speaker phone while he followed Ed Schell's blue window van east out of town, on US 62/39. He told Caroline what he was doing, and why he was doing it, and she said only, "Be careful, Michael," before switching off.

The black-topped road curved and rose and dipped over the hills of the countryside. Businesses lined the way – an auto dealer, a lumbermill, a farm implement outfit and some retail shops. After only a few miles, the van turned south into the farmland on TR-351, and Branden followed, holding back somewhat on the turn.

The road intersected with TR-310, and there they turned east again. A winding and hilly route took them to TR-354, and at a long, sloping field of cut hay, Ed Schell turned right, into a gravel lane.

Branden approached the gravel lane slowly, and he watched as the blue van climbed the hill to a brown-shingled farmhouse at the top, standing out in front of a line of tall pines. The entire house was trimmed with white. It looked as quaint and dark as the gingerbread houses that his grandmother used to make.

The fields on either side of the gravel lane had been mowed recently, and the low and long, pale-green mounds of cut hay were drying in the sun. Branden was able to stop about thirty yards short of the lane. He still had a clear view of the farmhouse, one-hundred and fifty yards up the slope of the long fields. He parked beside the culvert, climbed out with a pair of binoculars from his glove compartment, and leaned over with his elbows braced on the front hood of the truck, to put the binoculars to his eyes.

As the Amish family was getting out of the van, Ed Schell hastened around to the passenger's door, to help Donna down from her seat. She leaned heavily on his shoulder and she walked with tender care, as if her knees were troubling her greatly. Ed got her van door closed, and he escorted her to the small front porch of the house. There he helped Donna on the steps. When she had reached the porch, she turned around to sit facing out over the sloping field of hay, on a wooden bench that had been constructed with stout planks and concrete end pieces. She breathed heavily while she sat there, and she watched with exhausted disinterest as Ed followed the Amish people up the porch steps. She was rubbing at her sore knees and meddling anxiously with the bandage on her hand.

Once Ed had the four Amish people inside, he came back down the porch steps, took one suitcase at a time into the house, and came out with a plastic tumbler of water for Donna. She thanked him and drank it without making any further remarks, and she remained on the bench when Ed went back inside. Donna was still wrestling with pain. She rubbed continuously at her knees. Branden took the opportunity to study the exterior of the house.

There were two stories on the house, with four large windows across the front of the second floor, and two smaller windows on the first floor, flanking each side of the porch door. A metal garage sat back from the house. Attached to the ginger-brown siding of the house, there was a three-legged metal tower, with a complicated wire TV antenna at the top, rising to something like five yards above the peak of the roof. The electric service and a phone line were fastened at the right front corner of the house, near the roof line.

Lace curtains were drawn back in one of the upper windows, and a light was switched on there. At another window of the second floor, the curtains were also pulled to the sides, but no light came on in that room. Each of the windows remained closed, and as hot as it was that afternoon, Branden trained his binoculars down to study the foundation around the house. As the closed windows suggested, on the left side of the house, he found the air conditioner that he expected. Beside it stood a brown metal box, with a thick black power cable running into the basement. This he assumed was an emergency generator.

Away from the house, also on the left, there was a cylindrical tank for natural gas. Electricity, phone, air conditioning, TV, lace curtains and central heat, he thought. Not an Amish house.

As the professor watched from the road down below, Ed Schell started carrying bags of groceries from the back compartment of the van, up the steps and into the house. He had made five trips by the time he got it all inside. Donna pushed up from her bench as he came up the steps with the last of his bags, and she opened the door for her husband, before she followed him inside.

Ten minutes later, the Amish woman came out to sit on the porch bench. Instead of her conservative black Amish attire, she now wore a mint-green dress, full length, with black hose and soft black shoes. She had a plain white apron in front, tied at her waist. These were Mennonite clothes. Instead of a full black Amish bonnet, she wore a simple lace prayer disk pinned to the hair bun at the back of her head.

The young girl came out behind her. She was dressed in similar Mennonite attire, but instead of a simple prayer disk on her head, she wore a white prayer Kapp with string ties. She sat beside the woman, and she leaned her head against her shoulder. The mother put her arm around her daughter, and she drew her closer. She lifted her hand and kissed it. The girl wiped tears from under her eyes, and she spoke a few brief sentences to her mother. Each time that she spoke, mother answered her at length, seeming to explain matters with her words and hand gestures.

The Amish man, perhaps in his mid-forties, came out next. He was dressed in a checkered shirt and plain blue jeans. He wore white cotton socks and new cross-trainer shoes. He sat on the porch steps, and he took out a cell phone to make a call. The call was brief, and he made several other calls, similarly brief. Finished for the moment with his calls, he slipped his phone into his jeans pocket and pulled a plastic card from his shirt pocket. It was the size of a driver's license. He studied the front and back of the card, and he held the card close, to read the information on the front of the card carefully. He turned around to display the card for his wife, and they seemed pleased with it. They seemed to admire it. Then he came down the steps with his phone, placed a call, and talked on his phone, while he walked around the corner of the house, disappearing to the rear of the property.

Next, Ed Schell came back out to the front porch. He spoke briefly to the Amish woman there, and he came out to the driveway and got into his van. He turned around in the gravel drive, and he started the van down the long lane of the hill.

The professor got quickly back into his truck, and he drove past the hay fields before Schell had come more than halfway down the lane. After he had crested a low hill, Branden turned around in a neighbor's drive, and he followed Ed Schell back toward US 62/39. The van was moving fast, and Branden allowed himself to fall back from it. As he drove, he pushed a speed dial number that rang in the sheriff's office.

"It's me again," he said.

"Where?"

"Out on TR-354. The Schells have a house out here. Two stories, at the top of a long field."

"Why is that important?"

"The Amish people that I told you about? Well, they're now wearing Mennonite clothes. They've changed. They're using a cell phone. I'm following behind Ed Schell's van. Staying back."

"Is he coming back to Millersburg?"

"That's my guess. He seems to be done out here. For the time being, anyway."

"What do you need from us?"

"Property records. Have Rachel search for property that the Schells own out in the country."

"Rachel has already gone home. Stan has taken more convalescence leave."

"Can you call her at home?"

"I'll try."

"I'm going home, too. Have Rachel call me. If she can't find that the Schells own any property out here themselves, she should search to find out if their church owns any property."

"Really, Mike. What has you following the Schells like this?"

"The Amish people."

"That's it?"

"Also, why are the Schells boarding these Amish people out here in the country? And why have they changed to Mennonite attire?"

"OK."

"And the plates on the van, Bruce? They're from Iowa. That's a little bit strange. I'll give you the digits. Can you run them for me?"

"Sure, Mike, let me know what happens out there. But look. Missy has ruled that Lydia's death was an unintentional homicide, and Meredith Silver obviously can't stand for charges. We're still interested in Silver's apparent suicide. But all you've got there with John and Mary Yost is a domestic dispute. So, we can't devote any more resources to this. The sheriff's office is stepping away from this. OK? If you want to hunt for Mary Yost, it'll be on your time. We can't keep it going as an official inquiry any longer."

"I'm surprised," Branden said. "There's a lot here that I want to chase down."

"I understand, Mike. You can certainly do that. But I'm closing the Mary Yost case on my end."

"Can you at least send some of Lydia's things over to the house? Like all of the rest of her diaries?"

"I think you already have a lot of them, Mike."

"Yes, but I want them all. And maybe her laptop, too? And can you send me that recording you made last night of Mary Yost's phone call? There's something there that I'd like to pursue."

"I'll send Rachel with it all. Once she's run those plates for you."

"And the real estate records, Bruce. Don't forget the real estate records."

"Why have you got such a bug for this thing, Mike?"

"I owe it to Lydia, to find out what has really happened to Mary. And it rubs me wrong that the Schells are boarding Amish-turned-Mennonite people out in the country. It just rubs me wrong, and I want to look into it. I really want to know what's going on with Mary Yost."

"OK, Mike, but like I said, we're closing the Mary Yost case here. We need to step away from it."

- - - - - - - - - - - - - -

Once Branden had gotten his truck back to the Light-Path Ministries boarding house, the nearest parking spot was three blocks away from the house. He parked, got out, locked up and came forward along the sidewalk. The blue window van from Iowa was parked again in the boarding house driveway. Branden stopped a block short of the boarding house, and he leaned against the trunk of a large oak on the tree lawn across the street. He was thinking about the brown-shingled farmhouse, now occupied by Donna Schell and an Amish family of four, dressed purposefully in new city Mennonite clothes.

The farmhouse had looked old. Long ago, a family had been raised there. Maybe more than one family over the years. Had it been Amish? Now, certainly, it was not.

219

He had seen no farm equipment on the property, so the fields must be leased to neighbors. These were fields of cut hay for the animals on adjacent farms. Feeling rather melancholy, the professor imagined that once there had been children there. Swing sets, trampolines, volleyball nets, and wading pools. He imagined the chatter of young voices, children at play.

OK, the Schells were not who they had claimed to be. Not entirely. They were more than that. At the country house, they had affected the transformation of Amish people into something new and different. Were they doing more than just preaching modernism at their church? But that was the point, wasn't it? They were evangelists.

At the Schells boarding house, Ed Schell came out onto the side porch with two people, a married couple the professor surmised, who were holding matching suitcases.

Ed gave the woman a hug, and he shook the hand of the man. They all went down to the blue van on the driveway, and they stowed their suitcases in the side door, on the floor between two of the bench seats. They formed a circle beside the van, held hands, and offered a prayer. Then the couple got into the van, with the man driving, and they backed out of the driveway. Ed Schell stood at the top of the driveway to wave goodbye to them. Then Schell turned and went slowly back into the boarding house.

Branden obeyed his instinct to follow the couple in the blue passenger van. They traveled north out of town, on SR 83. At Wooster, the van turned west on US 30. Branden followed as far as the exit for US 250 to Ashland, and there

220

he broke off his route, as the van continued west on RT 30. Driving back to Millersburg, Branden wondered. Was the blue van headed back to Iowa?

As he came into the northern edges of Millersburg, the professor was also thinking on another matter. Where had the Schells' young children been kept during the evening when Ed and Donna had been away from home? One was merely an infant, only eight weeks old. Were the people from Iowa such close friends of the Schells that they could be trusted with the children? Evidently, they were. They had stayed at the Schells' boarding house with the Schells' young children, while Ed and Donna had escorted the Amish-turning-Mennonite family out to the country house. Now Ed was home again, without Donna.

The professor pursed his lips and shook his head slowly. He felt himself frowning as he thought about it. In how many ways was Light-Path Ministries something more than just a gospel church?

Chapter 24

Friday, September 1
8:30 PM

After dinner, Caroline admitted Rachel at the front door and led her back to the kitchen table. Rachel was considerably shorter than the average person, and knowing this, the Brandens kept a stepstool for her in the corner of the kitchen. Rachel pulled it out and used it to climb up to a familiar seat at the Brandens' kitchen table. She laid printout pages on the table, and she asked Caroline, "Is Mike here?"

"He'll be down," Caroline said. "Why is Bruce pulling away from the Mary Yost case?"

"Really, there isn't any case."

"Aren't Niell and Lance going over to Fort Wayne to get her phone?"

"No, that has changed," Rachel said. "They're going to mail her phone to us, now."

"Michael is still interested, Rachel. I have to say, so am I. We're not convinced that Mary would leave her family behind."

Rachel tapped a finger on her printed page. "I found some things. Mary might have had some encouragement. She might have had a lot of help, getting out of her sect."

The professor appeared from upstairs and asked, "You've got the Iowa plates?" He sat down beside Caroline.

Rachel slid her printed pages across the table to him. "That van is owned by a church, Mike. It's the *Church of True Believers*, in Omaha. It has Iowa plates, but this church is just over the border in Omaha, Nebraska."

Caroline said, "That church name puts it right out there, doesn't it? Nothing subtle there."

"Omaha?" the professor asked, more as a comment than a question.

"It gets better," Rachel said. "The Schells do own that property that you found, out on 354. They own their church building and their boarding house in town, too. But the Omaha church is listed as co-signers on the mortgages."

"Just for the house on 354?" Branden asked.

"No, for all three properties. The Omaha church. They call it the CTB for short – The Church of True Believers."

"Why would they be co-signers?" asked Caroline.

"I checked their website," Rachel said. "They list a number of missionaries that they support in the U.S. They call them 'domestic missionaries.' The Schells are just one of them. They consider the Schells to be their missionaries to the Amish people in Holmes County. The CTB is a big church. An evangelical megachurch."

"The Schells aren't just locals?" Branden asked.

"No, and it gets better. The CTB also owns nearly a dozen houses outright, all around the country. They are all near interstates. I printed out one in Fort Wayne and another in Davenport. They're all small houses, two bedrooms and three, but these are the two that are close to Interstate 80."

The professor said, "Omaha is right on 80, too."

"Right. You take US 30 over to Fort Wayne, and that puts you at the first house, after an easy one-day drive. It's another one-day trip up to I-80 and then over to Davenport. The third day gets you to Omaha. I'd guess that their blue van has made this trip before."

Branden laid his hands flat on the tabletop, and he drummed out a beat with his thumbs. He stared at his hands for a while, and then he looked up at Rachel. "Missionaries?"

Rachel nodded, held a pause and then asked, "Do you still want Lydia's things?"

"Yes, and her laptop," Branden answered, still absorbed in thought.

Rachel popped off her chair and retrieved a satchel from just inside the front door where she had dropped it. She hoisted it up to the tabletop and climbed up to her chair again. "The laptop doesn't have a password. You can see all of her searches, files and emails, but it's mostly just college stuff."

"It's the diaries that are going to be the most interesting," Branden said. "I need the last one, especially."

Rachel pulled several more of Lydia's diaries out of her satchel. "There's a lot in there about Ed and Donna Schell," she said. "And this 'Dithy.'"

"Meredith Silver," Branden explained.

"Makes sense."

"What about them?"

"Well, were these friends of Lydia's?"

"Yes, good friends," Branden said. "Why?"

"You'll see, Mike. I don't think she was very happy with them at the end."

- - - - - - - - - - - - - -

As he read the entries in Lydia's last diary, the professor became increasingly concerned. He was even somewhat agitated, and several times he called Caroline into his study to show her some of the entries.

"It's the midwives, Michael," she said on her last visit. "She was trying to find the midwife that Mary would use."

Perplexed and also stubborn to make sure of his conclusions, the professor read several of the last passages again. On a Thursday, several weeks before classes had started, Lydia had scribbled:

> *This is not right for Mary. She's the mother of seven children, and leaving her church is not the right answer. I thought they were helping her cope. Would they really advise her to leave him? That's what they were telling her? It's too radical. Donna and Dithy? Why? They should know better. It's right for me to get out, but not for Mary.*

She's a member of her church. She'd be
shunned. Find Mary! Where? And what
about her baby? There is Esther, too.
Where are they? Where would Mary have
gone?

The diary contained other types of entries, about the
coming semester, about Audi her boyfriend, and about
meeting the girl Susan who would be her new roommate.
There were several entries about the classes she was to take.
Branden's class on *Slavery in the Americas* was mentioned.
Also, she was very much looking forward to taking her
second economics class from her favorite professor.

Then on a Wednesday, still a little over two weeks
before the start of classes, Lydia had written:

Still no news. She's been gone over a week,
now. John seems worse than ever. Did they
actually get her talked into this? Donna!
Dithy too. What were they thinking? It's a
radical solution. Way too radical. I can't
believe she'd go this far with it. Talk to the
babies. It's so quiet there, up on the hill.
Call Dithy. Talk to the little babies.

On Monday August 21st, Lydia had made a list titled: *Check Midwives*. In the list, she had seven names, and the first five had been crossed off, as if she had already talked with those. But at the end of the list, there were still two names, each with an address near John and Mary Yost's farm: *Vera Erb* and *Hannah Yost*. Then following this list, there was another entry:

> *Mary. Midwives. There are only two more to check. Maybe she's already delivered. So that would have to be reported, right? Check how midwives report births. Do they have to? Do they <u>always</u> do that? Check state records. How soon do they report a birth? Amish childbirths, in private homes - who would know? Maybe slaves were like that? Ask Professor Branden in class. Did they report slave baby births? Are all Amish births reported? Maybe not. Midwives - only two more to check.*

- - - - - - - - - - - - - - -

And so it was that well into the night, the professor worked at his computer, on the internet. He immersed himself in a search inside the labyrinthian website for the

Ohio Department of Health. In the clickable link to the Office of Vital Statistics, he read the legislation on requirements for reporting and documenting live births. He read the various and detailed reporting requirements for doctors, physician's assistants, health care professionals and clinicians. The separate and specific requirements for hospitals, ERs, medical clinics and walk-in urgent care facilities. Reporting requirements for births in various locations, including private or commercial vehicles of any variety, whether on the way to the hospital or not. Whether attended by paramedics, officers, relatives, midwives or passers-by. Then in one of several layered subcategories, he found the requirements for midwives who were registered with the state and certified.

It was a vast and endless swamp of rules and regulations, and the professor was beginning to regret the muck and the mire of the state's live-birth data system. But this was precisely what he needed to find, now. This was what he needed to do. Wade through the vast and endless miasma of state records on Ohio live births.

This had also been Lydia's reasoning, he realized. It had been the reasoning behind her questions about records of slave and Amish births. Because if Mary were to be found, a record of the birth of her eighth child would provide a route to finding her. That is what Lydia had been trying to do, and that was, the professor had concluded, the best thing he could do now, too.

When Caroline called him to breakfast for the third time, she did it by coming up the steps to retrieve him. She cleared her throat in the upstairs hallway, moved into his study and stood behind him. She rested her hands on his shoulders, peered in from above, and read the display for his computer. The descending tabs for his search read: Ohio Department of Health/Data and Statistics/Birth/Birth Data/Ohio Resident Live Births/2006 – present. It was the kind of arcane organization that only a government bureaucrat could devise. It was the kind of complex system that only an experienced government wonk could use.

On the professor's screen, there was a government "chart generator," with over a dozen birth types to be designated before any search of the state records could be initiated. Plus, filters were required for age, race, pre-natal care, length of gestation, year of birth, etc. and Caroline, befuddled to think that any of it could be useful, said to her husband, whose shoulders were bent with strain, "What can it possibly give you, Michael? Dates? Numbers? Names?"

"Just the numbers," the professor said wearily, clicking out of his browser. "Any kind of birth, anywhere in Ohio, sorted by County. But then, it'll give us only the *number* of those specific kinds of births. Otherwise," - he spun his chair around and stood up - "there's a mind-numbing hierarchy of legalities and rules that makes it pretty much impossible for a non-professional to use the data. It's the government. What did I expect?"

Caroline took his elbow and led him over to the steps. When she had him downstairs and seated at the kitchen table, she said, "You look a little dazed."

Branden arched his spine and sat himself up straighter. "Midwives," he grumbled wearily, "are supposed to file a Certificate of Live Birth within seventy-two hours of a delivery."

Caroline sat at the table across from him, waiting for him to say more. "Michael?" she prompted after a prolonged silence.

The professor looked thoughtfully at her, silent for yet another moment, and then he explained it to Caroline, saying, "Lydia was right here, at this point in her thinking. She thought she could find Mary by finding a record of her new baby's birth. But Lydia had been farther along with it, too. She asked me about births to slave women. As in: 'Who would know, if they weren't reported?' She was wondering about similarities between Amish babies and slave babies, as far as birth records were concerned. Only the immediate families would know. She was searching for Mary, and she was already thinking about an unregistered birth. So, if we're going to find Mary and Esther Yost, the key is going to be her newborn child."

"Lydia had a list, right?" Caroline said.

Branden nodded. "There are two more left to check."

"OK, Michael, but Mary is not in Holmes County anymore."

"The midwives here might know something. I don't know where else to try. I'd be happy if we could just understand a reason for this. Her midwife might be able to explain why she left. Really, other than this, I don't know where else to try."

"Fort Wayne, Michael. Or the CTB in Omaha."

"Sure. If the sheriff were still interested. He'd have the resources to search for her."

"Michael, if she's still alive, I don't think she wants to be found."

"We'll just check this one last angle," the professor said. "We'll just spend the weekend on this. Then we'll let it go."

Chapter 25

As the Brandens were backing out of their garage Saturday morning, Dr. Evelyn Carson pulled her silver Prius up to the curb out front. The professor parked his truck, and he and Caroline got out to greet the psychiatrist on the driveway. They offered a place to sit inside with coffee, but Carson declined.

"I can't stay," she said on the driveway. "I have morning appointments. I stopped to let you know that John Yost has not improved. I spoke with Bishop Yost this morning, and even he agrees that John is not ready to go home."

Branden asked, "Have you been able to help him at all?"

"We've talked some," Carson said hesitatingly. "He's not accepting any medicine, but he has moments when he'll talk. If I ask him about Mary, he cries."

"Is he more than just depressed?" Caroline asked.

"That's his main problem. He was suicidal. Maybe he still is. I got the bishop to agree to take his shotgun away, before he goes home. So, there's that at least."

Branden asked, "Are you going to continue treating him?"

"If the bishop will let me, yes. But if John won't talk with me, I'd like him to get some good counseling from

232

someone else. I think it'd do him a lot of good. Anyway, he's not completely rational on the question of his wife."

The Brandens waited while Carson studied the pavement at her feet. After a pause, she looked up and said, "Normally, I would never tell you this. It's a matter of doctor-patient confidentiality. But when they're a danger to someone else? Well, I'm obliged to tell someone. You can decide if you want to tell the sheriff."

"He's a danger to other people?" the professor asked.

Evie nodded. "And he's irrational. At least on this one point. On the one hand, he insists that his wife would never leave him. On the other hand, it got so bad between them that they were having shouting matches. He told me about that this morning, when his bishop was standing right there with us. John feels remorseful about it now, but he has been depressed for so long that I don't think he understands how bad it was between them. Bishop Yost was quite surprised by it, though. He got a really good look at how thoroughly depressed John is."

"What can we do?" the professor asked.

"Maybe talk with the bishop?" Carson suggested.

Caroline asked, "What makes you think that'll do any good, Evie?"

"Like I said, the bishop heard some surprising things this morning. I think he's really surprised about John."

"What would we tell him?" the professor asked.

"Tell him about medicine, Mike. Tell him about antidepressants. If I could just get John started on

233

something. He needs something for anxiety, too. I think in two weeks we'd be able to show the bishop some significant progress. I just need him to tell John that it's OK to start with some medicine."

Evie Carson held a pause. She looked down at the pavement again, shook her head and sighed. Looking up to the Brandens, she said, "I shouldn't be telling you this. I certainly wouldn't tell Bruce Robertson. But in my sessions with John, he obsesses over two themes. First, like I said, he doesn't believe his wife would leave him. Well, something like that. He speaks Dietsche. I don't always get it all. I don't know. It's something more like saying that 'she *didn't* leave me.' Not so much that he doesn't believe it, but that it didn't happen. And second, he muttered something about graves several times. Graves on his farm. I don't know. I'm not sure I got it right. But the bishop heard him plain enough, and he was quite surprised by it."

Branden said, "You should tell the sheriff."

"I wanted your advice," Evie said, nodding her head. "I'm not sure it means anything. Please don't talk to Bruce about this. I need more time with John to understand what he means. I think he's muttering and crying about graves on his farm."

- - - - - - - - - - - - - -

As Evie Carson was pulling away from the curb, Bishop Alva Yost arrived in his black buggy. The Brandens showed him inside, to the living room, and the three took seats there. Without any preamble, while shaking his head, Yost said, "John is not any better. He's actually worse than I realized. What alarms me the most is his muttering about graves. He says '*Grawbes*,' plural, as in more than one."

Carefully, the professor eased forward in his upholstered chair. "Bishop Yost?" he asked and then paused. "Do you think John has killed his wife?"

Yost frowned. He scratched at his chin whiskers, and he shifted nervously in his chair. He held a long pause, considering, and eventually he said simply, "No."

The professor thought it worth pressing, and he asked, "Are you certain of this?"

The bishop sighed out a hesitant, "No."

"What then?" the professor asked. "What does that mean?"

"It's unthinkable," Yost said quickly. "It's just not possible. I know things were bad, there, and I know now how deeply depressed John really is. But, no. It's just not thinkable."

Branden pressed again on this point, saying, "But what does that really mean? You hesitated."

The bishop considered his answer for quite a long couple of minutes. His thoughts registered honestly in his expressions – first unsure of himself, then searching his memories, with his eyes shifted up and to the left, and finally reaching a conclusion. "Before recently?" he started. "Before Lydia left us?"

The bishop halted and seemed to hesitate with his next words. The Brandens held silence, to let him continue. Eventually, the bishop spoke. "Before Lydia," he said, "I'd have been certain of myself. But she got something started in my congregation. There were questions. I could tell that some of my people had doubts, after Lydia left us for your English world. I held the line, but some of my people really did pester me about her. They wanted to know if she were really lost. They wanted to know if she couldn't repent and come back to us."

Carefully, the professor asked, "Did you put a *Mite* on her? Did you tell your people to shun her?"

"No," Yost answered. "She had never taken vows to join the Amish church. So, shunning wasn't appropriate. Shunning? No. But we did want her to come home to us. We very much did want that."

The professor said, gently, "She never would have done that, Bishop Yost. She was never going to go back to living Amish."

"But, how do you know that?" the bishop asked. "How could you really *know* that?"

Branden nodded. It was a reasonable question. Instead of providing an immediate answer, he said, "There's a letter on her computer, Bishop Yost. She wrote it to you, but she never sent it."

"Can I still read this letter?" Yost asked.

Branden said, "Yes. Wait right here, just a minute. I'll print it out for you."

When he returned to the living room, the professor handed Yost two printout pages. The bishop read the letter while sitting there. At first, he seemed only curious. Eventually, as he read, he was shaking his head. Before he had finished, he was shedding soft tears, down his cheeks and into his white beard. He composed himself, dried his tears with a bandanna from his side pocket, and asked, while holding the pages forward, "May I?"

Branden nodded wordlessly, and the bishop read the letter aloud.

Dear Bishop Yost. Alva. First, let me say, "Thank you," for the wisdom you shared with us, while I was growing up in your congregation. I was listening. I heard you. On a certain level, I knew all along that you were right. I knew that you are a kind and righteous man.

The English world is a strange and somewhat frightening place. You have always been right about that. They are often conflicted, arrogant, and malicious. But here at the college – and elsewhere, I imagine – they do honestly search for knowledge and for truth. I find this to be admirable, and I think you would, too. You'd have to keep an open mind at first, because there is so much surface banality in their society, and I fear you'd never be able to get past that. But, if you gave it an honest try, you'd find honor here, and sincerity, too.

It began for me with starlight. You said once in Gmeinshaft one Sunday that all we needed to know about the stars was that they are beautiful, and that God put them each right where he wanted them to be. And you asked us, "What more do you need to know than that?"

Well. Bishop Yost, that was the start of it for me. I know you didn't intend this, but that was when I began to ponder all the other questions, too.

How do airplanes stay up in the sky? How do we know about mathematics? What is water? Where does it come from, and what composes it? Then, what are the objections to automobiles? Why must we all dress the same? When is a father ever wrong? Why must babies die, when the English have such wonderful medicines?

So, can you see it, Bishop Yost? Can you try to understand why Amish life was never going to be enough for me? Can you please answer your question honestly? "What more do we need to know?"

*Well, for me, Bishop Yost, it is
everything. I want to know <u>everything</u>. Surely
that is not a sin. Knowledge is not an enemy
of God. Knowledge brings light, and it is the
light that sets us free to find our limits. Light,
Bishop Yost. For me it was starlight. At age
ten, I knew that I was not truly an Amish
person. Here at college, I am finally
discovering who I was always meant to be.*

   *And it is OK, Bishop Yost. You
needn't worry about me. I am not lost. I
know I can never go back home, but really - I
am not lost.*

- - - - - - - - - - - - - -

   Bishop Yost did not speak. He sat with the letter
held loosely in his lap, with his eyes closed. His lips pursed,
as if he were searching for words, but he didn't give voice to
any of them. Eventually he dried his eyes and rose from his
seat. He stepped woodenly to the front door, and he held his
place there, with his hand resting on the doorknob. The
professor came over to him, and he laid a hand on the large
bishop's shoulder, saying, "I'm sorry, Alva. What can we do
for you? Can you rest here a moment longer?"

   Slowly Alva turned back into the living room. He
walked slowly back to his chair, and he sat there with his

239

eyes open, but not focused on anything other than his thoughts. His expression framed a state of bewilderment on his face. There was sorrow in his eyes. Branden sat next to Caroline and said, "Please don't think that you failed her, Alva."

Alva looked first at Caroline and then at the professor. "If the failure is anyone's, Professor, it is mine."

Softly, Caroline said, "She was happy here, Bishop Yost. She had found a place for herself in the world."

Yost nodded. He drew a ragged breath. He began to weep again, and Branden came to his side, to kneel beside his chair, and he said, "Lydia was not lost to you, Alva. She was not lost at all. That's what she wrote to you. You can see that, can't you?"

Solemnly, the bishop nodded. Seeming as weary as the ages, he whispered, "My brother has also lost his way. John. He's just as lost as Lydia is. As Lydia *was*. I don't know how to help him. So, he'll be lost, too. How is that not my failure?"

"We have been talking with Dr. Carson about John," Branden said, rising. He sat again with Caroline on the sofa. "She believes that she can help him."

"Your psychiatrist lady is wrong," Alva said. "John would not hurt anyone. He's not dangerous to anyone."

"He might be dangerous to Mary," Branden replied gently. "Maybe that's why she left him."

Yost squared his shoulders and sat up straighter. "That would be a church matter, Professor. It's something I should deal with privately."

"We would like to help you find Mary," Branden said.

"We are not violent people," Alva said. "But we are a private people. And a man and his wife? That's a private family matter."

"He's depressed," Branden said. "It's not his fault. It's not a failure of character. It's a specific medical condition. His brain chemistry is all wrong. He needs medical help."

"I am Bishop," Yost said hesitantly. "I'm *always* supposed to know what to do. I'm supposed to know how faith can cure all ills. We live by faith. If it is God's will . . ."

His assertion died off in consternation. Perplexity was the expression on his face. "I've held the line on faith for so very long."

Branden asked, "Does faith not allow for medicine?"

With his brows, Yost framed a question.

"There are medicines that can help him, Bishop Yost." Branden continued. "Antidepressants. Anti-anxiety meds, too. They can help him. He doesn't have to be miserable all the time."

Tentatively, Yost said, "Our faith is supposed to be strong enough."

"I have a friend," Branden said, "whose faith is stronger than anyone I know. He has colon cancer. Does faith demand that he die with it?"

"We are not to question God's will."

"Yes. I know. But there is an operation that can save his life. Would you advise him not to have it? Would that be the proper thing for him to do?"

"People do die, Professor. Who are we to question that?"

"I think you have missed the point. God himself has made this surgery possible. Who are you to question that? Lydia's letter must have opened your eyes a little bit."

Behind closed eyes, Yost studied the matter. When he opened his eyes, he appeared chagrined. He appeared to doubt himself.

Branden said, "Just tell John that he should try the medicine for three weeks, Alva. Let him try it as an act of faith. Perhaps God has allowed this. Perhaps God has allowed medicines to be developed. Perhaps it is God's will that John should be well again, and that he should be a better father and husband. Perhaps it is God's will that they not suffer any more in that family."

The professor saw the moment when Bishop Yost relented. It was evident in his expression and his breathing. His shoulders took a slump as if he were releasing tension. His face softened as if he were thinking now as a person, not as an autocrat. His lungs drew a deep and long breath, which he released as a sigh.

"Bishop Yost," the professor said. "Take your buggy back into town. Tell John that he can try Dr. Carson's medicine. Just for three weeks. You've seen how troubled John really is. You can *just try* the medicine. If it isn't God's will for John to be well, you'll know soon enough."

242

Chapter 26

At Weaver's Marketplace on County Road 235, there was a black SUV, looking out of place and maybe a little bit lost, parked on the gravel lot with its nose pressed in against the old split rail fence that bordered the one-acre cemetery adjacent to the store. The cemetery's headstones - some as old and bleached as the bygone centuries - had taken a lean, as if the winds and rains of the ages had rendered them weary. The grocery store by contrast looked new, bright and colorful, with large outdoor signage fastened to the side of the building and a black and yellow placard standing beside the road, advertising the store's daily specials. Here was the anachronistic contrast so typical of Holmes County – the new and bright, parked next to the ancient.

The professor pulled in beside the SUV, and he surveyed the old headstones before he shut off his engine. "Strange," he said. "I've never paid any attention to this little cemetery. I've never been in this little store, out here in the middle of nowhere."

Caroline said, "He was sad, Michael. The bishop was sad to have read Lydia's letter."

"Yes," Branden said, "but also distressed. Lydia put it on his shoulders that he was the one who had gotten her started. She was only ten at the time."

"Plus, Michael, I think he's more worried about John than he lets on."

"He's worried about Mary, too. We need to find her."

The two climbed out of the white truck, and as she closed her passenger's door, Caroline asked over the cab of the truck, "Do you suppose he has people searching for her, too?"

The professor started for the entrance to the store and said, as he walked, "If he's smart, yes. He'll have had people looking for her for several weeks."

At the hitching rail, closer to the store's front door, there was a single plain black buggy. Its rusty iron wheels had scored narrow tracks into the gravel of the parking lot. The tracks were wavy, as if the buggy horse had been unsure on its feet – slow and weary - and the driver anything but hurried.

The black fabric carriage, dusty and sun bleached, was entirely unadorned. Its ill-kept and boney horse had its head hanging down toward the gravel, trying to crop some of the grass that grew under the rail. But the short reins on the bridle held fast to the hitching rail, and the horse looked too weary and frustrated to bother any further with the strain of reaching down against the pull of the leather straps.

Leaning against the end of the hitching rail, there was a new-looking woman's bicycle. It was of the cross-country style, with wide black tires and a black graphite frame. A white wicker basket was attached to the front of the handlebars.

"A Mennonite bicycle," the professor remarked as he led Caroline into the store. "And a Schwartzentruber buggy."

"I feel sorry for the horse," Caroline remarked as she followed him into the store.

Inside, there was a black-clad Old Order Amish woman sorting through a stack of red apples on a table display beside the front door. She glanced up briefly at the two English arrivals, her round and plain white face framed by her black bonnet, but she quickly turned her attention back to her basket of apples. The professor eased past her in the aisle and noted that the apples the woman had selected for her basket were, for the most part, the bruised and nicked ones.

He led Caroline down a short aisle of bulk flours and beans, all put up in clear plastic bags with yellow twisty ties. "Typical,' he thought. Bulk foods with a minimum of packaging. He progressed to the back, and he stopped beside a Mennonite woman at the glass-fronted cheese cooler, who was giving her order to two young Amish girls behind the counter.

To the left stood three English women in colorful summer dresses, waiting for service at the far end of the meat display. The professor was amused to see their metropolitan impatience, and he turned to watch them. But when he heard Caroline speak to the girls behind the cheese counter, he broke off his surveillance, smiling and shaking his head.

Over the top of the cooler, Branden said to the counter girls, "I'm with the Sheriff's Office," and he held up his badge.

One of the two girls came over to him, wiping her fingers on an old towel. She waited wordlessly behind the display for Branden to speak.

The professor put his badge case away and said, "We'd like to find Vera Erb. She's a midwife out here. Your store is the only address we have for her."

The Amish girl arched a brow. "She used to work here. She died last week. Sorry."

"Unexpected?" Caroline asked.

The professor noted that the Old Order Amish woman, with her bruised red apples near the front door, had turned to listen.

"Not really," the counter girl said to Caroline. "It wasn't unexpected. She was ninety-seven."

"Just old, then?" Branden asked. "Nothing suspicious?"

"Just old," the girl said with an awkward smile.

The Old Order Amish woman pushed out through the store's front door. She had left her basket of bruised red apples sitting on the display table. The professor turned to watch her leave, and when he turned back to the counter girl, she said, "Miriam steps out when a place gets too crowded with English folk."

Branden asked, "Was that Miriam Yost? The bishop's wife?"

The girl nodded. "The bishop likes apple pie. I mean he *really* likes apple pie. But Miriam only buys the bruised ones, because she knows we'll give her a discount."

The girl glanced down toward the three English women in their showy summer dresses, gave a nod toward them, and said, "Anything else, then?"

Caroline said, "We want to speak with Hannah Yost. Can you tell us where she lives?"

The counter girl smiled, nodded, and took out paper and a pencil, saying, "I'll draw you a map. Really, it's just up the road."

Chapter 27

A gentle rain, little more than a rolling hill-country mist, was wetting the Brandens' windshield as they left the bishop's house. They drove north on CR 235, up and down over the hills toward the Wayne County line, heading deeper into Bishop Alva Yost's Holmes County countryside.

A gray cover of clouds had settled close to the ground for a rest-of-the-day drizzle. Low pockets between the hilltops were shrouded with a dreary fog. The available light was little more than a pale gloom, dispelling all chances for the casting of shadows. It could have been mistaken for the twilight of a bleak and colorless late November day, except that the temperature was hanging in the low seventies.

The professor set his emergency flashers to blinking, and he slowed his truck to a crawl while Caroline read off the numbers on the mailboxes beside the road.

"That was it," Caroline said eventually, and the professor stopped, backed up on the blacktop, and turned into a long gravel driveway. The mailbox read: Lucas and Hannah Yost. Just as the Brandens cleared the pavement, a heavily loaded logging truck sped by on the road behind them.

Glancing back anxiously at the lumbering truck, Caroline said, "That truck could have hit us. It's too dangerous, Michael, traveling out here in this fog."

"We'll just try," Branden said. "Maybe we'll also have some luck with this last midwife."

The yard and driveway were deserted as they parked beside the white wooden house. The horses and buggies were put up out of sight, and the barn doors were all closed tightly. The swing set and sand box on the front lawn had been abandoned in the rain by the Yost children.

"They'll all be inside," the professor said as he stepped up onto the front porch. Caroline followed and stood back as he knocked on the heavy wooden door. They waited, and then he knocked a second time.

It was a ten-year old boy who eventually pulled the door open from the inside. There was silence behind him in the house, and the interior there seemed unnecessarily dark and gloomy to Professor Branden. All the house's heavy purple window drapes had been closed. No lights could be seen at the windows. When the boy opened the door, there was an orange kerosene glow from indoor lanterns.

The lad stared out at the Brandens with a stone-rigid face, and he didn't speak. Branden gave it a long ten count, to wait for the boy to say something, but the lad said nothing as he stood impassively at the door.

He was dressed in black Amish garb, and his bowl-cut blonde hair worked with the reserved absence of mirth in his expression to give him a somber Dutch-boy look. When Branden hadn't spoken, the taciturn boy looked back into the dark room and seemed to be searching for instructions from an adult. A voice, nearly inaudible, sounded softly behind him. The stolid lad nodded toward the voice, turned slowly back to the Brandens and started to close the door.

"It's important," Branden said into the interior of the room. "We're trying to find Mrs. John Yost. I believe you know her. She's missing, and I think you know that. Mary Yost. Mrs. John Yost. We're looking for her midwife, to try to find her."

From a dim corner of the front room, a figure in black slowly emerged. The blonde lad surrendered his position at the door to his father, and there stood a black-clad man with a bushy gray beard, looking as grave as a funeral director.

"We know," the man said stiffly, "that Mary Yost is missing. Several of us have been trying to find her."

"Can you step out onto the porch here?" the professor asked. "I am Michael Branden, and this is my wife Caroline. Lydia Schwartz was my student at the college in Millersburg."

Lucas Yost nodded. "Lydia Schwartzentruber was known to us. She lost her way."

"She just wanted to go to college," Caroline said, stepping abruptly forward.

Surprised that she would speak up so readily, Branden framed an apologetic smile for Yost and said to him, "She was my student."

"College is not for us, Mr. Branden. We keep to the simpler ways. Should a child be smarter than her parents?"

Caroline shuffled a few steps forward on the porch, and the professor turned back to her, to remind her of caution. She didn't respond to Yost, but Branden realized that it was a near thing. He could see that the instinct to argue with the man was fixed in Caroline's eyes.

He turned back to Yost and said, "Can you please tell us if you have seen Mary? Her baby is due, and your wife is a midwife in the church. And Mary has her daughter Esther with her. We are concerned."

"We have not seen her," Lucas Yost said, stepping back from the door. He put a hand on the edge of the door and began to close it on the Brandens.

The professor pressed in closer to the screen. His nose was practically touching the mesh. "Please, Mr. Yost. John is your brother. So is Alva. We just want to find Mary. Alva should want you to help us with that. The sheriff took a phone call that makes us believe she's in Fort Wayne."

Lucas Yost began again to close the door to Branden. While it was still closing, Yost pronounced a judgement. "If Mary has left her family, then she has lost her way, too. If she's in Fort Wayne, then she'll have to make her own way home. She's a member of the Amish church, so if she doesn't come home, she'll be *mitcd*."

Through the screen, Branden said, "Does she know people in Fort Wayne? Or even in Indiana? If this is a waste of time, I should know that. Who would she be visiting in

Fort Wayne? Are there midwives there to help her? And how would she have gotten herself over there?"

"I don't know," Lucas Yost said impassively. "Most of our Indiana relatives have settled near Indianapolis. There aren't any Yosts in Fort Wayne."

Branden stepped anxiously in place. He resisted an urge to reach out for the latch. He resisted the impulse to pull the screen door open and push himself inside the house. "She was at a motel, Mr. Yost."

Yost lifted his shoulder with a weary shrug. "There are recruiters, Professor. They do a lot of damage. They are aggressive. They help weak souls flee the church. They give them rides, clothes, and a place to stay. Maybe you should ask these English people about Mary Yost. If no one can find her, then maybe she has had some help. You English are responsible for this. Lydia is dead because of you English."

Caroline tried a line with the stubborn man. "Please, Mr. Yost. We'd like to talk with your wife. If she hasn't seen Mary, then maybe she could tell us something that would help us find her. I know you are trying to find her, too. But we would just like to ask your wife some questions. What harm would that do?"

Lucas Yost stared blankly out through the screen at Caroline. Fog seemed to roll up onto the porch and obscure him. He seemed to recede like an apparition.

Caroline held his stare and said, "We'll just take a minute or two, Mr. Yost."

"Take a seat out there," Yost said. "I will send her out. Once you have finished, I want you to leave us alone."

- - - - - - - - - - - - - -

With an infant daughter taking a breast in her arms, Hannah Yost came slowly out onto her front porch. She had a modesty towel laid over the child's head. On a hickory rocker between the professor and Caroline, Hannah sat down carefully with her child.

Using a casual tone, Caroline asked, "How old is your daughter?" The Brandens had agreed, while waiting for Hannah to appear, that Caroline should take the lead in the conversation. They had rehearsed some of the issues that Caroline should try to raise with her. Caroline was dressed in a plain blue, calf-length skirt and a white blouse. Her long auburn hair was up in a bun. All things considered, it was the most conservative outfit that Caroline could present with such traditional people.

With her child in her arms, Hannah settled back on her chair and looked to Caroline to say, "I don't know your names." She also looked to the professor to say, "Midwives?"

Caroline answered. "My name is Caroline Branden. We want to find the midwife that Mary Yost would use. This is my husband Michael. He's a teacher at Millersburg College. He's also a deputy with the sheriff's office. We started by asking at Weaver's store about Vera Erb. But they told us that she died recently."

Hannah nodded, closed her eyes, smiled, and said, "Ninety-seven." She opened her eyes to Caroline and said again, "Vera was ninety-seven. She lived a good life."

To encourage the conversation forward, Caroline asked, "Was she good at midwifing?"

"One of the best. She was with me when little Sarah here was born."

"That must have been recently," Caroline said. "I mean, your child is very young."

"She's only four months old," said Hannah. "We have several midwives in the church. Vera was one of the best."

"We have a list," Caroline said. She handed the page to Hannah. "Are these your people?"

Hannah glanced only briefly at the list. "Yes," she said, handing the page back to Caroline. "We're down to only these, now. But some of the younger women are helping. For training."

"Do you ever use doctors?"

"Maybe if it is an emergency. But probably not."

"Would Mary use a hospital?"

"Probably not."

"So mostly the women are traditional? With their deliveries, I mean."

"Yes. A child should be born at home. That is best."

Caroline shifted forward in her chair and leaned in closer to speak softly to Hannah. "We're trying to find Mary Yost."

Again, Hannah made no reply.

"Do you know where she is, Hannah?"

"No."

"Do you think she left him?"

"No."

"Well, something must have happened."

"We don't know. She was in a Bible study with a neighbor lady. She was starting to pester her husband with awkward questions about scriptures. It wasn't a proper way for an Amish wife to behave."

"Questions about the Scriptures?" Caroline asked.

Hannah nodded. "And about our traditions. About the ways we choose to live."

"Like with using midwives?"

"Oh, not really. That's just common sense. She might have had questions about our traditions, but she didn't doubt the Scriptures. Nothing like that."

"Then traditions?" Caroline asked. "She questioned your traditions?"

"Some of them," Hannah nodded. "We keep the old ways. We are the last peoples who do that. We are the remnants. We are the only ones left. It is our duty to be the remnants."

"That sounds like the topic of a sermon."

Hannah smiled as if remembering something fondly. "The preachers tell us the right ways to live."

"Do they tell you that you can't use hospitals?"

"You are a modern person?" Hannah responded.

"Yes."

"Do you consider yourself to be well educated?"

"I think so."

"Then tell me, Mrs. Branden. How can a disease stop itself?"

"Are you talking about vaccines?" Caroline asked.

"Yes. Tell me. How can a little bit of measles stop a lot of measles?"

"That's how vaccines work," Caroline answered. "They are beneficial. Think about it. We don't get the three-day or seven-day measles more than once, right? That's because the illness causes our bodies to produce antibodies, to fight against the disease. And that's what vaccines do. They give us the antibodies we need to prevent the disease. So, if you get measles once, that's it. Your done with measles for the rest of your life."

"We think vaccines do more harm than good."

"What about mental imbalances? They can be alleviated with medication."

Hannah shook her head with confidence. As if recalling a familiar sermon, she seemed to recite a passage. "If God himself has made us, who are we to alter that with chemicals?"

"Hannah, we alter ourselves with chemicals every day. Food. Aroma therapies. Spices. Folk remedies. Tobacco and wine. These are all chemicals."

Hannah shook her head again, reciting something long nurtured in her traditions. "Food is given to us by God. Medicines are made by man. And if they sometimes do some good, they also do great harm. More harm than good, we believe. Just read the side effects from any of your modern medicines. They're worse than the maladies that they are supposed to cure."

"Sometimes, perhaps," Caroline said.

"The bishop knows best. So do the preachers."

"And the women who die in childbirth?" Caroline asked. "The ones who could be saved in a hospital?"

"If it is God's will," Hannah asserted.

"Mary Yost is missing, Hannah. She is due to deliver her child. We think she is in Indiana, now. Does she know how to find a midwife there?"

Hannah shrugged her shoulders. She stood and waited for Caroline to stand beside her. "You have your list of midwives," she said, terminating the interview. She moved toward the door. She reached out for the latch on her screened door, entered, and with her infant still in her arms, she turned back to talk to Caroline through the screen, saying, "She'll use a midwife. Wherever she is, Mary will find a midwife to help her with her delivery."

Chapter 28

Saturday, September 2
2:10 PM

"She really didn't tell us where to find Mary," Caroline complained.

The professor shrugged and took another bite of his sandwich. They were parked at Weaver's Marketplace again. They had bought cheese, apples, premade sandwiches, a can of cashews and bottles of water. As they ate lunch in the truck, the rain was still falling. The professor had his engine running, with his wipers swiping the windshield intermittently. "This midwife angle is not going to work out."

"Is that it, then?" Caroline asked. "Are we just going to quit?"

Branden shook his head. "There's another angle, here. The Schells. I want to show you their house over east of Millersburg."

"You think this is tangled up with them?"

Branden nodded. He finished his bottle of water, and he put his truck into reverse. "Just wait until you see this house. I want your opinion. There is something there that troubles me."

The professor backed around on the gravel and turned south on CR 235. After crossing TR 606, he continued south through the countryside, eventually crossing 62/39 to the Schells' gingerbread house on the hill.

The professor drove past the brown house slowly, so that Caroline could get a good look at it.

The house was framed by the tall pines behind it, and the ginger-brown structure with its white accent trim looked dark and lifeless in the gloom of the rain. And it looked outdated. A battered white passenger van, equally outdated and marred by heavy use, was parked at the top of the driveway.

Farther along past the house, Branden turned around in the driveway of a neighbor and came back to the property to park a bit short of the long sloping field of hay in front of the house. He kept his engine running, with the wipers swiping the glass. The rain was falling more steadily now. It panged incessantly on the thin roof of the truck. It spattered with force on the windshield. The brown-green stubble of hay in the field beside them was also taking a thorough drubbing from the rain, and over the racket, the professor remarked offhand, "They must have taken it up this morning."

"Michael?"

"The hay. They had just cut it the last time I was out here. Friday, at dinner time. They must have cut it Wednesday or Thursday, then let it dry yesterday. They got it up just in time. To still be dry, I mean, before the rain. You can't stack wet hay in a barn."

Caroline pointed to the house at the top of the hill. "That's the Schells' house?"

"Yes."

"Who owns the white Amish-hauler?"

"The Schells, I think. It was parked at their boarding house yesterday."

The front door of the brown house opened from the inside, and Donna Schell stepped out onto the porch and popped an umbrella open. Ed Schell came out behind her, and he held her elbow as she took the steps gingerly.

Once down to the sidewalk, Donna paused there under her umbrella, and she bent over to rub at her knees. Ed went back into the house. He came out carrying their infant Annie. The newly-turned Mennonite woman stepped out too, holding little Sophie Schell's hand. She also opened an umbrella on the porch.

Ed took Donna's umbrella in his one free hand, and he ushered her toward the van. While on the walkway, Donna was speaking earnestly about something, as she trailed behind Ed. Annie lay asleep in her father's arms, oblivious to the noise of the rain and the words of her mother.

Again, Donna needed Ed's help to manage the ascent to the passenger's seat. All the while, as she settled on her seat, Donna kept talking to him. For his part, Ed was nodding his agreements with everything that Donna was saying.

The companion woman got Sophie up into the side door of the van, and she helped Sophie buckle her seat belt on the bench seat. After she was buckled herself, she took little Annie from Ed, and she strapped the infant into a child seat between her and Sophie.

Ed turned his van around in the driveway, and he drove them all down the long sloping hill. On TR 354, he turned left on 310, headed presumably back toward the village of Millersburg. Donna was still talking, but now she was frowning deeply.

"Something's wrong," Caroline commented. "Donna's not happy about something."

The professor wrinkled a frown and scratched at his beard. He shook his head to refocus his thoughts. "There are three more people still here," he said. "There is this woman who just left with the Schells, and then there's going to be her husband and two children. And this woman who left with the Schells? Did you notice that she was not dressed Old Order?"

"Yes," Caroline said. "So, this is some kind of halfway house?"

"I think so. That's what I thought you would say, once you had seen the setup here."

"Then where did they come from, Michael?"

"Could be from anywhere. Iowa, Indiana, or right here from Holmes County. The point is, this is what the Schells are doing. And I don't think this is their first time."

"This can't happen very often, Michael. This is rather extreme."

"Right."

"There are still lights on in the house," Caroline observed.

"Then let's just ask them about this," Branden said. "Let's just go up there and ask them directly."

- - - - - - - - - - - - - -

Once Branden had parked his truck in front of the brown house, the lights started turning off inside. The Brandens popped out and ran in the hard rain, up onto the front porch. No one answered the door when Caroline rang the bell. She pulled the screen door open and knocked loudly on the inside wooden door. No one came to the door.

Taking a thorough soaking for their troubles, the Brandens tried the back door. Nothing. Then the professor cupped his hands to the glass and peered into a kitchen window. He could see no one inside.

Back in their truck, dripping rainwater onto their seats, Branden said to Caroline, "We really ought to carry umbrellas."

"Or towels," Caroline answered with a nervous laugh. "Why won't they talk to us?"

"I don't know."

"Who's going to know anything about this, Michael?"

"Cal Troyer," the professor said, starting his engine. "We'll ask Cal. If anyone knows about this, it'll be Cal."

"Are they breaking any laws?"

Branden considered the question. "I don't know. But Meredith's death? I'd bet any amount of money that this has something to do with that."

Countering, Caroline said, "Meredith had just caused the death of Lydia Schwartz."

"It was in her note, Caroline. It was a line saying, '*we* should have never started any of this.'"

Chapter 29

Saturday, September 2
7:05 PM

After dinner, the professor parked his truck in the gravel lot between Cal's church building and the parsonage, and as soon as he and Caroline were out of the truck, they heard a woman's voice inside the house. The rain had stopped, and the sound of her voice carried indistinctly in the humid evening air, so that her exact words were unintelligible. But the professor did recognize the voice.

"That's Alice Shewmon," the professor said as he rang the bell at the kitchen's side door.

Rachel Ramsayer opened the door, and with her brows raised in a quiet sigh, she gave a long-suffering shrug of her shoulders. She stepped back to let the Brandens inside, where Alice Shewmon was standing with Cal, who was leaning back against his kitchen sink, looking perplexed.

Cal seemed pleased to see the Brandens. He said, "Hello, welcome," and he stepped out and around the taller Shewmon and pulled a Jello snack out of his refrigerator. When he turned around to his three guests, he said rather tiredly, "Can I fix you anything? Coffee? Juice? I've been on Jello and clear liquids all day."

The three declined a snack. Instead, Caroline spoke to Alice Shewmon. "Are you OK, Alice?"

Alice turned to Caroline. "Guess I'm a little worked up."

"OK," Caroline said. "Is this about the Schwartzentrubers again?" She held a chair out for Alice at Cal's round kitchen table, and Alice sat down and scooted in. She pulled her long black ponytail around to the front of her, and she tugged on the ends, seeming distracted enough to want to pluck some of the long strands from her head.

"These Schwartzentrubers," Alice said with a weak and anxious smile.

Caroline sat and asked, "Have you been back to see the Yost children again?"

Alice nodded. "At their grandparents' house."

"And?"

Laughing, Shewmon said, "And these are not modern people."

"No," Caroline said. "Not even a little bit."

"Well, I just want to work around that, somehow. Cal's been telling me that it's nearly impossible. I'm just not ready to accept that, I guess."

The professor took a seat at the table. Cal sat there, too, with his cup of Jello. Rachel already had a glass of apple juice poured and set out for him at the table.

Rachel said, "Is apple juice OK, Dad?" and Cal gave a weary nod.

Looking skeptically back at Shewmon, Rachel left the room.

Alice took the opportunity to press her discussion with Cal. She pushed her long hair around to the back, and

265

she seemed to have acquired some new and sharper focus. "These people talk like they've got the secret to life, or something," Alice said, "but they're just archaic. That's all. I just need to know why. Can you tell me why?"

Trying to smile, Cal managed only a hint at mirth. He chuckled weakly. "I *have* been telling you, Alice."

Professor Branden interjected. "They value their traditions as much as their faith, Alice. They live by the traditions of their ancestors."

Cal swallowed a spoonful of Jello, drank from his glass of apple juice, and shook his head. "That's only part of it, Mike."

Alice made a sad smile. "I don't understand this. It goes against everything I've been taught. Against everything I believe."

"No doubt," Caroline said.

Cal sighed and tried again. "Just think of it as pacifism, Alice. I'm sure you can respect that."

Alice stood and said, "OK, but I'm going to try to talk with them again. I'd be so much happier if I could just get the children vaccinated. I'll go out to see the bishop, to explain the science to him."

- - - - - - - - - - - - - -

Once Shewmon had left, Caroline said, "I sympathize with her, Cal. All their old ways – their traditions – do cause harm. Illness, accidents, genetic disorders. I mean, the list is endless if you really are honest about it. Everything from sanitation – their outhouses? – to John Yost in the hospital, who won't take medicine for his depression? That's extreme. Contagion, epidemics, accidents, childhood deaths? Really, Cal, aren't too many of the headstones in their cemeteries the headstones for young children?"

Cal held a tender smile. Gently, he said, "Don't let it make you crazy, Caroline. You've lived in Holmes County long enough to know all of this. Don't over-think it. It'll take a long time for any of this to change. And then the change will have to come from within the framework of their faith."

"Well," said Caroline slowly, "I think Mose and Ida Schwartzentruber need some of your wisdom on that point." She gave out a little laugh. "Probably John Yost, too. And Mary Yost, if we can find her. We think the Schells might be the key to that."

"Oh?" Cal asked.

The professor scooted his chair closer to the table. He leaned over the table on his elbows, and he addressed Cal as if taking him into a conspiracy. "We think they're running a rescue mission. An underground escape route to help the Amish who want to get out. To get out and live English. Have you ever heard of anything like that? Ever hear anything about recruiters?"

Cal nodded. "One church, south of here. In Knox County, several years ago. But here with the Schells? Well, I guess I wouldn't be completely surprised."

Branden said, "We think they have a safe house down in southwest Berlin Township. South of 39. The house is owned by a megachurch in Omaha, and they list the Schells as their missionaries."

"This is rare, Mike," Cal asserted. "People like this take an extreme position. They're zealots for evangelism. They consider their work to be sacred. It's not really all that common. So, the Schells, you think? They're like that? Why do you think that?"

"I saw them," Branden said, "taking a young Amish family out to their safe house. In a van owned by *The Church of True Believers*."

"Is this the Omaha connection?"

"Yes."

"Then, if you're right," Cal said, "the Schells serve as feeders for the Omaha church. And there will be a network, spread around the country, to help get Amish converts safely away from their families, and to get them started living as English people."

"Is it legal?" Caroline asked.

"Yes," Cal said. "Unless evangelism has become illegal, and nobody's told me."

Said Branden, "There might be underaged children involved."

"Like who?"

The professor gave a glance to Caroline. She nodded. The professor answered Cal's question. "Like Mary Yost and her little Esther."

"And a newborn child," Caroline added. "Mary could have delivered her child by now."

Cal pondered the question and asked, "How is this related to the death of your student, Mike?"

"We don't know," Branden answered.

Shaking her head, Caroline rose from the table, and she whispered a tentative, "No, something's not right."

She got a glass out of the cabinet over the sink, and she ran out water for herself. Sitting back down with it, she said, "It still doesn't work for me, Michael."

"What?" Cal asked, looking first to the professor and then to Caroline. "What doesn't work for you?"

"I don't believe," Caroline said, "that Mary Yost would leave all of her other children behind. Voluntarily, I mean. I just don't believe it."

Cal asked, "What if she had encouragement?"

"From the Schells," the professor said.

"Yes," said Cal. "With this Omaha church."

"And the Culps," the professor said.

"Who?" Cal asked.

"Paul and Nancy Culp. In Parma. They're marriage counselors. Psychologists."

Cal asked, "Were they working with Mary Yost?"

"They were waiting for Mary to come up to Parma on the bus," the professor answered.

"How are the Schells connected with this?" Cal asked.

"They're the ones who put Mary Yost in touch with the Culps in the first place," Branden said. "They sent Mary up to Parma on a bus."

"And?" Cal asked.

"And she disappeared," Branden said. "She never made it to the Culps. She never made it to the hotel that the Schells had arranged for her near the bus route."

Shaking his head, Cal said, "This is tangled. You're talking about a network."

"Probably," Branden said. "The Culps, the Schells, the Omaha people. Setting up a disappearing act for Mary."

"Alice Shewmon," Caroline said, "won't have any trouble believing that Mary wanted out of her church. And out of her marriage. Alice won't have any trouble believing that at all."

"This is extreme," Cal said again. "Evangelism is one thing, but breaking up families? That's extreme."

"Is it possible?" Branden asked.

Cal nodded. "If they are zealots."

"Who?" Caroline asked.

"Any of the three," Cal said. "Or two of the three, working together."

"Or all three," Branden said. "An extended network."

"This would be rare," Cal said. "And if any of it is true, someone has been lying to you. Except . . ." Cal hesitated with a thought.

"What?" Mike and Caroline asked simultaneously.

"What?" Caroline asked again.

"If they are zealots, they wouldn't be able to conceal it. They'd be proud of it. They'd admit to it, if you pushed on them hard enough. They'd want to own it."

"If they are zealots," Branden echoed.

Cal smiled. "That's a pretty big '*if,*' Mike."

- - - - - - - - - - - - - -

Standing outside on the gravel parking lot beside his truck, the professor asked his wife, "So, how do we push hard enough on them? And who do we push on?"

"If it's a network," Caroline said over the roof of the truck, "one would tell the others."

"I think Cal's right," the professor said. "They'd want to own it."

Caroline shrugged her shoulders. "They might tell you what they did, Michael. But they'd probably never tell you where Mary is. They'd go to jail before they would tell you that."

Nodding, the professor said, "Yes. If they're that extreme."

Caroline pulled the passenger's door open, and on his side, the professor slid in behind the wheel. He put the key into the ignition, but he did not start the engine.

Instead, he sat in the dark, drumming his thumbs on the steering wheel. He shook his head and frowned. He looked over to his wife and asked, "How did we get this far along? Thinking this way, I mean?"

"If Cal is right," Caroline said, "you just have to push a little, to get them to admit to something."

After a silence, while the professor started his truck, Caroline said, "We wanted to drive with Cal up to Cleveland, Michael."

The professor switched off his engine, and Caroline waited in the truck while Branden rang the kitchen's side bell again. When Cal opened the door, Branden said, "We're still going with you up to Cleveland, right? On Wednesday?"

"They called," Cal said. "They want me up there Tuesday night."

"Even better," Branden said. "We'll all go up, Tuesday after dinner. Caroline will stay there with Rachel. I have classes on Wednesdays."

Cal nodded. "I don't know a time for the surgery. All they'll tell me is that I'm scheduled for Wednesday morning. So, they want me available, in case they take me first thing. It could be five AM."

"I'll come back up to see you Wednesday after dinner."

"I'll be there," Cal said. "Don't know what condition I'll be in, but I will definitely be there."

272

- - - - - - - - - - - - - -

While they were driving back home, the professor's phone chirped with the sheriff's coded tone. Branden handed his phone to Caroline, and Caroline answered it. She verified that it was Robertson, and she immediately switched him to speaker phone, saying, "Michael is driving, Bruce. You're on speaker phone."

"Mike," Robertson started, "John Yost has been croaking out gibberish with Evie Carson. In the hospital. Well, some of it is gibberish, anyway. But he's talking about graves on his farm. He's crying and grumbling about graves. We're going to search the place tomorrow."

"OK, wow," Branden said. "That's a surprise. You don't want to do something yet tonight?"

"Tomorrow, Mike. I told the bishop tomorrow. We have his permission to search the farm. I think he's as worried about John Yost as we are, now. But tonight, let me meet you at your house. It's on the way. I've got an idea."

"What?" Caroline asked.

"I need you to go out to the Schwartzentrubers' with me."

Caroline said, "It's rather late to be knocking on doors, Sheriff."

"I've got an idea," Robertson said. "This can't wait."

"They might not answer the door at this hour," the professor said.

"What's your idea?" Caroline asked. "Maybe if I go out there with you?"

"That might help," Robertson said. "I don't know for sure. But I've got that recording I made of the woman who called my phone from Fort Wayne. I'm talking about the woman who said she was Mary Yost. I'm going to play it for Junior and see what he says about it. I've just got a hunch."

Branden said, "I thought you were letting this drop, Bruce."

"Yeah, well now John Yost is muttering to Evie Carson about graves, Professor, and I've got this one little something that's been bugging me."

"Who told you about John, Bruce? Evie?"

"No, it was the bishop, actually. He was just here. I told him we wanted to talk to John Junior, and to Mose and Ida Schwartzentruber, too, and he was agreeable."

"We can go out there," the professor said.

"Then I'm going, too," Caroline said. "It's late. You need to let me be the one who knocks on their door."

Chapter 30

At first there was only the slightest movement in the long purple curtains of the porch window at Mose and Ida Schwartzentruber's farmhouse. On the porch, standing to the left of the window, for the third time, Caroline knocked on the front door. Branden and the sheriff had remained in Robertson's Crown Vic, which was idling at the side of the porch with its lights off.

While watching the window, Caroline knocked again on the wood door, and there was a flicker of flame at the narrow split between the window curtains. Then there was a faint orange glow. The glow increased and moved away from the split. After another knock, Ida Schwartzentruber pulled the front door open and held her kerosene lantern up above her eyes, to peer out at Caroline from behind the crack in the door. The flickering orange light of the lantern bathed old Ida's lined and craggy face with the irregular shadows of a Halloween eeriness. Nowhere in her expression or posture was there any hint of a welcome for Caroline. To emphasize this point, she reached to the latch on the screened door, and with a soft click, she locked the screened door in place.

Through the screened door, Caroline spoke self-consciously. "I'm sorry, Mrs. Schwartzentruber. I am really

275

very sorry about this. I know it's late. But this is important, and I think you will want to help us."

"Help you with what?" Ida asked with a throaty, sleep-infused whisper. "Why are you here?"

"We have a phone call from Mary Yost. She said she was over in Fort Wayne. But I don't think she would have gone there, and the sheriff," – Caroline gestured toward the Crown Vic, and Ida unlocked the screened door and stuck her head out of the door to look over at Branden and Robertson – "thinks you can help us. We think that you or John Junior could listen to the phone message."

"How is that possible?"

"The sheriff made a recording of the phone call. We can play it for you. You can listen to what she said. It won't take very long, Mrs. Schwartzentruber. You'll have helped us very much. You'll have helped us find your daughter."

Pensively, Ida considered Caroline for a very long and silent time. She put her head out again, looking to the side of her front porch, and she studied Branden and Robertson sitting in the Crown Vic. She said, "Wait," and she carried her lantern back into the house. The light disappeared with her, and Caroline was left on the porch with nothing but the moon to illuminate her position. She stood awkwardly and self-consciously in place, and she waited in the dark.

Then at the door, Mose Schwartzentruber appeared with the lantern. He was barefooted and dressed all in black. He held silence for a moment, as if the circumstance required careful thought. Eventually he said, "A phone call?"

"Yes, a phone call that the sheriff recorded. We want you to listen to it."

Behind Mose, Ida appeared again. Mose was holding the lantern at shoulder height, and Ida stood back, so that the glow of the flame partly obscured her to Caroline. From there she said, "We don't know why this can't wait until tomorrow."

Caroline considered that and nodded. "I know," she said. "It's late. But we are worried about Mary and Esther, and if you take just five minutes to listen to the phone call, it'll help us very much. We want to find Mary and Esther. You can help us with that. You can help us a lot, just by listening to a few sentences that she spoke when she called the sheriff."

Mose asked, "Can you play it for us here? Or does it need the electric? We don't have the electric."

"We can play it here, Mr. Schwartzentruber. You'll hear Mary's voice. It will help us. It will help her. Please."

Mose nodded solemnly. He held rigidly to his place behind the screened door. Caroline turned and descended the porch steps. She walked down them carefully in the darkness, and she walked over to the Crown Vic. She took Robertson's phone from him, and she carried it back to the front door. "I'll tap the icons," she said, "and it will light up. Then I can make it play a recording of Mary's voice."

Mose nodded, but he didn't otherwise reply. He waited while Caroline prepared the phone. He watched impassively as she called up the file and chose the playback feature.

Mary Yost's words issued out of the phone, and Mose did not seem startled. The words played out just as Mary and the sheriff had spoken them:

>*We're fine, Sheriff.*
>*Where are you, Mary?*
>*That doesn't matter. We're both fine. I'm having some labor now, so I can't talk.*
>*But, we're fine.*
>*You need help? Let us help you.*
>*I have a woman with me.*
>*A midwife, Mary?*
>*A nurse. I'm fine. I can't talk. What? OK. I need to hang up, now.*

Caroline switched the recording off. Mose stared out at her with mild puzzlement showing in his expression. His eyes narrowed, and he seemed bewildered to Caroline. He pulled Ida farther back into the room with him, and with the lantern between them, they spoke to each other in Dietsche dialect. Leaving Mose standing back a few paces away from the door, Ida came forward with the lantern to face Caroline through the screened door, and she asked, "Can you play that again?"

Caroline did, and Ida turned around to Mose, shaking her head wordlessly. Mose disappeared with the lantern. Ida stood at the door and watched placidly out at Caroline. After a couple of minutes, Mose reappeared with John Yost Junior, who was dressed in his full black denim attire, with even his vest buttoned in place. He was barefooted, and his face showed deep imprints from his pillow.

Mose nodded to Caroline, and Caroline asked, "Again?"

Mose nodded a silent yes, and Caroline played the recording again, this time with Junior standing there to listen. Junior listened to it all. He turned to his grandfather Mose and pulled him back into the shadows of the front hallway to confer with him.

When Junior came back to the door, he spoke out through the screen to Caroline, saying only, "That is not die Maemme's voice. That is not my mother."

Chapter 31

It was well into the early morning hours before Sheriff Robertson and Professor Branden had made their plans and placed their phone calls. When they got to the Schells' boarding house, Robertson parked his Crown Vic on the driveway, behind the Schells' battered white Amish-Hauler van, and the men stepped up onto the side porch in the dark, to knock on the door. Caroline had earlier argued that this was not a door where she was needed. They had her best advice, and she had helped them make their plans, but this wasn't the door of a skittish Old Order family out in the country. There wouldn't be any need to soft-peddle the interview.

Everything had been discussed. Two deputies had orders to interview the Culps first thing Monday morning, and they had already left for a hotel in Parma. Deputies Ryan Baker and Dave Johnson were to go Monday morning to Omaha, to interview the pastors at the *Church of True Believers*. "Now," the sheriff had declared, "we've really got something, Mike. We finally have something to investigate."

Branden knocked a few times on the Schells' side door, and then Robertson took to pounding the door with the heel of his hand. A light switch was finally thrown in a downstairs room, and there was a rustling behind the closed door. Softly, they heard a woman pleading, "Please don't wake the children."

Branden spoke through the door. "Mrs. Schell? This is Mike Branden. We need to speak with you."

There was a soft click behind the door, with the opening slap of a dead bolt, and through the closed door, Donna asked, "This can't wait until tomorrow?"

"We need to speak with you," the professor repeated.

"We?" A second click sounded from behind the door. There was a bit of a rustle at the lock on the doorknob.

"I'm here with Sheriff Bruce Robertson," Branden answered.

A man behind the door asked, "Is this about Lydia Schwartz?"

"Ed?" Branden said. "It's only partly about Lydia. We're really here to ask about Mary and Esther Yost."

Faintly, Branden heard a back-and-forth whispering from behind the door. Then he heard clearly when Ed said to Donna, "Are you sure?"

Donna spoke as she turned the knob. "It's late, Professor. Do you have any idea?" The door opened a slight amount, and Donna asked, still shielded behind the door, "Why can't this wait until morning?"

Now Robertson came forward. "It's Sheriff Robertson, Mrs. Schell. Just give us a minute."

"Do you have a warrant?" Ed Schell asked from inside. "Do we need a lawyer?"

"You aren't suspects in any investigation," the sheriff said, surprised by the legal maneuver. "We just want to ask you about Mary Yost. You sent her up to see the psychologists in Parma."

"Are they OK?" Ed asked as Donna opened the door completely.

Together the Schells stood in their bathrobes, on the other side of the threshold. Ed threw a switch on the wall to his right, and a yellow porch light came on above the heads of the men on the porch.

"The Culps are fine," Branden said in the yellow light. "It's not so much about them, other than the fact that Mary was supposed to talk to them."

"And she didn't," Ed said, nodding. He stepped back from the doorway, waved the men inside, and said, "Please be quiet. You know. The children."

Inside in the hallway, Robertson said, "We're trying to find Mary Yost, folks. Have you seen her? Have you heard from her?"

With quizzical expressions, the Schells looked to each other. Then Ed turned to face Robertson, saying simply, "No."

"Do you know people in Fort Wayne?" Robertson asked.

"No," Donna said.

"Really?" Branden asked.

"Well, maybe a few people," Ed said.

Robertson asked, "Would you be surprised to learn that Mary Yost had gone over to Fort Wayne?"

"In her buggy?" Donna asked. "That's a fairly long trip in a buggy."

"Or maybe she got a ride?" the professor asked.

"We don't know about that," Ed said. "Why are you asking about Fort Wayne?"

"Do you own property over there?" Branden asked.

"No," said Ed, and Branden looked to Robertson for the next question.

"Someone," the sheriff said, "called us from Fort Wayne."

"Really?" Donna Schell asked.

"Yes," Robertson said, nodding solemnly. "But she said she was Mary Yost, and John Junior has just told us that the voice on that call is not his mother's. Do you know anything about that? Because clearly it is not Mary Yost who called us."

Again, the Schells exchanged puzzled expressions. Then Donna said, "I saw her Friday afternoon, a week ago, when I put her on the bus. Up in Wooster."

Robertson asked, "Was that to travel up to see the Culps? To talk with the marriage counselors?"

"Why, yes," Ed replied. "We thought she could really use their help."

"Help with what?" Branden asked.

"Why all the questions?" Ed asked.

"We're worried," Robertson said. "Her sister Lydia has died, and Mary is now missing. Then also you thought her home life was bad enough to warrant counseling with psychologists from out of town. Is that all a coincidence?"

"I suppose it is," Ed said. "You don't think the woman who called you was really Mary Yost?"

"Her son, John Junior, told us," Branden said, "that it was not the voice of his mother on that call."

"You must have recorded the call," Donna said.

"Well," Robertson said and hesitated. "Well, yes, I recorded the phone call. I had gotten one earlier from this woman, but all she did then was leave a voice mail message."

Ed rolled a smile across his lips. "You didn't play the voice mail message for Junior? You could have done that a lot sooner."

"I guess I could have," Robertson said. "But this call was more recent, and I just went for that. I didn't think this was the kind of squabble that a sheriff ought to get into. You know, a family squabble. But it doesn't matter. It's the same voice on the earlier voicemail, and on the phone call I recorded, and John Junior says that the voice is not his mother's."

"That's curious," Ed commented nervously.

Branden asked, "She's Old Order, right? Where do you suppose she got a phone?"

Ed shrugged his shoulders and lifted his flat palms. "Your guess is as good as mine, Professor."

Branden nodded and turned for the steps. Robertson held out his hand to shake Ed Schell's with a "Thank you, folks," and he descended the steps with the professor. Ed was closing his door when Robertson said, with a contemplative tone, "I don't know, Ed."

The sheriff came back up the steps, leaving Branden down on the sidewalk. Under the yellow light again, Robertson said, "Really Ed, if you put it all together, we think someone is helping Mary hide."

Donna used an incredulous tone to say, "You think us? Really, you think we're helping her?"

"It's a thought," Robertson said.

"We tried to give her the help that we thought she needed," Donna said with a trace of heat in her voice. "We've already told you that."

"Yes," Robertson said. "You've told us that. You put her on a bus, Mrs. Schell. To go see the Culps for marriage counseling."

Donna gave a simple nod of her head. Ed said nothing.

Branden asked, "Was her little Esther with her?" He came back onto the porch to stand with the sheriff.

"What?" Donna asked.

"Yes, of course," Ed responded at the same time.

Branden shot Robertson a look and shook his head for the sheriff. The sheriff stepped forward, and the professor stepped back. This they had planned. An aggressive tone for Robertson was also something they had planned for this eventuality.

"I want to know," Robertson intoned authoritatively, "where Mary Yost is."

Looking spiked with anxiety, Donna folded her hands in front, saying, "We really don't know."

"I don't believe that," Robertson insisted. "I've got deputies at your brown house out on TR 354. What are they gonna find?"

Ed pulled gently on Donna's elbow to move her back a step, and he came forward as if guarding her. "We haven't done anything wrong, Sheriff," he said.

Robertson pressed on, speaking to Ed Schell. "What are those Amish people out there gonna tell us, Mr. Schell?" He turned to Donna and said, "What are those people gonna say, Mrs. Schell?"

Donna suffered a rosy blush in her cheeks. "We're helping them," she said meekly. "We are missionaries, and we're just helping them."

Branden asked, "And your Omaha church?"

Ed spoke up quickly. "They are not involved."

Robertson asked Donna, "Are these Amish people, or English?"

"Who?" Donna asked, as if confused.

"At your brown house, Mrs. Schell. Amish or English?"

"Christians," Ed said, standing up straighter. "They are just Christians, now. Mennonites. We've done nothing wrong."

Stepping forward, Donna said, "We're helping them. We're just helping them. There's nothing wrong with that."

"Like you helped Mary and Esther?" Robertson asked.

Evenly, Ed said, "We're just trying to help people."

Robertson eased back a step and said, "Sorry for pushing, folks. I just needed to know."

The sheriff stepped down off the porch. He was headed for his Crown Vic when Ed Schell said, "That's awfully rough treatment, Sheriff. For good people who are just trying to help."

Robertson tilted his head at that, turned back to Ed and said, "I'm sorry, Mr. Schell. Sorry that you don't like it."

"But not sorry to have done it?" Ed challenged.

"Sorry," Robertson said as he came back up the steps. Branden was still on the porch.

"It's OK, Ed," Donna said. "They're just doing their jobs."

"Just a few more questions," Robertson said. "And then we'll get out of your hair."

Branden addressed Donna. "You told us that it was just Mary who traveled to Parma on the bus."

Donna stammered a bit. "I must be confused. I guess I really don't remember."

Branden arched a brow. "It's rather an important detail, Mrs. Schell."

"I'm all flustered. It's late. Can't some of this wait until morning?"

Robertson said, "Yes, sure," and he pulled lightly on the professor's elbow. The two men went down the porch steps again, and Robertson paused there to ask, "How would it be if we came back at 9:00? First thing in the morning, I mean. How would that be?"

"Why?" Ed asked. "We've answered your questions."

Robertson came back a few steps toward the porch. Speaking up to the Schells, he said, "We are just worried, folks. We need to be certain that no one has hurt Mary Yost. And there's the matter of the little girl Esther. Surely you can understand that. We need to be certain that no one has hurt them."

Donna bristled a bit and said, "We haven't hurt anyone. We're not like that."

Robertson spoke up aggressively. "Is Mary Yost still alive?"

"What?" Donna gasped.

"How would we know?" Ed asked.

"OK," Robertson said as he came back up the porch steps. "OK," he said. "But we're still worried. There's already been one tragic death in that family, and no one can tell us where Mary is. Or little Esther."

"You should look to her husband," Donna said anxiously.

"We've got to ask the questions," Robertson said. "We started with you two, because you are close in town. We'll also talk with the Culps, in the morning."

From the side walkway, Branden pressed a statement forward. "The *Church of True Believers*," – he came up onto the porch to join the sheriff – "owns a house in Fort Wayne."

"So?" Ed asked. "There are a lot of houses in Fort Wayne. Churches do own some of them. That's certainly not illegal."

"Do you know anything about this church's house, Mr. Schell?" Branden asked.

"Of course not."

"They also own the brown house," Branden said, "The one that you all went to, over south of 39. The house where you took four Amish people just this Friday. Is that just a coincidence? Because they're listed on the mortgage, along with you."

"This is starting to get annoying," Ed said.

Roughly, Robertson asked, "Do you know where Mary Yost is, Mr. Schell?"

Forcefully, Donna said, "What kind of question is that?"

Ed pulled again on Donna's elbow, but she resisted him, saying, "They are safe, now, Sheriff. You've asked your questions. Now really, you need to stop this. It's insulting. And like we said, it's late."

"Safe from what?" Robertson asked.

Ed showed a touch of heat. Sternly he started to exclaim, "Safe from . . . . ,"

"Ed!" Donna shouted, stopping him.

Sternly, Branden said, "You've been lying."

Robertson angrily said, "Don't you realize how much of our time you've wasted?"

Ed stood tall, and Donna wore a satisfied smile. Robertson stepped down off the porch, and Branden followed him.

- - - - - - - - - - - - - - -

Once they had driven off in the Crown Vic, Branden said, "We need to go at them again."

"No doubt," the sheriff said gruffly.

"I don't trust anything they've said, Bruce. I don't trust anything that I thought I knew about this case. For all I know, Mary Yost has been dead all along."

"You're talking about a situation where a dozen people are involved in a conspiracy, Mike, here and in Parma, Fort Wayne and Omaha."

The professor held silence and shook his head. "We're still going to search the Yost farm?" he asked eventually.

"Count on it, Mike. First thing tomorrow. The bishop is expecting us."

Chapter 32

By the time Professor Branden had reached the Yost farm on Sunday morning, the barnyard between the horse barn and the farmhouse was tangled with the sheriff's vehicles. Branden knew he was there to watch. That would be his role. Chief Deputy Dan Wilsher was managing a sizeable crew of deputies. Captain Bobby Newell led his detectives Pat Lance and Ricky Niell. He would have done enough, the professor figured, if he just kept the impulsive sheriff company.

Robertson's Crown Vic had been the last to pull into a spot, and Branden parked his truck behind the Crown Vic, on the Yost farm lane coming in from TR 606. Because of the congestion of vehicles, Branden was thirty yards out from the barnyard when he locked his doors. He walked past Robertson's sedan, and he also passed a pickup truck that had a small trailer for dirt bikes attached to the hitch. The dirt bikes had already been removed from the trailer.

A cruiser was parked in front of the pickup, and Ricky Niell was seated behind the wheel, talking on his cell phone with his windows down. As he passed by him, the professor heard Niell say, "Dr. Evelyn Carson, please. She'll be in John Yost's room." Branden made a mental note of that and continued forward.

291

It was already warm at the farm. Another hot day, the professor told himself. There's today, still. Time to work the case. Then a full Monday, with its classes, office hours, appointments with staff, and a department chairperson's monthly conclave after dinner.

In the barnyard at the back of the farmhouse, the sheriff and Chief Deputy Dan Wilsher were talking with two uniformed deputies, Ryan Baker and Dave Johnson, who were seated side by side on an off-road, four-wheeler ATV of the type that hunters use, with two seats and four large knobby tires. Stacked in the back compartment of their ATV, behind the tall steel roll bar, there were shovels, pickaxes, hoes and handsaws. Also, there was one chainsaw in a hard, yellow plastic case.

A larger trailer for two ATVs was parked with its tow truck beside the horse barn. The second of its two ATVs, the one not occupied by Baker and Johnson, was not in the barnyard any longer. Tracks for its wide tires angled out of the barnyard and ran over to the side of the house, where Branden had found the trail that led to the slaughter pit first, and then to a spot on 606 opposite Meredith Silver's ranch house. Beside the trailer, Wilsher was talking on his hand-held radio, while Baker and Johnson listened.

"How far are you, Lance?" Wilsher was saying. "At the bridle trail yet?"

"Yes, Chief," Pat Lance replied on the radio. "It crosses the creek beside some Sycamores, and it leads back into the woods."

"Is it wide enough for one of our four-wheels?" Wilsher asked. "I can send Daniels and Wilson."

"It's just a bridle path, Chief. Little more than that. I can't tell how wide it is inside the woods, but it goes past the creek, runs through the forest, and comes out on a hill, to a clearing at the top of the property. That's where the headstones are. Up at the top. But I can't tell how wide it is. It may take a dirt bike to get up there. Through the forest, I mean."

"Have you flown over all of the cornfield yet?" Wilsher asked into his handset.

"Most of it. I'm taking it back now, to finish that. But I flew up to the clearing at the top of the hill, beyond the woods. It's got two simple stone markers. There's tall grass up there, and I can't get down low enough to read any inscriptions."

"Where's Captain Newell, Lance?"

"He's taking my video feed on his laptop. He's parked in his cruiser at the end of the lane. Well, at the far curve in the lane."

"Bobby?" the Sheriff Robertson asked into his own radio.

"Yes, Sheriff. I'm recording everything she sends me. We haven't found anything other than those two graves at the top of the hill."

"OK," Robertson said, "when you've finished covering the cornfield, have Lance send it up over this slaughter pit in the other woods, along the professor's trail."

"OK," Captain Newell replied. "OK," Lance agreed.

Turning to Branden, Robertson said, "We're using a drone to search from the air. Lance is the best we have at running it. She flies it like a stunt pilot. Maneuvering, I mean. She's a bird. A natural."

"Those woods are pretty dense, Bruce," the professor said.

Robertson nodded. "We're going to cover most of that ground on foot, once we've done what we can with the drone and the vehicles."

Robertson turned to Baker and Johnson in the ATV. "Did you hear Lance?"

Deputy Ryan Baker nodded, saying, "Take the bridle trail across the creek and up through the woods."

Dan Wilsher spoke up. "But if you can't make it through, Baker, I'll call the dirt bikes back, and you can give it a try with one of those."

Baker cranked a coughing start out of his ATV, and he drove off down the farm lane, toward the first turn that would take him east, to the trail where Lydia Schwartz had died.

To Wilsher, Robertson said, "You squared away here, Dan?"

Chief Wilsher smiled and said, "Of course."

Turning back to Branden, the sheriff asked, "Care for a walk, Professor?"

"The slaughter pit," Branden said, and he led Robertson over to the path.

As they took the path through the woods, off to their right and deeper into the woods, the growls of two dirt bikes filtered back through the trees to Branden and Robertson. As they continued along the path, Robertson said, "We're searching everywhere, Mike. We haven't found anything, yet."

The two men quickly reached the slaughter pit that Branden had discovered on Thursday evening. Deputies there, with the second ATV, had already excavated the bones of farm animals from about four feet of soil.

Robertson asked, "Do we need a backhoe here?"

"We need to go slowly," one deputy said. "Shovels and picks."

"Then stay on it, Brett," Robertson said to him. "Go deep here and then put in other shallow holes around the clearing, to see if there are other burial places."

"Sir," Brett said to acknowledge his orders.

Pointing to the ATV, Robertson asked Brett, "OK if we take this out on 606? Over to find the edges of the Yost property?"

The deputy nodded and said, "We won't need it for several hours, Sheriff. But we could use some help here, if anyone gets free."

The sheriff lifted his radio. "Bobby?"

"Sheriff?"

"When Baker and Johnson get down from the grave markers on the hill, send them over here to help with the digging."

"Where?"

"It's on the trail that leads away from the house. It's on the other side of the house."

"OK, Sheriff. Lance and I will be done soon, too."

"Find anything?"

"Nothing."

"Then I'm going to take the professor up and down 606. I want to see how far the Yost farm extends."

Captain Newell didn't immediately reply. "Bobby?" Robertson said, and Newell said, "Wait one."

Sheriff Robertson stood with his radio up to his lips. Thirty seconds later, Captain Newell said, "There's a clearing in the corn field. Lance has her drone over the top of it now."

"How big?"

"Ten by five. Enough for four or five people to crowd in together."

"Let me know," Robertson said.

"We're walking into it now."

"About where is it, Bobby?"

"Thirty yards from 606. Twenty back from the farm lane, on the east side of the field."

"Wait there, Bobby?"

"OK."

"Mike," Robertson said, and he got in authoritatively behind the wheel of the ATV.

Branden ducked into the seat beside the sheriff. "You remember how to drive these?" he asked Robertson.

Robertson laughed. "Better than you, Mike. At least I won't get myself stuck in the mud."

"That was forty years ago, Sheriff."

"More like fifty," Robertson said and chuckled. When he started off toward 606, the four-wheeler jerked with the abrupt start that the sheriff gave it. It snapped their heads back. With an awkward grin, the sheriff shook his head and glanced surreptitiously at Branden.

The professor grabbed the hand bar in front of him, and he smiled and laughed. "Really, Sheriff? Whiplash? There isn't even a manual clutch on these anymore."

- - - - - - - - - - - - - -

Out on 606, the sheriff had the ATV up to thirty. He pushed down harder, but that was the fastest speed he could get out of the machine. They passed the farm lane leading down to the farmhouse, and then quickly they had passed the other end of the U-shaped lane, where Robertson was supposed to have turned in. He braked to a safe speed, spun the wheel, and brought the little machine around in a tight circle on the blacktop, to enter the dirt lane.

The lane was rutted where Monday's rain had soaked the ground, and Robertson was forced to drop to a crawl as the wheels dipped in and out of the deep tracks in the hard-dried mud. He stopped where he figured that Captain Newell had told him to, and he said to Branden, "This about right?"

Branden said, "Good enough," and the two men climbed out of their seats.

Robertson led into the corn. After twenty to twenty-five yards, they found Newell and Lance. Lance was still holding the remote controller for her drone, and Newell was holding an empty beer bottle. As Robertson and Branden approached by crossing one row north into the corn, Newell pointed at the litter on the ground and said, "Beer, cigarettes and marijuana, Sheriff. The kids come here to party."

"Teenagers," Robertson said. "Anything buried here?"

Newell kicked at one of the low-cut stalks of corn. "Nothing. No holes. No loose dirt."

To Lance, the sheriff said, "Where's your drone?"

"I landed it back at the house, Sheriff. On a flat roof extension of the horse barn."

"Can you put it back up again?"

"Sure."

"Then search over the woods beside the house. We're digging out a bone pit, there."

"Sheriff?"

"To see if there are any other burial spots in the woods. To see if there's another clearing, I mean."

"We've been over that, Sheriff," Lance said.

Robertson nodded. "Let's go over everything a second time."

"Yes, but first, we're going to need to charge the batteries," Lance replied.

"How long will that take?"

"Maybe an hour, if we just take it back to Mt. Hope. For the electricity, I mean."

"OK, do that," Robertson said, and he took the professor back to the barnyard on the ATV.

Daniels was off in the woods again on his dirt bike, continuing to search the rest of the forest lands. Johnson and Wilson had gone back to Mt. Hope, to get food and water for the whole team. And Ryan Baker, standing beside one of the dirt bikes, was waiting to report to the sheriff.

"There are two small headstones," Baker said. "Small ones, with brief inscriptions, up on the top of the hill."

"Small graves?" Robertson asked.

"Can't tell, Sheriff. The surrounding area grew over with tall grass, but the graves are clear. The headstones weren't any larger than they needed to be."

"What inscriptions?" Newell asked Baker.

"One said, 'baby girl Yost, three weeks,' and the other said, 'baby girl Yost, four months.'"

"The graves of children?" Robertson asked.

Baker nodded. "Infants, Sheriff."

With a measure of tired frustration, Robertson asked weakly, "Do we need to dig them up?"

"We could just wait to ask John Yost about it," Baker suggested. "And ask Mary Yost, if we ever find her."

"Or," Robertson said, "we could ask Mose and Ida Schwartzentruber, across the street. They'd know if young children died here."

"That's the best idea," Branden said.

Robertson kicked at dirt and rolled his gaze up toward the sky. He closed his eyes, muttered an invective

299

and said, "We've been over most of it, Mike. We're not going to find anything."

"She was talking to the babies," Branden whispered, not really hearing the sheriff. "Lydia was just up there on the hill, talking to the babies."

Chapter 33

Sunday, September 3
2:30 PM

"Sheriff," Ricky Niell said. "I don't know if this is good news or not. I've been on the phone with Dr. Carson. Two things."

The sheriff was standing with Professor Branden beside the Crown Vic. Search efforts at the Yost farm were finished. Many of the sheriff's people had already loaded equipment and left for Millersburg. Gray clouds lingered, a vestige of yesterday's drizzle, and equally gray was the sheriff's mood. When Ricky had spoken, the bulky sheriff had been ruminating on the question of Mary and Esther Yost.

"What, Niell?" Robertson grumbled, scratching distractedly at the gray flat-top bristles on his head.

Niell hesitated, and the sheriff sighed and said, "Sorry, Ricky. What have you got?"

"This afternoon, Sheriff, Dr. Carson is going to bring John Yost back to Bishop Alva Yost's house over west of here."

"And the second thing?"

"Bishop Yost is waiting for you in his buggy, Sheriff. He's down at the end of this lane."

Robertson drew in a cleansing breath and blew it out as a long, perplexed whistle. "Let's go, Mike," he said to the professor, and the two walked out to where the bishop was waiting on the blacktop.

Alva was standing beside his black rig. His horse was restless, and the muscles and tendons in its legs were jumping and flexing. Accordingly, Alva was holding tightly to the ends of the reins, which he had looped around the brake lever in order to keep the rig immobile.

Directly on walking up, the sheriff said, "Why is John going to your house, Mr. Yost? Why not send him home, to be here with his kids?"

"We are going to try the medicine for depression," Alva declared. "I'm not sure about it, and it's not our way of doing things, but the gibbering that John has been doing in the hospital about graves? Well, your Dr. Carson convinced me to try the medicine."

"That is very good," Branden said, smiling.

Yost shrugged his massive shoulders. "I didn't realize how bad he had gotten. I understand better why Mary left him. He was dangerous like that, with his shotgun and this depression. And I didn't realize how neglected his family has been. The condition of his farm is an embarrassment to us. He'll stay with me for three weeks, while the congregation works to clean the place up. And we'll try the antidepressant. If it works, then he can bring his children home to his farm. In the meantime, the children will stay with their grandparents."

Robertson asked, "What made you change your mind?"

Yost pulled a weak smile that linked into an arched brow. "Dr. Carson explained his depression to me. She explained the chemical things that are missing from his brain. She said that the antidepressant medicines will restore the brain chemicals that he is supposed to have."

"He'll get better with the medicine," Branden offered. "It will ease his burdens."

Yost nodded. "Dr. Carson said that '*he'll pray better*,' and that's more important to me than his burdens. We all carry burdens."

"But John's are excessive," Robertson said.

"I agree," Yost said. "He'll pray better, and his family needs his prayers. And right now, I don't think he could manage a simple, '*Thank You, Lord*' at dinner time. So, we'll all keep his farm going for him, and he can rest at my house while he gets started on the medicine. We're going to give it three weeks to see if the medicine works."

Branden asked, "Would you consider letting Alice Shewmon visit the children?"

"Is this the Social Services lady?"

"Yes. Alice Shewmon."

Alva shook his head with determined sadness. "She'll be just as bad as those Schells."

"Why do you say that?" Branden asked.

"We know how they preach division. Your Social Services lady will be no different."

"Alice isn't interested in that sort of thing," Branden said. "She'll just want to make sure that the children are safe and healthy."

Yost bristled. "That is *my job*, Professor. We do not want the government pestering us about our families. Maybe you could tell that to your Miss Shewmon. Tell it to those Schells, too. If it weren't for them, don't you think Mary would still be home with her family where she belongs?"

Robertson pushed in closer to Yost. "Do you know where she is, Bishop Yost?"

Yost answered calmly so far as his tone was concerned. But there was intensity flashing in his eyes and conviction set in his jaw. "Everyone we know has been contacted, Sheriff," he declared. "We've been mailing letters since the day they disappeared. The whole Amish world knows about Mary and Esther Yost. If they were anywhere to be found, we would have found them by now. Unless she's with you *English* somewhere. So, no. The Schells are not welcome here. Dithy Silver used to be a friend, too, but she should have stayed out of our business. I'll be announcing all of this to our people next Sunday. We are not going to have anything more to do with the Schells and their ministry."

- - - - - - - - - - - - - - -

As the bishop's buggy disappeared over the rise, Robertson was kicking a toe at the blacktop pavement of 606. The professor stood beside him, watching the familiar workings of the sheriff's mind – first an unconvincing smile and then a frown – an arched brow and then a wrinkled brow – thoughts and ruminations passing across the big sheriff's eyes. Here were the signs of a determined decision - conclusions, convictions, resolve. The sheriff had reached a pivot point in his thinking. Branden knew from the set features of the sheriff's jaw that these new intentions would be unopposable.

"Mike," the sheriff said at last, "it's the Schells. They haven't told us the truth. I don't think they've told us the truth about any of this. Mary and Ester? The Culps? Meredith Silver? We haven't been getting the truth. It's like the bishop said. If the Amish themselves can't find Mary, then she has to be with the English somewhere."

Branden nodded concurrence and said, "I tend to agree with you, Bruce. I've been thinking along these lines since I first saw their house."

"What?" Robertson said distracted. He turned to face Branden and asked again, "What house, exactly?"

"The brown house in the country," Branden answered. "The gingerbread house with Amish-turned-Mennonite refugees."

Chapter 34

Sunday, September 3
7:10 PM

On Millersburg's Courthouse Square, on the first floor inside the old red brick jail, Branden and Robertson stood in the observation room between Interview A and Interview B. Pat Lance sat talking with Donna Schell in Interview A, and Ricky Niell sat talking with Ed Schell in Interview B. Late that afternoon, and then after dinner too, each of the Schells had seemed both calm and definite about the details. They had seemed content to be talking, and to be making a true statement, finally, of what had really taken place with Mary Yost. They had each stepped away from the story that Mary had gone up to Parma to counsel with the Culps. They were no longer floating that tale. It had all been a fabrication, designed to steer the search away from Mary's true location.

"So far their stories match," Robertson said to Branden in the middle observation room. With his back to the professor, he was watching Pat and Donna through the one-way glass into Interview A. Professor Branden had arrived only recently. The interrogations had been underway since five o'clock.

The professor for his part was watching Ricky Niell through the opposite one-way glass. "Are they lying now?" Branden asked Robertson without turning. "Or were they lying before? Did they have Mary for all three weeks, or just for the one night?"

"They're both saying it was the whole three weeks, now, Mike. Their statements match now. Mary stayed at their halfway house for three weeks. She stayed at the brown house over south of SR 39. They say that she didn't want Lydia to know, but they also say that they always encourage their 'runners' to avoid contact with their families, because they're so often tempted to go back home after a couple of weeks. Anyway, she delivered a baby boy there. On Monday, two weeks ago. They both say that now, Ed and Donna. And they're claiming that Mary left in a taxi on Thursday that same week. She took Esther and her infant boy with her."

"She was actually leaving the Amish church?"

"Apparently."

"You're handling them pretty gently," Branden observed. "Are you going to let Pat and Ricky push on them?"

"I don't think so. Not yet, anyway."

"Why not?"

"I'm waiting. I'll go at them harder if their statements start to diverge. But so far, they are aligned. In every detail."

Branden turned around and joined Robertson, looking in on Pat Lance and Donna Schell. Robertson turned the wall dial to increase the volume on the room's speakers.

"We gave her all our cash," Donna was complaining to Pat, looking genuinely and believably chagrined. She had her hands open flat on the table, with her palms facing up, as if making a plea.

Lance stood up slowly. "We've contacted your church in Omaha."

"What?" Donna asked. She stood abruptly on the other side of the table. "I don't want them involved in any of this!"

"Sit down, please," Lance said smoothly.

Donna remained on her feet. She became suddenly agitated. Her cheeks were taking a flush, and she was shaking her hands nervously in front. "I can't have you pestering the Omaha people about this!" she crowed out. "We'll lose our funding!"

"Sit down," Lance ordered.

Donna sat, and Lance sat across from her again.

"You're going to need to explain that," Lance said, scooting her chair closer to the table, and taking up a notepad and pen.

Donna took an old tissue from a side pocket of her dress, and she held it up to her eyes. She pulled the band-aid loose on her left hand and scratched nervously at her healing burn wound there. Upset for the first time that evening, Donna held an unfocused gaze on the tabletop and cried softly, "They don't know about Lydia. About Meredith. We'll lose all our funding, if they learn that people have died here. They think it was just Mary that we were involved with."

They had been talking for over two hours since dinner, which had consisted of nothing more than a pizza and a glass of water. Now Donna was starting to show signs of fatigue and frustration. She dabbed the wadded tissue at her eyes, tried to reaffix the band-aid on her palm, and looked up at Lance.

"I need to call Omaha," she insisted earnestly. "I need to explain. We can't lose our funding. This is the worst thing that could have happened."

She looked intently into Pat Lance's eyes, and her focus seemed to shift to a new thought. "When can we get our kids back?" she asked. "How do I know they're OK? Really, Detective Lance, I think we've been here long enough."

"They're fine. Alice Shewmon is staying with them at your house. Remember? You can get back to them when we are through here."

"I think we've been here long enough. I think we've answered all your questions. I don't know what more I can tell you."

Her band-aid loosened again, and she pulled it off and wadded it up. She tossed it into a waste can in the corner and said, "I want to go home, now."

"Did you really give Mary Yost all of your money?" Lance asked in stride.

Donna nodded solemnly, interested now in this new topic. "We cashed a check. We gave her everything we had. This is the heart of our ministry. We just couldn't do anything else. She wanted out so badly. You wouldn't believe how horrible it was for her. She begged us to help her get out. He was dangerous. He was completely oblivious to her pain. And you wouldn't believe how expensive this ministry is. Really. It's astonishing. So many people need our help. We've usually spent everything by the third week of the month. We were going to ask the pastors in Omaha to increase our funding. But now? What can we do now? They won't trust us after Lydia and Meredith have died. They're going to cut us off, and then we'll have nothing."

"You've still got your Sunday collections," Lance offered. "At your church."

Donna shook her head. "It's not really that much. We don't take in all that much. We can barely get by on it. I've just got to call Omaha."

"Soon," Lance said.

In the observation room, Robertson switched off the microphone button for Interview A. "Ed Schell says pretty much the same thing," he said to the professor.

They turned around to the glass into Interview B in time to see Ricky Niell leaving the room. Ed Schell was standing glumly in a corner, at the far end of the room's rectangular table. The door into the observation room opened from the hallway, and Ricky stepped inside. To Robertson he said, "He's not too happy that you sent deputies out to his house in the country. And he's pleading the pauper. Says they're out of money."

"Same thing from Donna," Robertson said.

"Do their stories really match, now?" Branden asked. "In all the particulars?"

"They do now," Robertson said. "Ricky?"

Niell ran the list, holding up a new finger for each point. "Mary moved in with them four weeks ago. That was three weeks before Lydia died. She didn't want Lydia to find out what she was doing. She had decided to leave the church. To leave her husband. She delivered a baby boy two weeks ago. On August 22nd. Smooth delivery. No complications. And she left in a taxi that Thursday, a week and four days ago. They gave her their last penny, and she left with Esther and her new baby boy. On Thursday, August 25th."

"Lydia died a week ago," Branden said. "Mary had already left? Is that what they're saying?"

Ricky nodded. Robertson said, "Yes. They're saying the same thing."

"And what about the Culps? Are you going to pursue that angle?"

Robertson nodded. "Tomorrow morning. Plus, we've already interviewed this James Matt you told us about."

"Anything there?"

Robertson shook his head. "Matt doesn't too much like the Culps. He blames them for breaking up his marriage. He wants them to pay for the damage to his truck, if you can believe that."

"What about their connections with the Schells?" Branden asked.

"Donna gave them some referrals, from time to time," Robertson said. "Nothing beyond that."

311

"And the Schells?" Branden asked. "You consider that Ed and Donna are telling us the truth, now?"

Robertson shrugged his shoulders and turned to look in at Donna and Detective Lance. He put his hands in his coat pockets and fumbled a bit with his keys. Then he turned back to Branden. "They're on the same page, Mike. But it's not the same story that they floated last week. Either they're finally telling the truth, or they've had time to square their stories."

Branden shook his head. "They're still lying about something. I'd guess it's their connection with this Omaha church."

Robertson asked, "What makes you think that?"

"A blue passenger van, Sheriff. A blue van and phone calls to you from someone pretending to be Mary Yost."

"You want to try something, Mike?"

Branden nodded. "Which of these two do you think is the poorest liar?"

- - - - - - - - - - - - - - -

Lance left Donna alone in Interview A, and she joined Ricky and the sheriff in the observation room. On the other side of the one-way glass, the professor sat talking with Ed Schell in Interview B.

"You really focus on the Schwartzentrubers, don't you, Ed."

"Yes, of course," Ed said with a measure of pride. "They are clearly the most backward. I ought to know better than anyone. It's a miracle that my parents got us out of that sect."

"And you consider yourself to be a missionary?"

Schell did not reply.

"Doesn't matter," Branden said. "The *Church of True Believers* considers you to be missionaries to the Amish."

Again, no reply came from Ed.

"That's a little bit strange, don't you think? I mean, aren't missionaries usually sent overseas?"

Ed smiled. "You don't have to live overseas to have a wrong understanding of faith."

"A wrong understanding of faith," Branden enunciated carefully. "Who understands their faith wrongly? The Amish? I mean precisely, Ed. Who?"

"Well, Schwartzentrubers, surely," Ed said. "Others, too."

"Well, you see, Ed. That's something that has bothered me since I began to understand what it is that you and Donna have really been doing."

With a dismissive smile, Ed said, "I don't think you understand at all, Professor."

"I think I do, Ed."

"No, you don't. You wouldn't be harassing me if you did."

313

"We're just talking, Ed."

"No! You're like the others. You really don't get it."

"I'll listen, Ed. You can explain it to me. Really, I'd like to understand."

Loudly, Schell declared, "They are not practicing faith the right way, Professor!"

"What are they missing? You still haven't told me."

"You can't just *do it*, Professor. You really have to *believe it*."

Branden leaned in to glare across the table. "There was no taxi, Ed."

"What?"

"There was no taxi for Mary and her two children."

"You've lost your mind, Professor."

"You said they went off in a taxi, but it was a blue van from CTB in Omaha. You could have just told us the truth. But you knew you had done something wrong, and you started lying about Mary from the first night you came over to my house."

"Taxi? What in the world?"

"Mary and her two children are in Omaha. It's rather obvious that they traveled there in a blue passenger van owned by the CTB. You could have just told us that. You could have just told us the truth."

"Really, that's a small matter, Professor."

"You lied to cover the truth. That's an indication that you were aware of your criminality. But there's more."

"Do I need a lawyer?"

"Again, you're aware of a crime. Just by asking that, you admit that you are fully aware of a crime. I suspect you've been covering for CTB. Someone there is going to be charged with hindering a law enforcement investigation. You will probably be charged with that, too."

"What are you talking about? Nobody . . ."

"Stop! Stop before you make it worse. Someone made phone calls to the sheriff, pretending to be Mary Yost. I suspect it will have been one of your confederates at CTB. That's criminal interference. Do you want to tell me who it was who made those calls?"

Schell had nothing to say.

Branden stood and pronounced a judgement. "Worse than anything, Ed? You broke apart a family because they don't agree with *your* definition of faith."

"You don't know anything about this sort of thing, Professor."

"No, I suppose not," Branden said, sitting down again. "But I can see that the Schwartzentrubers are living their faith every day."

Haughtily, Schell asked, "What kind of faith is that?"

"Faith isn't real unless you're living it every day, Ed. The Schwartzentrubers are actually living their faith every day."

"They just follow their rules, Branden."

"No, I don't think so," the professor said. "And I can tell you something else, Ed."

"You're a real expert, now, Professor?"

"On this point, yes. Until it has been tested, you can't know that your faith is strong."

"How would you know anything about a test of faith?"

"Cal Troyer, Ed. Cal Troyer is teaching me this right now."

Ed Schell harrumphed. He looked disconcerted. He seemed overwhelmed with anxiety.

"Tell me this, Ed," Branden said. "When you knew Mary Yost needed help, why didn't you just go to the bishop? You could have started by talking with the bishop."

Schell adjusted himself on his chair nervously. "He wouldn't have listened."

"Are you sure?"

"He's a Schwartzentruber, Professor. Of course I'm sure. I know first-hand what I'm talking about."

Branden smiled snidely, hoping that it would look like an accusation to Ed Schell. "They're too backward, Mr. Schell? The Schwartzentrubers? How about this? Alva Yost is going to let John Yost take antidepressant medications. Is that good enough for you, Schell? Are you sure that the bishop wouldn't have helped you with Mary? Because if you aren't sure about that, then you've wasted two lives, and broken apart a family, for nothing."

Schell stammered. "I. We. I."

"Starting to see it, Schell?"

Ed's face took a blush that must have put uncomfortable heat into his cheeks. He curled an eyebrow, thinking it through.

Branden pressed forward. "One last thing, Schell. I just want to know one last thing."

"What?" Schell asked weakly.

"Meredith Silver wrote that you made a promise to Mary Yost. She wrote it just before she died. As if that were the only reason Mary was willing to leave her family. What was it, Ed? Your promise."

Ed Schell groaned. Head down, he said, "We promised Mary that we'd get the other children out, too."

"How in the world did you expect to make good on that promise?"

Schell put his head in his hands and leaned over with his elbows on the tabletop. "I don't know," he whispered. "I really don't know."

- - - - - - - - - - - - - -

Branden joined the sheriff and his detectives in the observation room. In Interview A, Donna was finishing another cup of coffee. Tired and distracted, she sighed heavily and tossed her coffee cup into the trash can in the corner of the room. Nervously, she scratched again at the wound on her left hand.

In Interview B, Ed Schell was pacing nervously from one end of the room to the other. He didn't look happy.

317

Robertson said to his people, "They've been mixed up in this from the beginning. They've been lying on so many levels that it's astonishing."

Branden said, "They've been trying to keep us from finding Mary Yost."

"Yah, well they've done a pretty good job of that," Robertson exclaimed.

The professor drew closer to the glass and said, "Wait, are any of you seeing this? It wasn't an oven rack."

"What?" Robertson asked.

"The band-aid," Branden said. "She took it off, and now she's scratching at her palm."

Robertson came forward, too. "The band-aid?"

The professor said, "She had that wound the first night they came over with Cal. It was late Monday night, after Lydia and Meredith had died."

"Mike, what are you talking about?"

Branden explained. "She said she burned her hand on an oven rack. But dollars-to-donuts it was a revolver. She burned her left hand on a revolver's cylinder gap."

"Donna shot Meredith Silver?" Ricky asked.

Robertson guffawed and said immediately, "Ricky, I want you to get an evidence case."

"Which one, Sheriff?"

"Doesn't matter. A yellow one. A big one. I want to be able to pull out a bunch of equipment. And Pat, get the fingerprint reader and its laptop out of the squad room. Then I want you both to carry it all in and drop it on the table in front of Donna Schell."

When it was arranged as the sheriff wished, Robertson entered the room shaking his head and wearing a deep frown. He advanced immediately to the trash can and retrieved the coffee cup that Donna had pitched out there. He also pulled out the band-aid, and he bagged each of them separately. He was using a blue nitrile glove, and he made a show of handing the items back to Niell.

"Detective Niell," he said, "I want the print from this cup sent to this laptop as soon as possible. Also, I want DNA from this band-aid."

Niell backed out of the room with an accusatory smile at Donna Schell.

Robertson sat across the table from Donna and said, "We've always wondered about a second set of prints on Meredith Silver's suicide note. I think we're going to clear that up right now."

Donna issued forth with a nervous laugh. "What in the world?"

Robertson arranged the fingerprint reader in front of Donna and said, "Lay your four fingertips on the glass, Mrs. Schell."

"I don't have to do that!" she exclaimed.

Evenly, Robertson intoned, "Either you clear this fingerprint comparison by giving me your prints, or I intend to charge you with the murder of Meredith Silver."

"What? What? I mean, why? Why would you think . . . .?"

"Your fingertips, Mrs. Schell. On the glass."

"I don't want to."

Robertson held a pause. He studied Donna Schell's anxious expression and said, "Donna Schell, you're being charged with . . ."

"OK! OK! They're my prints. I was there. I picked it up and read the note."

"And the gun?"

"What?"

Robertson shook his head disdainfully. He reached into the yellow evidence kit and pulled out a cotton swab. He also retrieved a sample bottle, which he set on the table between them. "I believe you shot her, Mrs. Schell. I believe that if I use this test for gunshot residue - and believe me it doesn't wash off that easily - I'm gonna find that you shot the gun that killed Meredith Silver."

"I don't have to sit for this!" Donna complained.

"You don't know anything about revolvers, do you Mrs. Schell?"

Indignantly, Donna said, "I don't know what you're talking about."

Robertson nodded and smiled. "The professor saw it first. The burn on your hand, there. You see, the gun fire doesn't come out of just the front of the barrel, Donna. Revolvers are different from automatics. For revolvers, the fire sprays out sideways through the cylinder gap, too. That's how you burned your left hand. You were holding the revolver with both hands. Your left hand was covering over the cylinder gap."

"No!" Donna cried out.

"Mrs. Schell, you are being charged with the murder of . . . "

"OK! Stop! I didn't kill her. Oh, how could I! Sheriff, I tried to stop her!"

"You're going to have to explain that, Mrs. Schell."

"She had the gun," Donna said, now abruptly calm, as if she had been relieved of an unendurable burden. "When I got there, she was standing in the kitchen with the thing pressed up under her chin. She was muttering, 'I'm sorry. I'm sorry.' Time and again. I raced up to her and grabbed at the stupid gun. I don't know anything about guns. We wrestled over it. I got it out from under her chin, and then I stepped back. The stupid thing just went off while I was holding it. I don't know guns. I didn't know it could do that. We were wrestling for the gun. I thought I had saved her. But it just went off."

With that, Donna laid her head in her hands on the tabletop, and she wept. Robertson allowed her time to spend her grief out in front of him, and then he stepped around the table and lifted Donna gently to her feet. She stood willingly, and the sheriff waved at the glass mirror to bring his detectives into the interview room.

As they were leading her away, Robertson said, "Wait Ricky. Donna, there's one more thing."

Donna turned back to him with red, swollen eyes. "What?" she asked meekly. "What else can there be?"

"Donna," Robertson said. "What did you do with the gun?"

Donna seemed puzzled for a moment, looking like she had never once thought about this, and looking like she had managed to forget something that to her was immeasurably dreadful. Eventually she said, quietly, "I ran out the front door. I ran to my car. I had the wretched gun, and I ran into the back yard. I ran across the field behind her house, and I ran into the woods. Then I just threw the thing into the trees, as far as I could manage. I threw it into the woods behind her house."

Chapter 35

Monday, September 4
1:15 PM

In Professor Branden's office, Lawrence Mallory announced, "Kathryn Rausch is here, Mike."

Branden stood. "Show her in, Lawrence. Then you stay, too. I suspect this is about you as much as anyone."

As she entered, Rausch extended her hand and began by saying, "I've been hearing about you since I was a child, Professor. I'm very pleased to meet you at last."

Branden took her hand, offered her a seat in front of his desk, and took one there beside her. Lawrence brought in the chair from his desk in the vestibule.

"I knew your grandfather," Branden said to Rausch. "I knew him quite well."

"The General. I know. I envy you that. He was quite special."

"I understand you've been to see our President?"

"News gets around."

"Small campus. When we're not teaching, we work diligently to refine the lower arts of gossip and intrigue."

"I can't take much time here, Mike. Your museum? I understand there is some new thinking on campus about that."

Branden nodded and said, "It's the space that Nora Benetti needs for her new neuroscience major and its necessary labs."

"Mike," Rausch said, "the trustees don't like to determine academic policies. That's for the professors. If the college wants a neuroscience major, then it'll be our job to see that it happens smoothly."

"It's history, Kathryn," Branden said. "The museum is important because of the history."

"I wouldn't disagree with that, Professor. We actually want to do something about that."

"We?"

"My family. The General's family. We had pledged to increase the college's endowment at the end of this semester. Three million dollars. The Trustees have now been informed that that three million is going to be changed. I explained this to Nora this morning."

"Oh?"

"My people tell me that Benetti's proposed new major is very popular. You weren't going to have enough support among the faculty to keep your museum on campus. And it isn't just a few professors. There are alumni involved, too."

"I've been a little distracted. You know, a student died."

Rausch nodded. "I know. I'm sorry Mike. It's really very sad."

Branden kept a silent moment, and then he asked, "Three million?"

"Yes, Professor. It's now pledged for your new museum building. We'll build something off campus, but still here in the village. We're still going to give the money, but it'll go for your museum instead of the endowment. We're going to have a separate and proper museum building, just not on campus."

"I don't know what to say," Branden said. "Lawrence?"

"It'd be a thousand times better, Mike," Lawrence said, obviously pleased.

"You knew about this?"

"No, Mike, but I gave Ms. Rausch some of the information that I'd gathered here, and this all played out over the weekend. There hasn't been time to tell you about it."

Branden looked to Rausch and then back to Mallory. Lawrence said, "Mike, I didn't think our president was sympathetic to our museum. So, I just told Ms. Rausch what we really needed."

Again, Branden said, "I've been a little distracted."

Kathryn Rausch nodded and said, "We understand. It's going to be better, now. Lawrence is going to have a very nice office. Millersburg College is not going to abandon one of its most valuable traditions. Your museum is a treasure, and my family is going to make certain that you don't lose it. Academics change. History doesn't. We've withdrawn our money that was pledged for the general endowment, and we're going to use it to make a statement that my Grandfather would respect. I hope you can agree to that."

Branden's smile was as big as Kathryn Rausch's news. He couldn't find words adequate for the moment. Simply and earnestly, he just said, "Thank you."

"I'm flying to Chicago tonight, Professor. Then LA, San Francisco, and Atlanta. We're going to see if other trustees of the college want to participate. We're going to launch a drive for matching contributions. I expect that our three million will grow to something more like six million. That'll make up for what the college will lose, for its general endowment. Your president is not going to be disappointed. She'll still get her three million. She's going to be able to go forward with her renovations, sooner rather than later."

"Renovations?" Branden asked.

"It's the space, Professor. Your museum occupies important real estate on campus. Benetti has had her eye on it for a while, now. Neuroscience is going to need offices, classrooms, new professors, and those new labs, too. She had architectural plans drawn up for a preliminary study. It's nothing official, yet, but she has been moving in that direction. I don't think she was going to be much help to your cause."

Branden turned to Mallory. "You knew about this, Lawrence?"

"A word here. A whisper there. You know how it is, Mike. Small campus. Academic politics."

Branden arched a brow. He smiled and combed his fingers back through his hair. To Rausch, he said simply,

326

"Again Kathryn, thank you. Thank you very much. I don't know what to say."

Rausch stood and offered her hand again. "Trustees aren't always locked up in the *high towers*, Mike. We do see what's happening from time to time. And my Grandfather wouldn't too much appreciate it, if I didn't step in now to rescue your museum."

Chapter 36

Tuesday, September 5
5:20 PM

As the Brandens ate their dinner, Caroline said, "We've changed our plans a little for driving up to the Cleveland Clinic, Michael."

"Oh?"

"Cal is going to ride with Rachel, in her car. You and I will follow them. They want to get started a little earlier."

"How soon?"

"Well, now Michael. Finish here, and I'll load the car. Rachel and I have adjoining rooms at the hotel."

Professor Branden rose to clear their dishes. "You going to stay just Tuesday and Wednesday nights?"

"More, Michael. I'll stay with her during the surgery. No one should have to wait alone for that. Then I'll stay Wednesday night, and probably Thursday, too. They might send him home as soon as Friday."

- - - - - - - - - - - - - -

The professor was glum on the ride. Caroline drove, and he rode slumped in the passenger's seat.

"You're more tired than you realized," Caroline said. "You should have rescheduled your office hours."

"I'm not tired. I'm weary."

"Because of this case?"

"I guess."

"Meredith Silver confessed, didn't she? She wrote it in her suicide note. She shoved Lydia, and it was more than just an unfortunate accident."

"It was all unfortunate, Caroline. It was unfortunate from start to finish. The Yosts should have had some help. Instead they got bad advice from a couple of evangelical zealots. Plus, the bishop should have recognized the trouble they were having at the farm. He should have done something sooner to help them."

"And the Schells are going to be charged?"

"Oh yes. You can count on that."

- - - - - - - - - - - - - - -

In the Cleveland Clinic surgery ward, to the head floor nurse, Rachel said, "I thought he could stay at the hotel tonight. He'd be more comfortable at the hotel."

The nurse said, "We want to start prepping him tonight. They're going to want him in the OR by five AM."

"Why is he already sedated?"

"It's just a little Ativan, for anxiety. You can still visit. Talk. He'll just be calmer."

In the hospital room, they had provided Rachel with a step stool. She stood on it at Cal's bedside, to talk with her father. Mike and Caroline waited for nearly an hour before Rachel came out. When she emerged, she was crying. Caroline sat with her in the family lounge around the corner, and the professor went in to Cal.

Branden started with news. "Bishop Yost spoke with Mary Yost on the phone, Cal."

"I'd like to have heard that conversation," Cal said, smiling.

"He actually apologized to her. He explained that he's going to let John take antidepressants, and that convinced her. She's going to come home to help him with John. Pat and Ricky left for Omaha yesterday, to bring her and Esther home. Plus, she has a new son, now."

"A Schwartzentruber Bishop using a cell phone?" Cal said. "It must be the end of the world."

"He was gentle with her, Cal. Compassionate."

"Good."

"Nobody had told her about Lydia, and he was tender with her. I don't understand their Dietsche language, of course, but I could tell that he was treating her kindly. Giving her space for her grief. Consoling her."

"Tender," Cal said from a secluded place inside the Ativan. "Kind. Gentle."

"You're a little drugged up, Pastor. You can sleep if you want to."

Cal smiled. "So, this is how we end up Mike? In a sterilized hospital bed, with a tranquilizer drip?"

330

"This is not how you're going to end up, Cal."

"You don't know that."

"Neither do you, old man."

"Look who's talking, with gray in your beard like that."

Branden smiled and took Cal's hand. "Do you remember how we used to go fishing? We went all the time, Cal. They couldn't keep us off the water."

Cal's eyes closed, and he said, "I'll see you on the other side, Mike."

"The other side of surgery?" Branden asked. "Or the other side of life?"

Cal's eyes opened. "Does it matter? Doesn't the one follow the other fast enough to make the difference unimportant?"

"You'd leave a hole in the world, Cal."

"I can't keep my eyes open."

"It's OK to sleep, Pastor," Branden said.

Cal smiled with his eyes closed again. The last thing he said to the professor was spoken as a whisper.

"God is still on His throne, Professor. I shall not be dismayed."

Chapter 37

Friday, September 8
4:00 PM

They gathered on the grassy hilltop overlooking the
Yost farm, to bury Lydia beside the babies. The small
headstones of Mary's infant children, buried there years
earlier, were to be joined by a new stone, inscribed with
nothing more than the name Lydia Schwartzentruber.

The entire congregation attended. Strong deacons of
the church carried the pine coffin along the bridle path
through the woods, and up the long slope to the top of the
hill. Other men pulled Lydia's headstone along in a hand
wagon. There was a general drizzle over all of Holmes
County, and a soft sheen of water settled on the black wool
of the Schwartzentruber clothes, as Bishop Alva Yost
conducted the funeral service in German.

Mary Yost attended, leaning on her husband John as
she cried, and all their children stood with them, including
little Esther who had been to Omaha with her mother. Mose
and Ida Schwartzentruber stood among them, Ida holding
Mary and John's new baby boy Henry. Alva and Miriam
Yost attended with their children. His brother Lucas and his
wife Hannah Yost similarly were there, with all their
children. All the men of the congregation had gathered on
the hilltop, plus many of the women and children. Some
women and children of course stayed behind in the Yost
house, preparing food for the congregational dinner.

By the time they roped the coffin into the grave, water had puddled in all the dozens of stars that had been chiseled deeply into the face-plate of the wooden box. There were large stars and small ones, too, and they had been cut into the wood with great care. There were enough stars that Branden thought, as he watched the coffin disappear below the surface, that they constituted an entire constellation.

Branden and Robertson stood off to the side. They were not there to participate. They were there to witness and to testify to the tragedy and to the sorrow. They would not presume to have anything to say to the congregants. If they had spoken to John Yost, he probably would not have acknowledged them. The two English men were tolerated, though they were not particularly welcome. The sheriff and the professor knew this, and so they held to themselves. They spoke to no one.

After the mourners had trudged down the hill, and while four men were shoveling dirt into Lydia's grave, Branden and Robertson started down the hill. Quietly, they spoke to each other. The falling rain cocooned them under Robertson's umbrella. It muffled their voices and their footfalls. They enjoyed a measure of privacy as they made their way down the hill.

"Stars, Mike?" the sheriff asked the professor. "Schwartzentrubers tolerate no adornments at all, so what's going on with those coffin stars?"

Branden nodded. "They wouldn't be there if the bishop hadn't allowed them."

"Do you know what they mean?"

"Yes, they were special for Lydia. If the bishop chiseled those stars himself, then there are maybe only four people in the world who know what they mean."

"You gonna tell me, Professor?"

"Maybe someday. Right now, they're just Lydia's stars. It's a concession from the bishop. Or maybe an apology. I'll tell you someday."

After they had descended the path another twenty yards, Branden asked, "The Schells? What about them?"

Robertson touched the professor's arm and halted him under the umbrella. "You're a puzzle, Mike. Just tell me."

Branden shook his head. "I'll let you read a letter that Lydia wrote to the bishop. That'll explain it better than I can."

"You can just tell me now, Mike."

Branden shrugged. "Lydia wrote in a letter to the bishop that he had gotten her started thinking about the stars. What are they? Why are they there? Where did they come from? Like that. She told him it's why she wanted an education. It's why she left the Amish church. So, if he has put stars on her coffin, it's an acknowledgement of sorts. Now, what about the Schells?"

When they started walking again, the sheriff said, "Ed has been charged, but it's a minor crime, Mike. Interference with a law enforcement investigation. He'll never go to jail for anything."

"And Donna?"

"Charged with involuntary manslaughter. The prosecutor is convinced that she really did not intend to shoot Meredith Silver."

"I'd be happy if they both went to jail," Branden said. "Lydia and Meredith got tangled up in their ministry, and they both paid for it with their lives."

"Yes, I suppose so. Anyway, we found the revolver in the woods, where Donna tossed it. Her prints are all over it."

"Doesn't that pretty much close the case, Sheriff?"

"Not entirely. I'd like to charge someone at the Church of True Believers for those fake phone calls, pretending to be Mary Yost. But I don't think we'll ever find out who it was."

"No. Probably not."

"How about you? Are you done out here, Mike?"

"Actually, no. The bishop asked me to come out from time to time, to check on Junior."

"That's huge, Mike. You and Junior. The antidepressants. Talking on a cell phone with Mary, instead of shunning her. And hand-cut stars on a coffin. He's changing. For a Schwartzentruber, that's huge. It's a huge matter to think that Mary would have left in the first place."

"I think she was just trying to save herself and Esther."

Robertson shook his head. "You know what I mean. She broke away. It accomplished something good. The bishop is showing some flexibility because of her."

"Yes, and because of Lydia, too. I just don't expect him to go right out and buy a cell phone."

"Maybe in a hundred years, Mike."

"Maybe. What do you think Donna will get for manslaughter?"

"Sentencing is next week. I wouldn't want to predict."

"I wish she had given Mary Yost better counseling."

"No doubt. The thing is, Mike, she claims that Mary was really the one who wanted to leave. She insists that it was Mary's decision to leave. She insists that Mary had experienced a true religious conversion."

"Yes, but don't you think Donna and Meredith pushed her pretty strongly in that direction?"

"We'll never know. When does simple evangelism cross over into something more like manipulation?"

"Or into exploitation, Sheriff."

"Cal would know the difference."

Branden stopped on the trail. Robertson stopped beside him, holding the umbrella. The professor said, "Cal is the only kind of pastor that I'd trust to know the difference, and to respect it."

Robertson nodded solemnly. "How is Cal? When's he coming home?"

"Tomorrow, Bruce. He's not really doing too well, yet. He came through it hard."

"Has it spread? The cancer?"

"To his spleen. They had to remove that, too."

"He's not going to live forever, Mike. None of us is."

"Let's stretch a few more years out of it, Sheriff. I know a farm pond that has too many fish in it. Cal and I can hit it in the spring."

"I never understood the fishing thing."

"I know. It's just something that Cal and I used to do. After this, I'm going to make certain that we get back to it."

"Time is the only significant asset, Mike. Time with friends. Time with family. Maybe I'll buy a fishing pole."

"Between Cal and me, Sheriff, I think we can probably fix you up with a pole."

"Fishing?"

Branden nodded and smiled. "In the spring."

"Then that's a date, Mike. That's a firm date. But in November next year, I've got a little something planned with Missy."

"A trip?"

"You could say that. We're both going to retire."

Branden scoffed out a laugh. "And do what, Sheriff? Really, do what?"

"You said you liked Sarasota?" Robertson led.

"Yes."

"We're gonna start there, Mike. We're gonna find a place where it's warm. Someplace with water. Maybe buy a boat."

"I don't believe that, Bruce."

Robertson shrugged. "I'm going to help Ricky Niell run for sheriff in the fall elections."

"This is not a joke?"

"No joke, Mike. It's time I stepped aside. It's time for Missy and me to live somewhere warm. And it's Ricky's turn. Sheriff Ricky Niell. But, look, you and Caroline should come down with us. We can find a couple of places near the water, and see what kind of trouble we can get into."

The professor shook his head. "I need to teach, Bruce. Maybe a couple more years."

"You'd be missing out, Mike. I think Caroline would support me on this. Maybe I'll just mention it to her."

Branden frowned at first, but then he smiled with a happy light in his eyes. "Do you remember the day we met, Bruce?"

The rain puttered on the umbrella, and the sheriff smiled too, grandly. "Kindergarten, Mike. You were dressed in short pants and suspenders."

"I remember you teased me about that, Sheriff. I also remember that you were already quite chubby."

The sheriff kept his smile. "Cal was a regular little juvenile delinquent. A discipline problem, if you don't remember. Miss Sampson made him stand in the corner for ten minutes. I remember him there in his Mennonite denim, as if it were yesterday. I think he was crying."

"I remember," Branden said. "When he gets home, I'm going to find out if Cal does, too. The pastor, the professor and the sheriff. Little friends in Kindergarten. Who could have predicted how it would all turn out?"

"Small towns are built for life-long friendships, Mike. We were lucky."

"Yes Sheriff, and we were blessed."

Relevant Scripture Verses

From the Holy Bible, New Testament, The Apostle Paul's Letter to the Church at Ephesus:

Ephesians 2:8-9

[8]For it is by grace you have been saved, through faith – and this is not from yourselves, it is the gift of God – [9]not by works, so that no one can boast.

And then, from the general letter of James, to the twelve tribes scattered among the nations, Chapter 2, on the question of faith as evidenced by deeds:

James 2:24 and 2:26

[24]You see that a person is considered righteous by what they do and not by faith alone.

[26]As the body without the spirit is dead, so faith without deeds is dead.

Acknowledgements

I am grateful for the patience of my fans, who have waited too long for this tenth novel to be published. Thank you for your forbearance, and for the many fine letters you have sent me through my website, asking about my progress on this novel. Because of the sensitive nature of the issues, this is surely the most difficult topic that I have addressed. I have tried to write fairly and even-handedly about the lifestyle choices of the most conservative of the Amish peoples.

There are many people to thank, but let me especially mention Steve and Dawn Tilson, good friends and capable advisors, and Mr. Ed Schrock of Holmes County, Ohio.

Most of all, I am grateful for and indebted to my beloved wife Madonna, who is my most inciteful critic, my most effective muse, and my most cherished friend and companion.

Dedication

Dedicated to the patient fans of my Amish-Country Mysteries. Thank you for waiting. I know from your many letters that it has been difficult, and I can say only that I very much appreciate your patience.

Author's Note

Many difficult and puzzling questions arise when the various Amish societies in America are examined and compared. This is made especially obvious when all the numerous and different sects are brought fully into view. To the casual tourist, it may appear that the Amish people of America are rather homogeneous and unified. But to those of us who have made a study of it from the outside, the most astonishing discovery is the great number of different sects that exist within these diverse Anabaptist colonies. The division is often so complete that even a single congregation can sometimes be said to constitute a discrete sect unto itself. Across the spectrum from New Order Mennonite to Old Order Schwartzentrubers, the differences appear to be vast. Yet when one bishop's congregation is compared with another's, the differences can be minute. Even so, these small differences can become such critical issues that they will govern the decisions of bishops on whether or not to commune with neighboring congregations. For instance, the bishop of one congregation might permit gasoline hay baling equipment to be used, so long as it is pulled through a field by a team of horses, whereas a neighboring bishop might rule against gasoline hay balers altogether, whether pulled by horses or not. Over differences such as these, the one group might decide not to have fellowship with the other.

The consequences for Old Order congregants can be very great. Where one bishop permits the use of riding lawn mowers, another will not. A more liberal bishop might rule that riding lawn mowers may be driven into towns and villages, whereas a more conservative bishop will rule that travel over the roads must be done with horse and buggy exclusively.

This story is about the most conservative of all the Old Order sects – the Schwartzentrubers. I admire the fortitude and dedication of these people, and I am amazed by the steadfastness that is required to live according to their religious convictions. These are the people who refuse to make any reconciliation with the modern world. They hold religiously to the lifestyles and traditions of seventeenth- and eighteenth-century European peasants, and they will surely be the last of the Amish peoples to make compromises with the lifestyles and attitudes of *those English out there*. This ultra-conservative sect is just as solidly fixed in their old-world traditions as the past is fixed in the history books. Their farms are purposefully little different from the German farms that their ancestors had been driven from in the sixteenth and seventeenth centuries. They speak their own dialect at home and speak and read only High German in their bi-monthly Sunday services. These German services are always conducted by the congregation's sole autocratic bishop, with help from the preachers and deacons, to relentlessly emphasize not just the Gospel of Christ, but also the struggles, persecutions and martyrdom of the German *first families*, who fled the Fatherland to seek religious freedom in the Americas. And it is this religious freedom, guaranteed by the First Amendment of the U.S. Constitution, that now in the twenty-first century grants these backward-looking Schwartzentrubers the right as Americans, and the insulation from English society that is necessary, to live as mere peasants according to the oldest strictures on dress, behavior and lifestyle, in a world gone as modern as moon shots, cell phones and the internet.

It is necessary that I be honest with myself and my readers when writing about the Schwartzentrubers. With this novel, I hope to provide the opposing points of view that are necessary to allow my readers to form their own opinions about the culture and traditions of the Old Order Schwartzentruber Amish. I have endeavored to depict the conditions on a Schwartzentruber farm as I have many times observed them to be. Readers might be surprised at the primitive nature of these farms, but I have not written about anything that I have not seen firsthand in these communities. Regardless of one's opinion on these matters, it is essential to remember that the lifestyle that Schwartzentrubers have chosen is one that arises from deep and fervent religious convictions.

The Cover Image

The cover photo (Copyright © 2019 Paul L. Gaus, all rights reserved) is of two Schwartzentruber children walking along a road in the countryside near the setting for this story. The thin, parallel lines on the pavement at their feet are the noon shadows of electric lines that ran overhead. The image testifies to the span of five centuries that separates the Schwartzentrubers from the English who live among them.

The Previous *Amish-Country Mysteries* in Reverse Order of Publication:

9. *Whiskers of the Lion* – Plume at Penguin Group, 2015

8. *The Names of Our Tears* – Plume at Penguin Group, 2013

7. *Harmless as Doves* – 2011, Ohio University Press, and Plume at Penguin Group, 2012

6. *Separate from the W*orld – 2008, Ohio University Press, and Plume at Penguin Group, 2011

5. *A Prayer for the Night* – 2006, Ohio University Press, and Plume at Penguin Group, 2011

4. *Cast a Blue Shadow* – 2003, Ohio University Press, and Plume at Penguin Group, 2011

3. *Clouds Without Rain* – 2001, Ohio University Press, and Plume at Penguin Group, 2010

2. *Broken English* – 2000, Ohio University Press, and Plume at Penguin Group, 2010

1. *Blood of the Prodigal* – 1999, Ohio University Press, and Plume at Penguin Group, 2010

Resources for Readers

1. Author's Email Address: paul@plgaus.com

2. Author's Website and Blog: https://plgaus.com

3. Facebook's Community Page for The Amish-Country Mysteries:
https://www.facebook.com/Amish.Country.Mysteries/

4. Comprehensive Reference Work: *Unser Leit, The Story of the Amish*, in two volumes, by Leroy Beachy, Copyright © 2011 Goodly Heritage Books, 4324 St. Route 39, Millersburg, Ohio 44654-9681, (330) 893-2883

5. The Best Single Book on the Amish: *Our Amish Neighbors*, by Professor William I. Schreiber, Copyright © 1992 William I. Schreiber, a rare book that is sometimes still available at the Florence Wilson Bookstore, The College of Wooster, Wooster, Ohio. Alternately, it can also be purchased at many specialty bookstores, and at numerous online retailers.

. The musings of an Old Order Amish man, with comments
ıd observations on hundreds of important issues:
·denklich Happenings and More*, Volumes I and II, by
ⅴi L. Fisher, Copyright © 2013 and 2016 Levi L. Fisher,
asthof Press, 219 Mill Road, Morgantown, PA.

Made in the USA
Las Vegas, NV
05 July 2021

25976195R00204